BATTLE OF THE IRON GATES

REVISED EDITION

STEW ADAMS

CHAPTER ONE: THE PRISONER'S WARNING

'I'm here to see the prisoner.'

Arthur kept his voice level, his eyes on the three guardsmen, who'd tensed up at his arrival. His journey through the mountain fortress had led him deep underground, where torch-lit corridors wound their way down to the dungeons. In the guardroom, the three men had abandoned their card game, springing to their feet at his appearance. The nearest guard reached for a spear that was propped against the wall, while another snatched an unsheathed dagger from the table. The third faced Arthur empty-handed, though his fingers twitched toward the sword at his belt. Despite being caught at leisure, their swift reactions were impressive.

Armoured in plate mail and carrying a huge mace at his belt, Arthur halted in the entryway, raising his hands in what he hoped was a peaceful gesture.

The man in the centre spoke. 'Which prisoner, Sir...?' He was lean as a bowstring, and his worn leather armour and unshaven face made Arthur think he was an experienced sergeant. Not bothering with the usual flawless appearance that was demanded by officers, and ready to take the reprimands because of it.

'My name is Arthur, and I believe you only have one prisoner – Officer Phillip.'

The sergeant's mouth twitched. 'My apologies, sir, but Commander Ashworth left orders. Phillip is allowed no visitors.'

'Why not?'

'The commander did not discuss it with me.'

'No, I guess he wouldn't. Can you give me a guess, then?'

'I'm not paid to think, sir.'

Arthur huffed a laugh. This man was exactly the kind of soldier he liked, one who could refuse officious nobles without overstepping. Yet it presented a problem, because Phillip's information was vital. He stroked his beard, thinking.

'I am but a guest in this fortress,' Arthur said, 'and it would be terrible form for me to countermand the commander's orders. I'm not here to argue that. Instead, I will give you three an early relief. I will guard the prisoner for the next few hours, while you—' Arthur pulled a silver coin from his belt and flicked it towards them. The sergeant deftly caught it without breaking eye contact, '—will go to the nearest alehouse and have a drink. Then you can inform Lord Ashworth of my arrival.'

The three guardsmen regarded him solemnly. His plate mail marked him as someone of importance, despite the lack of other identifying marks. Arthur pulled one of the necklaces out from under his armour. Out of habit, his hand had pulled on the leather strap that held the likeness of his wife and child. With a frown, he reached for the one on the silver chain instead. At the end was the holy fire symbol of the Archangel.

'I think that's the First Templar,' one of the guardsmen said.

'I am indeed.' Arthur replied. 'Now off with you, go and enjoy your drink. The longer it takes for the commander to learn of my arrival, the more grateful I'll be.'

The sergeant held the coin for a moment longer before it disappeared into his palm. 'Thank you, sir, we shall.'

'We can't just—' the spearman began.

'Shut it, Hugh,' the sergeant snapped. 'We can't defy the orders of a Templar.'

'My apologies for putting you in this situation, but duty demands it.'

'Aye, the worst I'll get is chewed out,' the sergeant said. 'I've been chewed out before.'

The guard with the dagger had already sheathed his weapon. He glared at Hugh until the spearman reluctantly put up his weapon and moved out under his watchful gaze.

'The dungeon guards normally carry these,' the sergeant said, pulling a ring of keys from his belt. They jingled as he passed them over.

'Good man,' Arthur said, clapping him on the shoulder, and moved to unlock the door before they'd even reached the end of the hall.

The hinges squealed, revealing the interior of the dungeon. Thick stone masonry glistened with moisture, and the single barred window set high in the cell allowed only a sliver of grey light to fall across the straw-covered floor. Iron manacles hung empty. Phillip, long and willowy, had been spared their embrace as he sat against the wall with one leg propped up. The condemned man blinked against the torch-light, his bloodshot eyes sunken with exhaustion.

'Are they here yet?' he asked, shielding his face from the torch's glare.

'The savage horde led by a High Demon of hell?' Arthur asked lightly. 'No, not yet.'

'I told Lord Ashworth they are coming,' Phillip said, frustration clear in his voice. 'Every day I look through my window, and see no preparations. The soldiers just go about their business, as if they ignore it then the danger will just go away.'

Arthur chuckled. 'That's a good way to put it, actually. I don't know the politics involved, but I know Ashworth's never had a tough command and it's been over a decade since this fortress has faced any challenge.'

'It's about to have one,' Phillip spat. 'That stupid fool.'

'Stupid fat fool,' Arthur amended.

Phillip paused, studying Arthur. 'Who are you?'

'Arthur.'

Realisation dawned across his features. Phillip hastily got up, and managed a half decent bow despite the obvious stiffness in his muscles. 'I'm sorry, First Templar. I didn't know.'

'Sit down, man, I'm not the Archangel.'

Phillip looked around frantically, grabbing onto the only bit of furniture in the room – a lone stool with uneven legs. He presented it to Arthur, who ignored it.

'It won't be long until Ashworth waddles his way down here to stop me from listening to your heretic ways.' Arthur pulled a hip flask from his belt, unstoppered it smoothly, and took a long pull. The whiskey burned pleasantly, tasting of smoke and honey, before settling into a warm glow in his chest. He heaved a contented sigh. 'Forgive me, but it's been a long ride getting here.' He offered Phillip the flask. At the man's hesitation, Arthur added, 'Consider it an order – take a drink.'

Phillip reluctantly accepted the flask and sipped with the delicacy of a courtier, but it was still enough to send him coughing. In that moment Arthur glimpsed how young he really was. He couldn't be far past twenty.

'Good stuff, right?' Arthur said, taking the flask back. 'Now then, let's get to business. I've heard a lifetime of rumours, and your men are surprisingly tight-lipped about it all. Still, I need the truth.'

The man opened his mouth, then closed it. Then repeated the motion, giving the impression of a stranded fish. When he did finally speak, it sounded hesitant: 'Naberius is marching south with an army of over a hundred thousand men.'

Arthur waited, but the man stayed silent. 'Did you see it yourself?'

'Yes, Templar.'

Again, he didn't volunteer anything else. Arthur didn't have enough time to pull every word. 'You're sure?'

'Yes, Templar.'

'I'm not sure I can count that high. You're certain the army's that big?'

'Yes, Templar,' Phillip said, his words still clipped.

'And they're coming to this fortress?'

'By the Light, yes!' Phillip said with a raised voice, pointing towards the lone window. 'Naberius is marching south with a hundred thousand soldiers at his back, maybe as many as one hundred and fifty. When will you people see that?' Then his eyes widened, and he snapped his arms back to his sides.

Arthur grinned at him. 'When I saw this meek and defeated man, I wondered if I had the right person. But that fire is more of what I expected of the officer who defied his superiors and rode into hostile lands to scout out the enemy army that's about to descend on us.' The words relaxed the prisoner, until he looked almost bashful. 'Now you have a willing audience who will take everything you say seriously. Tell me the details; I need to know more. How far away are they? You mentioned their number – but are they all soldiers? How many are mounted? Are there more demons than just Naberius?'

Phillip stared at Arthur for a long time, relief easing the tension from his shoulders.

'It is difficult to get accurate numbers. I'd say at least ten thousand calvary, but I don't know whether they were heavy or light, horse archers or just scouts. Their camp was comprised of many nations and their organisation was … chaotic.'

Arthur nodded knowingly. 'I can imagine herding an army that big would have complications. Need a lot of food and rolling wheels to keep them serviced.'

Phillip's eyes grew haunted. 'I've never seen anything like it. Like some ravenous beast, they devoured towns and villages whole. Entire cities were nothing but burning husks in their wake, while they conscripted anyone within reach.'

'And they're headed here?'

Phillip considered, looking out the barred window and into the fortress courtyard. 'They may turn off, but I can't see what for. The roads to the sea get more treacherous the further south you come, and he's made no indication of heading towards Astaroth's fortress. I don't know where else he'd be going.'

Arthur nodded thoughtfully. They might be lucky and the army would focus on something else, but he doubted it. 'Deserters or dissenters?'

'There were plenty to begin with, but as the army grew…'

Arthur nodded. 'I can imagine those who objected were silenced, one way or another."

'That is the Light's truth.'

'Take another drink of that,' Arthur said nodding to the flask. The man looked down, surprised he still held the flask, and then he took another sip. There was less coughing this time before he passed it back.

'You can relax,' Arthur said. 'Your warnings have reached us, and our entire nation is mobilising. I came with the advance guard of the Citadel's standing forces, and soon this fortress will be bursting with armed soldiers.'

Arthur could see it: The man's shoulders that had been as tense as a drawn crossbow began to relax. Phillip's eyes darted around the cell as if to reassure himself of reality.

'An invasion by Lucifer's hound is generally something we take seriously,' Arthur said. 'We know what you've done to make this happen. The reports reached us, too – even the part about how your command imitated elements of the adversary's army to stir up resistance.'

'You heard about that?' Phillip asked, a tremor in his voice. He looked away, unable to meet Arthur's eyes. Word had it this man had committed crimes against innocents to incite retribution from the surrounding countryside. If even half the rumours were true, it would be enough to have him tied to a stake and purged with fire. But Arthur didn't want to press into that, at least not yet.

'What I don't know is why they're coming south,' Arthur said. 'Did you manage to find that out?'

Phillip had his eyes tightly closed, and didn't answer. Just as Arthur had begun to repeat the question, Phillip answered: 'I don't know. Naberius has been roaming the north for the last few decades, ever since he…' He trailed off.

'Yes, yes, ever since he slew the Archangel Michael,' Arthur finished. It had happened when he was a child, leaving Zadkiel as the last Archangel on Eden, and their last hope to hold back the Darkness. He shook himself briskly. 'The three-headed mutt is powerful, but he's also damn cunning. We know he's been searching for something up north, but the question is why has he suddenly turned his attention to us?'

'I don't know,' Phillip whispered.

'Well, if divine inspiration strikes, do let me know.'

The blasphemy caused Phillip's eyes to snap up to Arthur, as if he were unsure of what to make of him.

'We need to prepare for the coming siege. Behind our walls in the narrow choke of the pass we can stop them, but we need to be ready. For that I need more information. If you can't tell me his motivations then let's go with the others. How many soldiers are his, how many are veterans and how many are simple farmers pressed into service?'

Back on more familiar territory, Phillip considered before he answered. 'Those on the flanks, particularly the cavalry, are those loyal to him. Regardless of the loyalty of the rest, with the warlike nature of the northern kingdoms, I feel like they're moving with a lot of veterans.'

'That's what concerns me, but I would like more specifics—' Arthur began, but he was interrupted by heavy footfalls echoing down the corridor, followed by laboured breathing. 'Those boys must have drunk fast.'

'What?' Phillip asked, confused.

Arthur didn't answer, instead turning towards the doorway where the Fort's pompous commander now stood. Though only in his late forties, Lord Ashworth's fondness for fine wines and generous portions had taken its toll. His crimson face wheezed from the short descent to the dungeons, sweat beading on his brow despite the cool air.

'First Templar, I must protest your presence here.'

'Alright, no problem,' Arthur said. 'We'll finish this conversation later, officer.'

With that, he strode brusquely past Lord Ashworth, completely ignoring the man and enjoying hearing him stutter his indignation as Arthur headed for the stairs. If there was indeed an army bearing down on them, he wanted to go out and see it for himself.

CHAPTER TWO: THE IRON GATES

$\mathcal{A}$rthur moved through the halls of the keep, torchlight casting dancing shadows on the ancient stone walls. Over the centuries, the dampness of the mountain had seeped into the very bones of the fortress, leaving behind the musty smell of wet stone. His armoured footsteps echoed through the narrow corridors, accompanied by the laboured breathing of Lord Ashworth struggling to keep pace behind him.

The morning sun had barely crested the mountain peaks when he emerged into the main entry hall, Ashworth having fallen behind long ago. He strode past the massive oaken door that stood six inches thick – the keep's last defence should all else fail. As he stepped outside, Arthur shivered as a bitter wind howled around him, carrying the chilling bite of an early spring snow.

The courtyard opened before him like the palm of a giant's hand, bordered by walls that seemed to have grown from the living rock of the mountain itself. Spiralling staircases wound up through defensive towers, their arrow slits staring out like narrowed eyes. But it was the iron gates at either end that drew the eye – two sets of enormous double doors that gave the fortress its name. Arthur paused, staring at the gates. He'd been in such a hurry that he hadn't had time to appreciate the defensive marvels around him. Created by the Archangel Jophiel herself, they had been forged of some mysterious metal darker than iron yet lighter than wood, allowing them to swing easily on massive hinges despite their impossible size. In the mountain sunlight, their dull metallic surface absorbed the light, blending seamlessly with the surrounding keep as though the entire structure had been carved from a single piece of stone.

Half a dozen of Arthur's personal guard stood watch, but he saw none of the other Templars who had arrived with the advance guard. With the likelihood of the approaching army's arrival, his eyes traced the fortifications rising seamlessly from the mountainside, checking for faults or flaws. He felt a flutter of hope. If what Phillip had said was true, then these walls might be tested like never before.

A shadow detached itself from a doorway, resolving into Matthew's lean form. Stringy dark hair partially obscured sharp eyes that seemed to take in everything, while focusing on nothing. Despite his Templar plate armour, he moved with the silent grace of a mountain cat. In his arms he carried bundles of white furs and leathers streaked with charcoal – proper mountain gear. He shot a questioning look at Arthur.

'Yeah, I believe him,' Arthur replied to the unasked question. 'We'll need to go up into the mountains and see for ourselves.' Part of him hoped Phillip was wrong, but his gut could detect no lie there. 'Light, as if my legs aren't wobbly enough from over a week in the saddle, now we've got to climb a bloody mountain. I need another drink.' He paused, thinking about what they'd need on the peak. 'Where do they keep their supplies…?' Arthur broke off as Matthew pointed idly to a corner of the courtyard.

A few soldiers were arranging trail supplies – packs, climbing gear, and solid mountain boots were being laid out with military precision. Arthur couldn't help a smile. 'I was only gone for less than an hour. How in the hells did you organise all this?'

Matthew gave a nonchalant shrug.

'I forgot you were born here, weren't you?'

Matthew pointed further up in the mountains, where snow-capped peaks vanished into the clouds. Arthur followed his gesture. The trees looked like they barely clung to life at such heights, so he wondered how the mountain clans survived up there. Still, it would explain much about the man. 'I shouldn't be surprised.'

Before Arthur could continue, Lord Ashworth finally caught up to them, trying to speak but wheezing so heavily it was almost painful to watch.

'If we leave soon, can we still get up there before nightfall?' Arthur asked Matthew. Again, he ignored the commander. The quiet Templar lifted his face to the blue skies, nostrils flaring as if he were testing the mountain air. Though he frowned, he gave a slight nod.

'Good, I'll be along as soon as I can.'

'First Templar, there really is no need,' Ashworth managed between gasps. 'Phillip's lies have already … caused such panic … I had to have him isolated … pending a formal trial.'

'Best to be sure,' Arthur said, distracted. Then movement near the Keep's well caught his attention. Templar Peter was standing entirely too close to a young woman drawing water. Immaculately groomed with raven-black hair and dark, mischievous eyes, Peter cut a dashing figure that belonged more in a royal court than a mountain fortress. Even his plate armour appeared ornamental rather than functional, polished to a mirror sheen that caught the morning light. He whispered something in the woman's ear that made her face flush crimson.

'For the Light's sake,' Arthur shouted. 'Peter, we've been here less than an hour!'

The other Templar didn't immediately respond, taking his time in helping the woman with her bucket before bestowing a courtly farewell. Only then did he turn and make his way over, offering Lord Ashworth an exaggerated bow. 'My lord. I was merely becoming acquainted with the local populace.'

'Uh-huh,' Arthur said.

Peter's eyes fell on the mountain gear being assembled. 'Surely you don't want me to come up into the mountains with you?'

'Why would you want to go into the mountains?' Ashworth demanded.

'No, I've got a special task for you,' Arthur said to Peter.

'I'm almost afraid to ask.'

'Someone needs to prepare the fortress for the army's arrival, figure out how to house seven or eight thousand soldiers.'

'Templars!' Ashworth said, his voice growing hard. 'This has gone too far. You may be holy men, but I am a commander and this fortress is my charge.' The man seemed to have recovered his breath, while his face was still flushed red with anger. 'If you wish something, then it must be through my consent!'

Arthur gave a flick of his head to Peter, allowing the man an exit. The Templar gave a grateful smile. *Poor fool*, Arthur thought, *he's going to have to deal with this pompous fort commander all week. But for now, the man is my problem.*

For the first time, Arthur turned to face him. The man tried to meet his eye, but his gaze soon darted away. He was unused to being challenged, Arthur realised. It had caught him off guard, but that didn't mean he was a fool.

'I realise your concern, but we must take the word of this encroaching army seriously.'

'This is exactly why I have tried to quash these wild rumours. See the panic they have inspired?' Ashworth said with a wave of his arms. 'Our walls are high, our gates strong, and our garrison is ready.'

'I think even this place would have trouble against a hundred thousand.'

'The same army supposedly led by Naberius?' Lord Ashworth snorted. 'Preposterous. There aren't that many people in the entirety of the north. Besides, no force can breach the Iron Gates.'

'What did your own scouts report?'

Confusion flickered across the commander's features. 'Templar?'

'I would assume you have sent more scouts out to determine the truth of such rumours.'

The commander drew himself up, though the effect was diminished by his protruding stomach. 'You may be one of the Archangel's chosen, but I resent what you are insinuating. I have not been remiss in my duty – the patrols and scouts have been increased, and they have reported nothing.'

'Where are these scouts? I would like to speak to them myself.'

'They're out on patrol.'

'All of them? I must say your knowledge of the whereabouts of every single one of your own troops is quite remarkable.'

'There is no such army,' Lord Ashworth reiterated, wiping the sweat from his brow.

'I hope you are right, Commander,' Arthur said. 'If what he's saying holds even a hint of truth, you will answer to Zadkiel himself.'

Lord Ashworth paled visibly. 'The Archangel is coming here?'

'Yes, he is, with eight thousand soldiers and the rest of the Templars. I expect them here within the week,' Arthur said. 'You had best get along with Peter and help in preparing the Keep. Ensure it is worthy of his arrival.' Arthur could see the wheels in the man's eyes turning. 'If you'll excuse me.'

Arthur left before Lord Ashworth could even grunt a response, rejoining Matthew as he oversaw the supplies being packed into two bags. Yet before he could figure out a way to secrete a couple bottles of whiskey into his pack, a booming laugh echoed across the court-yard. The source was Wilfred, his massive frame making the very fortress doorway seem small. The Templar's wild black beard was braided into sections that did little to tame its savage appearance, while his huge battle axes hung on his back like deadly wings.

'I hear you're planning to climb Mount Moriah to spy on this army yourself?' Wilfred's booming voice echoed through the courtyard, bringing all activity to a halt.

'It's not necessary for you to—' Arthur began.

'But there might be fighting, yes?' Wilfred interrupted, his eyes gleaming with barely contained excitement.

Arthur sighed. 'There's a small chance—'

'Excellent!' Wilfred clapped his hands together. 'I will come!'

Arthur looked helplessly at Matthew, who shrugged – a gesture that spoke volumes from the usually silent Templar. With practiced efficiency he sorted through their supplies, his hands moving with the easy familiarity of someone born to mountain life. Each item was chosen with purpose – rope, pitons, extra furs, and trail rations disappeared into the packs. Within minutes, he had assembled a third set of gear that matched the other two.

Wilfred looked on with barely concealed impatience as Matthew led them through the Keep's winding corridors to a chamber tucked away from the main halls. The room was clearly meant for scouts preparing for mountain excursions – hooks lined the walls holding various bits of climbing gear, while sturdy benches provided space for changing. Racks of winter clothing stood ready, organized by size and purpose.

The mountain gear Matthew had prepared for them was a step up from what was on the walls – thick white furs, and heavy leathers streaked with charcoal for camouflage against the snow and rock. Each piece showed signs of careful maintenance, from the oiled leather straps to the meticulously-cleaned fur trim.

Arthur was grateful to be able to shed his plate mail, though he felt almost naked without it. The familiar weight of the steel had become like a second skin over the years. The winter clothing was surprisingly heavy in its own right, but offered much more freedom of movement. He tested his range of motion, swinging his arms and twisting at the waist.

Wilfred grumbled as he struggled to adjust the straps of his pack around his broad frame. The leather creaked in protest as he pulled at the buckles. 'How on earth are my axes supposed to fit along with all this?'

'You could leave them behind,' Arthur suggested, knowing the response before it came.

The large man's expression of horror – as if Arthur had suggested he abandon his own children – brought a smile to Matthew's normally stoic face.

Once properly outfitted, the Templars made their way along the keep's winding corridors and through the Iron Gates. The northern city spread out before them, its grey stone buildings huddled under the fortress walls like chicks beneath a mother hen. Their boots crunched upon the frozen ground as the bitter mountain wind cut through even their heavy furs, carrying the promise of snow.

Though the citadel's defences were impressive in their own right, Arthur couldn't help but admire the sheer tactical advantage of their position. The narrow mountain pass funnelled any attacking force down into a killing ground before the walls. No matter their numbers, the enemy would have no choice but to come at them head-on. The thought was both reassuring and troubling – if Phillip's warnings proved true, they would need every advantage they could gain.

Smoke arose from chimneys in thin columns before being torn apart by the mountain breeze. As they walked, Arthur's trained eye noted every defensive position – the murder holes above the gates, the overlapping fields of fire from the arrow slits, the carefully positioned choke points. His pack grew heavier with each step, but the weight was reassuring. They would need the food and clothing up among those cold peaks.

Yes, he thought grimly, *if war is coming, this is where we will make our stand.*

CHAPTER THREE: THE DARK TIDE

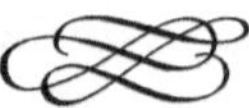

Ice crystals stung Arthur's face as the wind screamed through the mountain pass, its bitter fingers probing beneath his furs and leathers for any exposed skin. The thin air made each laboured breath burn in his lungs. His heavy pack threatened to overbalance him with every step, while loose stones skittered away beneath his boots. The rope around his middle had grown taut, a life-line connecting him to his companions as they inched their way up the northern face of Mount Moriah. All around them the mountain loomed like a sleeping giant, its grey-white shoulders draped in snow and shadow, blocking the afternoon sun from sight. Arthur's world had narrowed to the scrape of his boots on stone, the whistling wind, and the endless climb toward the northernmost peak that lined the pass.

Matthew led their ascent, moving with such natural grace that Arthur sometimes wondered if the man were a mountain goat. The quiet Templar navigated the treacherous mountainside as if born to it.

'Is it much further?' Arthur called ahead, his voice thin in the frigid air. 'I'm bloody tired!'

Matthew turned back, lifting his forefinger and thumb an inch apart. Arthur grunted in relief. He glanced behind him at their third member.

'How you doing back there?' Arthur called to Wilfred.

The big man grinned, showing the whites of his teeth behind his bushy black beard. Even in his white leathers that blended into the mountain, the other Templar looked huge and intimidating.

Arthur glanced towards the two tall pillars of rock, with a small opening in between. This gap led to their destination. He was so focused on it that he wasn't concentrating. His next step hit some loose gravel, and his feet began to slide. He reached out wildly, grasping onto a nearby rock, finding a grip through his deerskin gloves. Despite their fur lining, he could feel the chill of the rock seeping through. The contact steadied him enough to regain a sure footing.

'I'm fine,' Arthur said, waving away the other two men's concerned look. 'Let's get to the top.'

He clenched his fists open and closed in a vain attempt to warm them up. Then, more cautiously, he attacked the mountain one step at a time. His feet continued to slide on the treacherous footholds; their late start meant the sun had turned much of the mountain snow into ice, making the climb infinitely more difficult.

Arthur slid once more, almost twisting his ankle. Neither of the other Templars had noticed, too occupied with their own footing. *No one would know if I used the Light's power*, Arthur thought. He opened himself up to a sliver of the Light. Immediately he felt refreshed, as if waking from a good night's rest in a warm bed. The weight of his pack felt lighter, and the climb didn't seem so bad anymore. But he only took a few steps before he caught Matthew's disapproving frown.

'Alright fine, I won't use it,' Arthur said, releasing the Light. They'd agreed to conserve their power in case they needed to fight. Just as quickly as he'd felt revitalised, the newfound strength left him and he was back to being his mortal self. Grumbling, he followed Matthew's path as they zigzagged along the final leg of the trail.

To the side lay a narrow cave entrance, while in front of them were two massive pillars of grey stone. The gap between them led to the plateau that was their destination.

Arthur unhooked his pack, allowing it to slide to the ground while he stepped through the narrow passageway. Warm sunlight greeted him, and he immediately felt parts of him thawing as he took in the view.

Immediately in front of them lay the desolate mountain landscape, dotted by the occasional tree or shrub. Further down the slopes, forests of oak and beech spread like a dark green carpet, occasionally broken by streaks of lighter pine. Beyond these, the land opened into a patchwork of cultivated fields – winter wheat lending it a dull green hue, while others lay fallow in browns and greys. Thin wisps of smoke arose from scattered villages, their church spires reaching skyward like needles against the horizon.

Arthur stepped forward cautiously, one hand shielding his eyes against the brightness of the sun. The plain before them stretched for leagues, bisected by a meandering river that glinted like polished silver. Along its banks, clusters of peasant hovels and the occasional stone manor house dotted the landscape, surrounded by their fields and orchards. His eyes scanned every facet, but he could see no army.

'Nothing,' Wilfred growled in frustration, his breath forming clouds in the frigid air. 'Not so much as a dust cloud.'

Matthew moved to a different vantage point, scanning the network of dirt roads that connected the villages. These paths, little more than muddy tracks from this distance, wove between fields and disappeared into patches of woodland.

'Any signs, Matthew?' Arthur asked. Even before becoming one of the twelve Templars, the man had been a gifted tracker. His gaze shifted over the landscape like a hawk looking for prey. But eventually, even he shook his head.

'So what now?' Wilfred asked. 'Do we ride out to find them?'

'Even you would have trouble against that many soldiers,' Arthur said.

The gleam in the burly Templar's eyes hinted that he wanted to try.

'We set up camp. In a few days, Peter or one of the other Templars will relieve us.'

'Peter? There are no ladies to tempt him to come up here,' Wilfred grumbled.

Arthur pulled the hip flask from his belt, the metal cold against his fingers. The familiar taste of smoke and honey whiskey rolled across his tongue, warming him from the inside out. He offered the flask to Wilfred, who took it with a knowing grin. The other Templar knocked back a generous swallow, his beard failing to hide his appreciation.

The wind's howling filled the silence between them as Arthur took another sip, letting the warmth spread throughout his chest. Even the strongest spirits couldn't entirely ward off the crisp mountain air, but they made the bite more bearable. Besides, Arthur thought wryly, if they were about to witness the end of the world come marching through that pass, he'd rather not face it entirely sober.

'Alright, we may as well get settled in,' Arthur said. 'We're going to be here a while.'

In silent agreement, the three of them retreated past the pillars and into the narrow cave entrance.

The cavern's interior bore the marks of previous sentries, its rough walls softened by strategically placed furs and canvas that held the mountain's fury at bay. Stacked neatly against one wall was a generous supply of wood and coal. As Arthur stepped deeper inside, the howling of the wind softened to a whisper, and he set his mace aside before beginning to unpack.

Matthew crouched by the stone ring, the scraping of flint and steel accompanied a small spark. It took the man only a few minutes to get the kindling to catch, the fire throwing dancing shadows on the cave walls, its warmth fighting against the mountain's chill.

'I'll take first watch,' Arthur said, gathering up a woollen blanket.

Wilfred's grunt and Matthew's nod were their only responses as he left the cave and returned to the plateau.

The blanket helped against the biting wind as Arthur settled at his post, his eyes scanning the darkening horizon for any sign of movement. Specks of various people could be seen moving in the distance, but they were just ordinary folk returning from the fields. The monotonous tableau made his mind wander. He thought about his wife and boy. He reached under his winter clothing for the leather cords around his neck, and two pendants came tumbling out. The first was Zadkiel's holy flame, a symbol of his faith. The second was a silver medallion, worn smooth from years of touching. On one side, Sarah's likeness had been etched by a master silversmith, capturing her kind smile and the wild curls of her hair that she could never quite tame. On the other side was Richard's face, caught in that moment between boy and youth, a reminder of what he fought for. Arthur ran his thumb over the worn silver surfaces, feeling every groove and contour that had been deepened by his constant attentions. He devoutly hoped Phillip had been mistaken as he again scanned the horizon for the enemy army. If he wasn't, he couldn't help but wonder what it would mean for his family.

After hours of keeping watch with only the wind for company, Arthur saw Matthew appear carrying a roasted bird leg – smaller than a chicken but well-muscled.

'Where in the nine hells did you get that?'

Matthew pointed further up the mountain.

Arthur stared upwards, having had no idea that birds even lived on the mountain. Then the smell wafted over, and he grinned, trading the blanket for the food while he took a bite. The meat was crispy and flavourful – a feast compared to their hard rations. In the fortress it would have been tough and stringy, but with hunger as his sauce, Arthur could savour every bite.

'No point staying out here and being miserable late into the night,' Arthur said. 'Once darkness settles, come in and stay warm.'

Matthew gave him the thumbs up as he wrapped himself in the blanket.

Arthur returned to the shelter of the cave. Wilfred and Matthew had reset the hanging canvas and floor rugs to ensure the cavern retained its warmth. It felt almost cosy. Wilfred was running a whetstone over one of his battle axes, though Arthur could see no marring or burs on its perfect edge. The large man gestured toward a pot of simmering stew over the fire. Oats, hard cheese, dried strips of salted pork, and travel bread so dense it could break a man's teeth were stacked around it. Matthew had supplemented their supplies with dried apples and nuts gathered from the lower slopes. A small cask of pickled fish sat carefully away from the fire. Arthur hoped they wouldn't have to open it.

'Your boy,' Wilfred said, looking towards the Arthur's necklace. 'He a good warrior?'

Arthur smiled, thinking of his son, Richard. 'He will be.' Not yet ten, he was besting boys years older. 'And patient enough to still listen to me.'

'Must get that from his mother.'

Arthur grunted with amusement. His wife's face involuntarily popped into his mind, with her frizzy brown hair and kind smile. Less than a week ago he'd been with them, outside their humble wooden farmstead. Her sitting on a chair, mending some clothing, while Arthur and Richard planted the spring crop. Though the ground was hard, his enjoyment in spending time with them outweighed anything else. He remembered looking up and seeing the dust created by the mounted messenger. Instantly, he knew duty called. When he glanced over at Sarah, all he saw was her understanding smile. Somehow, that made the leaving all the harder.

'How are your children?' Arthur asked, trying to break free of the memory.

'Strong. Even the girls.'

Arthur had shared meals with Wilfred's family in the Citadel of Light, where their home perched above the weapon-smith's forge where Wilfred worked. Children had filled every corner of that house, running and laughing in such numbers that Arthur had lost count.

'How many children do you have now?'

'Unless my wife has given birth since I left, nine.'

Arthur blinked, then chuckled. 'An army of little Wilfreds at your back?'

Wilfred pondered for a moment, then his laugh thundered through the cavern like an avalanche breaking loose. 'Wouldn't that be a sight?' Wilfred said, a smile splitting his face. 'My children as my war band.'

'Enough to terrify even the bravest of our enemies.'

The man nodded. It took little encouragement for him to continue boasting about his children and their various quirks. Their conversation stayed light, as these missions could drag out and you didn't burden your companions with too much idle talk. After the chatter between them had gradually faded into silence, Arthur retired to his bedroll, pulling the woolly blanket over him. His final thoughts fell on Sarah and Richard before sleep eventually claimed him.

The three of them soon fell into an easy routine, with Wilfred and Arthur taking longer watches so that Matthew could hunt.

They passed the time in different ways. Wilfred would meticulously check his weapons, while Matthew would spend a lot of time out in the mountains. Arthur had enough whiskey for a week if he rationed, or for one really great night. When he considered taking the furs and rugs outside to beat them free of dust for the third time that day, he realised how bored he was getting inside the mountain cavern.

Around midday on the fourth day, Arthur had begun to stack rocks. He would find them outside, bring them in and use them like blocks, trying to get them as high as he could. When his latest creation crumbled because of the uneven stacking, he stood, frustrated, and exited the cave.

The usual mountain winds had given way to a dense white mist that cloaked the peak like a damp burial shroud. The fog was so thick that even the stone pillars flanking the cave entrance appeared as ghostly shadows, their tops lost in the swirling vapours. Beyond them, the world had vanished into an impenetrable white void.

Matthew stood nearby, his white clothing making him appear wraithlike.

'Hard to see the enemy in weather like this,' Arthur said. 'When you think it will clear?'

Matthew only shrugged.

'Well, I have been steadily losing my sanity in there. If I don't need to keep watch, I might just indulge in some of my private stash,' Arthur said, then paused. 'There's plenty to go around.'

Matthew shook his head, never taking his eyes from the dense mist.

'Suit yourself.' Arthur retreated into the cavern's warmth, pulling out one of his untouched whiskey bottles. It wasn't long before Wilfred joined him, the two Templars sharing the bottle in companionable silence as the fire crackled beside them. Even Matthew eventually settled down with them, accepting a few measured sips before passing the bottle back. The whiskey's warmth and the fire's glow soon lulled Arthur into a deep sleep against the cave wall.

He was roused from his drunken slumber by firm hands gently shaking his shoulders.

'What?' Arthur growled, his head pounding.

Matthew's response – a single word – cut through his hangover like a blade through flesh:

'Enemy.'

CHAPTER FOUR: BY BLOOD AND LIGHT

Arthur scrambled up from his blankets, barely registering the cold stone under his bare feet as he rushed out of the cave and towards the plateau's edge where the mists had lifted. The sight stopped the breath in his throat.

A living tide of humanity was sprawled over the countryside, stretching from forest to river like a dark stain across the land. Ranks of pike militia marched beneath their home banners, siege engines rolled ponderously behind them, and through the haze, standards fluttered in the breeze, while cavalry units moved along the edges like wolves encircling a herd of prey.

The rearguard seemed endless, with supply trains of oxcarts carrying provisions and fodder, workshops of siege engineers and smiths, and endless camp followers – merchants, craftsmen and servants. Even in the light of dawn, the campfires of those not yet marching dotted the horizon like fallen stars. Forges and cookfires sent columns of smoke to create a shroud above the host.

Arthur's mind tried to make sense of their sheer numbers and failed.

'Finally,' Wilfred bellowed beside him. 'A battle worth fighting.'

'For the Light's sake, Wilfred,' Arthur cursed, shying away from the sound while rubbing his aching head to stave off his reawakened hangover.

Matthew's grim expression spoke volumes as he surveyed the approaching apocalypse.

'Come, let us get back to the Fortress,' Arthur said. 'We have a siege to prepare for.'

The other Templars immediately headed back for the cavern. Arthur was grateful they were all practised military men, as their fire was doused, their supples stowed and packs soon hefted onto their backs. The rope between them was secured before they began the journey down the peak. Necessity forced Arthur's hangover aside. As they proceeded down to the base, the First Templar juggled their own numbers in his head. With the Fortress's garrison and the Citadel's standing army, they barely broke ten thousand, while some of their soldiers were hardly more than babes out of swaddling clothes. They needed more men. Fortunately, their cautious pace gave him the time to ponder how to overcome that problem.

The journey down took hours. The unsteady footing, and constant danger of falling down the mountain, had slowed them to an agonising pace.

By the time they reached the bottom the wind had completely cleared away the mist, offering a crystal clear view through the mountain pass and of the fortress that guarded it. The open ground was a thousand yards wide and over a league in length before the fortifications began. The outer walls of the northern city arose like a stone tide; square towers punctuated the walls every fifty paces, their arrow slits staring out like dead men's eyes. The northern city spread out behind these defences before giving way to the fortress itself.

Standing at the pass's narrowest point, where the mountains squeezed, the Fortress merged with the very rock itself. Its foundations were cut from the living massif. Murder holes crowned the battlements, while galleries had been carved into the upper cliff faces, creating positions that could rain down death from above while remaining virtually impregnable. At least, that's what Arthur had thought before he'd seen that army.

No one spoke as they walked under the massive outer gates that yawned before them. Ten inches of thick seasoned oak and iron reached towards the sky that served as the doors of the northern city. Frost and age had caused webs of fine cracks to spread through the mortar, but the walls still stood firm. Two more identical gates were open further along the wall, granting access to the northern city.

Arthur spotted a guardsman whose leather armour marked him as a step above the common soldier. 'You there, young man – your name?' The youth's acne-covered face made the term "man" feel generous.

'Hadrick, sir.' The young man straightened.

'Sound the alarm, Hadrick. The rumours about the enemy army are true. I want every soldier at his post and all officers and War Priests mustered inside the keep within the hour.'

The guardsman's eyes widened, but to his credit, he didn't baulk. 'Yes, Templar.' He spun on his heel, already bellowing orders as he ran.

Within moments, the bells in the nearest tower were swinging, their frantic pealing echoing through the canyon. The other bells in the city soon joined in, their ominous symphony carrying through the canyon like whispers of doom.

Matthew shot him a questioning glance.

'I know they're at least a week away, but what better way to prepare the inhabitants than to sound the alarm?' Arthur said, as he led them through the streets towards the Fortress while the northern city erupted into controlled chaos. Soldiers streamed from barracks and guardhouses, boots thundering on cobblestones as they rushed to their assigned posts. The air was filled with shouted orders and the clash of weapons being distributed. Through it all, the relentless tolling of the bells continued.

Women gathered children from the streets, hustling them toward shelter. Some carried bundles of supplies, others clutched family heirlooms. Their faces were tight with fear, but there was still a grim determination in their movements.

A mounted patrol thundered past, pressing the three Templars against a wall. The horses' hooves struck sparks from the stone as they raced toward the main gate. Arthur's gaze drifted to the surrounding buildings – deep blues, sun-faded yellows, weathered reds and blacks. The people had painted life into the grey stone of their homes.

By the time Arthur reached the Fortress, there were several hundred soldiers mustering inside. They were all wearing church colours, the white tabard with the silver flame of Zadkiel on the front. As they got closer, they saw Peter stepping out, still wearing his shiny breastplate, a long slender blade in his hand. His raven-black hair was immaculately groomed, and he looked almost like a prince posing in armour.

'Templar,' Arthur said. 'What's the latest news?'

'I was going to ask you the same thing.'

'The incarcerated officer was right – there's a horde of enemy coming towards us. We have a week, maybe more, to prepare.'

'How big is their army?'

'If we're lucky, we'll only be outnumbered ten to one.'

Peter paled.

Wilfred grinned. 'Means more to kill.'

'Light's above, is everything about bloodshed to you?'

The big man adopted a stupid expression. 'What else is there?'

To his credit, Peter recovered quickly, a small smile appearing. 'Well, I met a lovely young lass last night. And her sister has a thing for hairy brutes.'

'Does she now?'

'Templars,' Arthur said before their banter continued too far, 'we have a siege to prepare for. Matthew, gather the scouts. Find out everything you can about the enemy: numbers, readiness, how often they shit, no detail is too small. I want written updates to read with my every meal. Understood?'

Matthew nodded, then moved off.

'Peter, how many other Templars are here?'

'Luke and James arrived just after you left. I'm surprised they haven't already accosted you with their problems.'

Arthur sighed. The two Templars, distantly related, bickered like toddler siblings. Both were extremely competent, but their attitudes wore on him.

'Best get them out of the city then,' Arthur said. 'I want them to go south and scour every village and hovel, recruiting soldiers and hiring mercenaries. Have them go as far as Dentwall.'

The other Templar's smile grew frosty. 'I'll tell them.'

'Excellent, because after that, I want you to catalogue our supplies down to the last rusty blade. Whatever provisions we have, make them better. More food, more arrows, more men, more pitch and fire oil.'

'Why am I getting all the horrible jobs?'

'Because you didn't come up into the mountains with us,' Wilfred said. 'Too busy getting your hair fluffed.'

Peter considered it then shrugged, making no further complaints. He gave a lazy wave, beckoning over two messengers, to whom he relayed a series of instructions that included looking for the other Templars and asking them to come find him.

'Wilfred—' Arthur began.

'Don't even think of sending me off. I might miss some of the fighting.'

'Establish clear lines of command throughout our ranks. Every soldier, from officers to stable boys, must know who will lead them if their superiors fall. When men die, we cannot risk a broken chain of command.'

'Aye, I can do that.'

'And check our fortifications. I want any cracks filled in, any weak spots fixed.'

'I'm not too good at that,' Wilfred said.

'Then find someone who is.'

'What are you going to do?' Peter asked.

'See to our prisoner,' Arthur said. 'He knows better than anyone how to weather this storm.'

'You might have to wait,' Peter said. 'Zadkiel is in the cell with him now.'

Arthur froze, caught between relief and trepidation. The Archangel would strengthen their defences, but the danger posed to him was too much. They'd need to send him away to safety. Catching the others' expectant looks, he cleared his throat. 'Already? Good, then I can brief them both at the same time.' He turned to leave, then paused. 'I'll return in an hour if you have questions.'

'You've given us enough to keep us busy,' Peter said.

Arthur grunted in reply and strode toward the Keep. Soldiers who were still mustering in the main halls parted before him, allowing him to quickly descended the narrow spiral staircase to the familiar torchlit corridors.

As Arthur entered the guardroom, Zadkiel was just exiting the cell. He was in his mortal form, an unassuming man with light brown hair and a soft beard. He wore comfortable clothing of common make, that was more reminiscent of a baker or a miller's, instead of a being's who was the heart of the church itself.

Arthur had seen his true form only once – a towering figure in silver armour, white eagle wings tucked behind an impressive physique. He'd been truly resplendent, but today, the Templar was grateful for his simpler appearance.

'My lord!' Arthur exclaimed, stepping forward and embracing Zadkiel in a bear hug and lifting him off the ground.

The Angel grunted, stumbling back slightly after Arthur released him. An amused smile appeared on his face. 'Arthur, as always you are the epitome of etiquette.'

Once, Arthur would have expected to be struck by lightning for treating their church's deity so casually. But that was long ago. 'Got a reputation to live up to,' he replied with an answering smile. But his mirth quickly faded. 'You've spoken to Phillip?'

Zadkiel inclined his head. 'At great length. His story is a fascinating one – his goals align with the church's, while his methods – well, they leave much to be desired.'

'He really did murder those innocents, then?'

'Yes,' Zadkiel said sadly, 'That and more, much more. But he did it because he believed it was right, even though it damned his soul.' The

Archangel paused. 'But it does ask a pertinent question, what should be done with him?'

Arthur stared, his eyes flicking towards the door and back. Despite what atrocities the man had committed, he had led a rearguard against a vastly superior foe, not only increasing their own numbers but severely hampering the enemy's movements through sabotage and guerrilla tactics. 'We need every spear on the walls. It will give him a chance to earn some redemption.'

'I couldn't agree more,' Zadkiel said with a mysterious smile.

There was something about his expression that made Arthur suspicious. Then as realisation dawned on him the feeling quickly turned to horror as he realised the Archangel's meaning. Ignoring any sense of decorum, Arthur snatched at Zadkiel's sleeve, pulling it back. A fresh cut lined his inner forearm.

'You *didn't*,' Arthur whispered, already knowing the truth. He looked once more towards the door, wondering how the Archangel could have given the man such a gift. He recalled the ritual he'd undergone to become a Templar. If you drank the Archangel's blood, given to you willingly, you could access a portion of his power. Far beyond what a gifted Priest or Bishop could access.

'Rejoice,' Zadkiel said, 'for I have found the Twelfth Templar, completing your ranks for the first time in many years.'

'But he murdered children,' Arthur said.

'Are your sins so different?'

Arthur stared incredulously at him before he found his words. 'There's a difference between murdering the innocent and being a sellsword!'

'When I came across you lying on the floor of that tavern, passed out from consuming too much ergot and sprawled in a pool of your own vomit, I reserved judgement. When you had sobered up and we spoke, your spirit shone through and I deemed you worthy to become one of my ambassadors. And I see the same light in him. He has a sense of duty taller than any of these mountains. I have given him fresh purpose and new direction. With the Light's will, his quest for redemption will drive him to greater heights.'

Arthur continued to stare at the Archangel in disbelief.

'I ask that you take him under your wing and guide him in the ways of the Templars. With proper mentorship, he may find the redemption he so sincerely seeks.'

'One day, your understanding nature may be the end of you,' Arthur said. 'I'll show the whelp around, but you've got to do me a favour in return.'

'Oh?'

'Waterlord whiskey, and plenty of it. Consider it payment for this ridiculous task.'

The corners of Zadkiel's eyes crinkled as he struggled to hold back his smile. 'You should go to him.'

'And you should go help the rest of the Keep – we have a siege to prepare for.'

Arthur waited until the Archangel's footsteps had faded away before approaching the cell. Now, right before the siege, Zadkiel had made this man a Templar?

'The Light moves in bloody confusing ways.'

CHAPTER FIVE: BATHS AND BARS

Drawing a deep breath, Arthur pushed open the heavy dungeon door. The hinges groaned, but he lost track of the sound in the brilliant radiance that forced him to shield his eyes. Phillip stood frozen in the centre of the dank cell, holy light blazing through his prisoner's rags, spilling from his skin and eyes until the stone walls themselves seemed to glow.

'Heavens above, shut that off!' Arthur shouted.

Phillip looked outright bashful as the Light winked out.

White spots danced in Arthur's vision as his eyes adjusted to the torchlight. When they'd cleared, the new Templar stood staring at him, eyebrows raised in disbelief.

'Where does all the power come from?' Phillip asked in wonder. 'It's there, as easy as moving an arm or twitching a finger, and suddenly I'm exploding with energy.'

'Probably Zadkiel's sphincter,' Arthur said dryly. At Phillip's uncomprehending stare, he could only sigh. 'I've got a feeling my humour's wasted on you. Look, I'm no theologian – I just know it's there when I need it. The power feels endless, but it's not. You'll run dry eventually, and it takes its sweet time coming back.'

'But why—'

'I know you've probably got a million questions,' Arthur interrupted him. 'But I don't have the Archangel's patience. Walk with me and we can talk.' Arthur left the cell, pausing at the guardroom door to find Phillip hovering uncertainly behind him.

'Will you get a move on? We've got a fat fort commander to humble, a siege to prepare for and ale that needs drinking. You want redemption? This is your opportunity.'

The man stood rigid as a chapel statue, his movements mechanical and hesitant, but he eventually stepped out and followed Arthur.

'Where are we going?'

'You'll see.'

Arthur led the man up the stairs and into the halls of the keep. Here they stepped outside into a scene of controlled chaos. Dozens of officers filled the courtyard, some wearing armour, others in neatly pressed uniforms. Steam rose from their breath in the crisp mountain air as they conferred in hushed clusters, studying maps and dispatches. At Arthur's entrance, all conversation quietened to a whisper, then died entirely.

Zadkiel creating another Templar had nearly driven the siege from Arthur's mind, but the sight of his gathered officers brought him back to his purpose. He glanced back at Phillip.

'If you want to be a true Templar, watch closely. This is what we do,' he said, then turned to face the waiting crowd. Opening himself to the Light, he let its power carry his voice. 'Officers! You should hear this from me first.' Every eye was fixed intently upon him. 'Whatever rumours you've heard, know this – an army hundreds of thousands strong is bearing down on us.'

None of them gave shocked gasps, but a couple swallowed hard while others gave solemn nods.

'We have the walls, the Light, we Templars, and the Archangel himself. The pass will turn their numbers to nothing – we'll whittle them down like an axe against a great tree!' He let the words settle. 'Now we prepare; this is your moment to lead. You're the finest our army has to offer.' A few puffed out their chests and one man looked around, impressively. 'Your soldiers will look to you. Keep them busy, prepare for the siege. You are officers because you know what needs to be done. See to your commands, take stock of what's needed. What you can't fix, bring to me. Can I trust you all to do that?'

A chorus of nods and a murmur of assent rippled through the crowd.

'Good. Go, and may the Light guide your paths.'

The officers looked a little confused at his abrupt dismissal. Before they could recover, Arthur was already striding through their ranks, which parted without protest. Once free of the crowd, Arthur leaned back and whispered.

'Officer speeches are usually long, boring and without much point. Keeping it short is always a surprise.' Again Phillip didn't smile, and Arthur sighed. 'Fine, let's keep it simple. What did I do?'

'Inspired our soldiers?'

'Yeah, that was part of it,' Arthur said. 'What else?'

As they continued to walk, Phillip's face creased in concentration. 'That you can use the Light to project your voice?'

Arthur frowned, realising how naturally the Light came to him now. 'Yes, that's another lesson. But more importantly, I've faced nothing like this.' He caught Phillip's look of confusion and pressed on. 'Defending a fortress against a demon-led army that vastly outnumbers us? That's unfamiliar territory. But I cannot let that show. Instead, I project control, confidence, and most importantly—' he paused, '—I delegate.'

Phillip frowned so deeply that Arthur half-expected his forehead to crack.

'These people, more or less, are just as competent as I am. If I try to manage minor details, I will miss the bigger picture and get no time for myself. And that is exactly what we're doing now.'

Phillip's expression shifted between comprehension, confusion and deep thought, and it was almost comical to see. Arthur hid a smile as he led the man through the Iron Gates and into the southern part of the city. They made it a few blocks before Arthur found the inn he was looking for. He stepped inside the two-story building where the ground floor opened into a warm, inviting taproom. Rich oak beams crisscrossed the ceiling, darkened by decades of hearth smoke. Oil lamps cast a gentle glow over wooden tables and benches, while a massive stone fireplace dominated one wall, its crackling flames pushing back the mountain chill. The air was thick with the smell of roasting meat and freshly-baked bread.

A serving woman approached, her neat braid and spotless apron a stark contrast to the Templars' dishevelled state. She was clean in all the ways they were not, something she managed to convey as she eyed Arthur's mountain climber's furs and Phillip's prisoner's rags.

'What can I get for you, gentlemen?'

'Dinner, drinks, two rooms, some clothes for my friend here. Of fine make if you have them.' Arthur said. 'And some baths?'

The woman blinked. 'Is that all?'

'While you prepare the baths, we'll take some drinks. But don't worry, we'll stand. We wouldn't want to dirty your establishment in our current state.'

She smiled, her face lighting up with the expression. 'I appreciate that. But this is a mountain inn, used to catering to the scouts of the keep. Our baths are already hot, and we have replacement clothes for you while we clean,' she said, looking at Phillip's clothes, 'or burn … your other clothes. They're not fine, but they're comfortable.'

'We've come to the right place,' Arthur said to Phillip with a wink. The two of them followed the woman as she led them to the bath-house attached to the inn. It was a low-ceilinged room lined with copper tubs, steam rising from the hot water. Part of Arthur wondered at the practicality of keeping the baths constantly warm, but in the end he merely shrugged and began to strip. In less than a minute he was sinking into the water with a grateful sigh, feeling the heat seeping into his tired muscles. The water smelled faintly of herbs – lavender and rosemary – and the warmth melted away the tension he'd been carrying since spotting the enemy army. When he opened his eyes, he saw Phillip standing nearby, still dressed.

'Get in and clean yourself up, will you?' Arthur said. 'I promise that in the days to come, this will be one of your few fond memories.'

Though still reluctant, the other man dropped his clothes and got into the bath. A flicker of pleasure crossed his face before guilt chased it away.

Arthur tried his best to ignore him and enjoy his bath. They washed in silence, neither man willing to break it. After they were finished, they dried with soft towels and dressed in sturdy woollen tunics and fur-lined leather, the serviceable garb of mountain folk – plain but warm, with the familiar scent of smoke worked into the fabric.

Arthur led them back into the common room. He saw Phillip was still moving like a man awaiting an executioner's axe.

The serving woman met them. 'Everything went well?'

'It was grand, my lady,' Arthur said. 'We'll take our meal and ale now.' He flicked a coin from his purse to her. 'And there's another if I never see the bottom of my cup.'

She fumbled the coin, barely catching it before meeting his eye. 'We've got fresh venison stew with winter vegetables, bread still warm from the hearth, and sharp mountain cheese.'

'A feast for a king,' Arthur said, taking a seat at one of the tables. He could feel the warmth of the fire, and was relishing the simple joy of being warm when the woman returned with their ale. The froth was overflowing and escaping down the sides. Arthur immediately sipped the edges of the mug before the bubbles could spill much more. The ale was dark and rich, filling a hole within him. He leaned back, enjoying the sensations of civilisation, then looked up to see Phillip standing nearby, reluctant to sit down.

'Please sit; you're making it weird.'

Phillip's eyes darted around the room like a nervous sparrow before he finally lowered himself into the chair.

'Try to relax. You're acting like a youngster who's about to kiss a girl for the first time.'

The man swallowed before speaking, his voice stilted and monotone. 'The sins I have committed should mean punishment, not,' he waved his hands, 'this.'

Arthur stared at him, suddenly realising this whole mentor thing was going to be harder than he'd thought. 'Light, Elise handles this type of thing better than I do,' he muttered. 'But when your church's patron Angel gives an order, you bloody follow it.' He reached over and slapped Phillip. The crack echoed, snapping the man from his daze until his eyes finally focused.

'Drink.'

Phillip took a swig, spilling some on his new clothes. He tried hastily to brush it off.

'Alright. We need to get that divine awe out of the way or we won't get anywhere,' Arthur said. 'You are a Templar. That means much, and nothing at the same time. But I want your take. What are Templars, exactly?'

Phillip tried to speak, swallowing before finding his voice. 'They are an extension of the Archangel, paragons of Light and virtue. They extend the will of the church—'

'Yeah, yeah, enough of that,' Arthur said. 'We are men and women just like any other. I like my drink more than most, Peter will talk your own wife into bed if he can, Wilfred will ride a hundred miles for the chance of a decent fight, while Matthew has the conversational skills of a stone. You'll find the likes of us all soon enough. All eleven,' Arthur said, then amended, 'twelve now with you, have been recalled to the Fortress. You need to forget what the priests have taught you and understand that though we have been gifted divine power, we ourselves are not divine. Zadkiel saw something in each of us he believes is worthy of granting this power.'

Some of that stunned expression returned to Phillip's gaze.

'What we do is simple in theory, but hard in execution.'

Phillip looked almost afraid to ask. 'Which is?'

'Live up to the potential that he saw in us.'

The new Templar blinked, trying to understand the ramifications of such a statement. 'But my past...'

'Tell me what you've done, and I'll judge if your self-loathing is well earned.'

Phillip looked around, then dropped his gaze to his mug. Arthur waited, his steady gaze fixed on the man. He was halfway through his second ale before Phillip finally broke.

'I didn't just kill the innocents,' Phillip said. 'I needed to do more to inspire the populace to rise against Naberius. I … I crucified them. Staked out their bodies. Mutilated them in ways meant to enrage the people into fighting. Not just the men, but the women and children too.'

As Phillip spoke, Arthur could only visualise his wife Sarah and son Richard, imagining them staked outside their burning farmstead. Revulsion rose in his throat as he stared at the newest Templar, wondering for the first time if Ashworth had been right to throw him in the deepest dungeon.

Arthur had never been good at hiding his emotions. Seeing the disgust plain on his face, Phillip fell silent, eyes fixed on his mug of ale.

Luckily, the serving woman arrived just then with a large tray laden with steaming bowls of venison stew, thick slices of warm dark bread, and wedges of pungent cheese. The rich aroma of herbs and meat filled the air between them.

Instinctively, Arthur began to eat, but he found little joy in the meal. He pushed the bowl away when there was still half left. He looked at Phillip, and though the revulsion was still there, he'd brought it under control.

'If Zadkiel sees fit to grant you redemption as a Templar,' Arthur said, 'then I must do the same.'

'I shouldn't be forgiven so easily.'

'Light, you are not,' Arthur said with a harsh laugh. 'I've done plenty I'm not proud of, but you've crossed a line that can never be uncrossed. We cannot become what we fight against.' He drew a deep breath, mastering his anger. 'I now think I know why I was chosen instead of Elise.'

Phillip looked up, his brown eyes seeming haunted. 'Why?'

'Because I'll castrate you if you even think of doing something like that again!' Arthur surged to his feet, fists clenched. 'Even now, I want to take my mace to your skull for what you've done.' He swallowed hard, glancing at the ceiling.

'Light, give me strength,' Arthur muttered, aware of the silent taproom staring at him. 'I was chosen instead of Elise because you need someone hard, not understanding. Now listen well: When the fighting starts, don't throw your life away thinking a quick death will buy redemption. You committed these atrocities in village after village, didn't you?' His anger crystallized into a sharp glare. Phillip nodded, eyes fixed on the floor.

'Then your path to redemption must match the scale of your sins. Fight to save others, yes, but stay alive to bear that burden. True redemption must be earned with time, not a swift death.

'Take the coward's path and I swear by the Light, I'll hunt you down in the next life to extract the blood price.'

Something in his words seemed to steady Phillip. He straightened.

'Good, now drink. Tonight we're brothers, and tomorrow, your redemption begins.'

CHAPTER SIX: LESSONS IN LIGHT

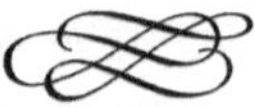

*P*hillip watched Arthur stagger from the tavern, disgust curdling in his gut. The First Templar – Zadkiel's chosen representative on Eden – couldn't even walk straight, requiring Matthew's silent assistance just to find his tent. Four nights it had been since Phillip's elevation to their ranks, and each had ended the same way. So much for joining an order of devout and professional warriors, he thought. The first night, he'd been in awe of the man and his righteous anger. But the more time he spent with him, the more he saw him as little more than a drunkard.

'He'll be fine,' Peter said, materialising beside him with a woman on each arm. The other Templar's dark hair was immaculate despite the late hour. 'Our dear First Templar has an impressive talent for sobering up when needed. Ladies, I'll have to catch up with you later – duty calls.'

The women pouted but departed with surprising grace. Phillip noted how Peter's eyes followed their retreating forms before turning to him with a practiced smile.

'Don't look so scandalised,' Peter said. 'Even holy warriors need spiritual comfort now and then.'

'Is everything a jest to you people?' Phillip asked.

'Not everything,' Elise said, approaching from the shadows. She was the first female Templar Phillip had ever met. A fit woman in her late forties, her salt and pepper hair was tied into a warrior's braid that draped down over her shoulders. 'When you've got a few greys and a child or two, you might understand better. But you are right, there are things that should be taken more seriously. The siege has stalled your military training and Arthur is too busy to see to it. Meet me here at dawn and we can train together. Until then, get some sleep.'

'Rest is for the dead!' Wilfred's booming voice carried across the courtyard as the massive Templar emerged from the same tavern. 'The boy wants to learn? Let's teach him now!'

'It's the middle of the night,' Phillip protested.

'Perfect!' Wilfred grinned, his teeth gleaming in the torchlight. 'The enemy won't always attack at convenient times. Peter! Elise! Let's show him how real Templars fight!'

'Let's keep it down. Our soldiers need their rest,' Elise said. 'But you're right; let's see what he can do.'

Before Phillip could object further, he was dragged into in the practice yard where the moon cast long shadows across the flagstones.

'Your weapon's the spear, yes?' Elise asked calmly, taking position to one side.

'An excellent choice,' Peter commented, stretching lazily. 'Though I prefer something with more … finesse.' He drew a slender practice sword with a flourish.

Wilfred snorted, hefting two wooden practice axes. 'Finesse won't save you when you're surrounded by a hundred enemies!'

'Show us your forms,' Elise instructed, ignoring the others' banter. 'While commanding the Light.'

Still apprehensive, Phillip embraced the Light, feeling its power flow through him. It was enough to illuminate his skin in the night air. When he steadied, he moved through his spear sequences. His movements were precise but occasionally jerky – the Light would surge unexpectedly, making his thrust overshoot or his parry come too strongly. The weapon felt like an extension of his arm in one moment, then foreign and unwieldy the next as the power ebbed and flowed through his muscles. He tried to maintain the steady golden sheen that marked a Templar's control, but patches of brightness still flared and dimmed across his arms with each move.

'Good foundation—' Elise nodded, '—but you're still thinking like a regular soldier. The Light gives us advantages, ones we must embrace lest it cause us limitations.'

'Limitations are for the weak!' Wilfred suddenly charged without warning, axes whirling. Phillip barely got his spear up in time to block. 'Ha! Good reactions! But you're too rigid. You need to flow with the Light!'

'Wilfred, must you always—' Peter began.

'Yes!' Wilfred laughed, pressing his attack. Phillip found himself giving ground before the man's onslaught. 'Nothing teaches better than fear of dismemberment!'

'Enough,' Elise called. 'You're teaching bad habits. Phillip, watch Peter's footwork – see how he uses minimal movement for maximum effect?'

Peter demonstrated, stepping into a tight sequence that made his practice sword whisper through the air. Each pivot flowed seamlessly into the next, his feet seeming to barely touch the ground as he wove between invisible opponents. The Light wrapped around him in a controlled sheath, intensifying with each precise strike but never flaring wastefully. His blade found its mark again and again while his body remained centred, as if he were balancing on a copper coin. Even his breathing stayed measured, the only sign of exertion being the steady golden glow pulsing beneath his skin.

'The Light enhances what's already there,' Elise explained. 'No need for excessive force when precision will do.'

'Bah! Show him how to fight multiple opponents,' Wilfred insisted. 'That's where it gets interesting!'

What followed was the most chaotic training session of Phillip's life. Wilfred would charge in with wild abandon, axes flying, while Peter would dart in with precise strikes at unexpected angles. Phillip would barely block a strike from Wilfred that should have shattered his spear shaft – only the Light flowing through the wood would keep it intact. Whenever Elise stepped in to demonstrate, she spun her practice blade in a move that covered fifteen feet in a single lunge, crossing the distance faster than any normal soldier could react. She showed him how to use the Light to sense incoming attacks, her skin glowing as she deflected three simultaneous strikes without even looking.

'The Light strengthens more than just your muscles,' she called, landing lightly after a leap that took her clear over Peter's head. 'It heightens everything if you let it.'

'Keep your Light steady,' Elise advised, as Phillip tried to fend off both Peter and Wilfred simultaneously. 'Like a candle flame, not a bonfire.'

'Break their formation!' Wilfred roared, somehow still bounding with energy. 'When you're surrounded, attack is the best defence!'

While Phillip was distracted, Peter executed an elegant disarming expulsion that sent Phillip's spear flying. 'Not everything requires brute force.'

'Enough,' Elise called finally. 'The sun's almost up.'

Phillip was drenched in sweat, his arms trembling. He'd learned more about fighting with the Light in this session that he had in all the days he'd spent with Arthur.

'Good show!' Wilfred clapped him on the back hard enough to stagger him. 'You might survive the upcoming battle after all!'

'He's not bad with that spear,' Peter admitted, 'though we'll have to work on his social graces. Can't have him scowling at every tavern wench like a disappointed priest.'

'The enemy approaches in force and you jest about taverns?' Phillip asked incredulously.

'Would you prefer for us to weep and gnash our teeth?' Peter replied. 'There's enough darkness coming without us adding to it.'

'Focus on what you've learned,' Elise said. 'Each of us serves the Light in our own way. Even Arthur ... even you.'

Her gentle words struck him like a physical blow. Phillip's throat tightened as memories surfaced – burning villages, screams in the night, all the orders he'd given. He'd thought becoming a Templar would wash away his sins, that rigid devotion would redeem him. Yet here was Elise, suggesting his past – all of it – might be a part of his path to serving the Light. He'd been so quick to judge Arthur's drinking, Peter's womanising, Wilfred's brutish nature, but who was he to cast stones?

'Speaking of our illustrious leader,' Peter said, looking up towards the Fortress. 'We should probably go and wake him. He'll want to inspect the new mercenary companies we have, and I've finally finished our supply reports.'

'I'll wake him!' Wilfred volunteered enthusiastically.

'Last time you did that, he nearly smashed your head in,' Peter reminded him. 'Let Matthew handle it – he's got the timing down to an art.'

Phillip watched them go, his feelings more conflicted than ever. Each Templar was so different from what he'd expected, from what he'd been taught they should be, and yet he couldn't deny their skill. He'd rarely been bested with weapons, but they'd humbled him a dozen times over.

In the distance, he heard Wilfred's booming laugh and Peter's smooth voice as he chatted to one of the late-night bar wenches. But Elise had remained behind, watching him thoughtfully.

'Arthur said something when he first became my mentor,' Phillip said. 'He told me you were better suited for this sort of thing.'

'I've had practice with my children,' Elise said. 'Templars are not so different. But for you, I think he is the perfect choice.'

'But he's a—' Phillip began, but hesitated.

'The Templars are brothers and sisters. No one else can carry our burdens or abilities. It means we must treat each other as intimate friends if we are to survive, so speak freely.'

Phillip considered his words. 'I just expected the First Templar of Zadkiel to act the part. We have an army bearing down on us, and he is drinking himself to insensibility every night.'

Elise smiled, though she did not answer him right away. 'What we are doing now is trying to snatch the last bits of joy that we can. I hope you enjoyed this night, because it is likely the last we will have together like this until it's all over. That is assuming we survive. None of us have forgotten, him least of all. And unlike us, he carries the burden of leadership, something that weighs heavily on him.'

Phillip frowned, thinking it through as the sun lit up the eastern horizon. Now they had stopped their exercises, the mountain wind was stealing the warmth from his muscles.

'I thought all Templars were of equal standing,' Phillip said at last.

'It is true that we answer to Zadkiel and no one else. Yet we defer to each other and our various strengths when there is a need.'

Philip stared at the woman for a long time. The tired fog of his mind was slow to come to terms with what she was trying to say.

'Is Arthur the eldest of you?'

'No, far from it,' Elise said. 'But we know each other well enough. Trust me when I say he is the best possible leader for us, and in time, you will see it too. I believe that is why Zadkiel had you apprentice under him.'

Before Phillip could answer, Elise continued: 'Come, I'll take you to your tent. You'll need some rest before the day begins.'

Phillip didn't protest, allowing himself to be led away while the Fortress was coming alive around them. Soldiers emerged from the southern gate to relieve the night watch, while craftsmen stoked forges and ovens.

'More training at midday,' Elise said simply. 'We'll work on channelling the Light more efficiently.'

Phillip nodded, waving farewell to her as he retreated inside his tent. He'd opted for a less luxurious setting, one more aligned with the officer quarters he was used to. Despite his misgivings, and the thoughts racing through his mind, his exhaustion from the night and its training session allowed him to fall asleep quickly.

He only slept a few hours, but he felt surprisingly refreshed when he got up. Outside the tent he could see Arthur standing, surrounded by a group of prosperous-looking citizens. The Templar's eyes were bloodshot but he was still speaking clearly.

Phillip crept closer, trying to overhear the conversation.

'When can you pay us?' one man was saying.

'It will be some months before you see the coin,' Arthur admitted. 'I will sign and seal the promissory notes, with a copy for each of you, to be forwarded to the citadel.'

'What you're asking,' a man with dark hair and of small stature said, 'it will ruin us if we don't get paid.'

Arthur gave a grim smile, his weathered face etched with shadows. 'I know, and part of me expects you to refuse. We're starving for supplies, scraping around for every bit of food and materiel we can find. Those murderous bastards will drown us without your help.' His voice dropped. 'If you need me on my knees begging, so be it. Our people's lives are worth more than my dignity.'

A woman who was short and plump showed a motherly smile. 'There is no need for that. You rescued my brother at the Seraph River, ensuring his goods were saved and returned to him after those bandits stole them. I know you are honourable, and I will give you my aid.'

The others around the circle slowly nodded, even the small, dark-haired man.

'Send me your prices, but please don't gouge me too much,' Arthur said.

'I make no promises,' the woman said. The others smiled, and slowly they all moved away. When Arthur was alone, Phillip moved closer.

'What was that all about?'

Arthur snorted. 'The craftsmen and merchants agreed to work on credit – keeping our forges burning, our arrows fletched and soldiers fed. The Citadel's debt grows deeper with each passing day, but the promise of future payment gives us survival, for now.'

Phillip frowned. 'Couldn't you just order them to do it under the power of a crusade or the Light?'

'It's an option,' Arthur said. 'But consent inspires them to work harder, and I feel like less of a bastard because of it.' Arthur sighed, looking towards the sun. 'Come, there's lots to do today, and I'd like to make it to the evening meal and ensure those stew sorcerers are serving something edible. But first, I need to have my morning argument with the quartermaster.'

Phillip followed the First Templar inside the Keep and into the command room. The man was surprisingly alert despite the previous night's excesses. He immediately looked over the reports and the map of the Fortress.

'Why is the inner keep still not yet supplied?' Arthur asked.

'Well, sir, the space—'

'Use the old grain storage rooms in the eastern tower. They're dry enough. If we lose the outer wall, we need the fall-back supplied and ready,' Arthur said. 'I want enough food and arrows cached in the inner keep to last a month.'

The quartermaster stared for a moment. 'Lord Ashworth's not going to like it.'

'Tell him to come find me if he has a problem. I'll be out south of the walls inspecting the mercenaries for the next few hours,' Arthur said, already leaving the room and heading back outside to where their horses were waiting for them.

Phillip silently followed him outside. He watched as Arthur greeted his own white stallion with a fond pat before mounting. The First Templar took no guards with him as he guided them beyond the fortifications and where the southern city sprawled across the plains like spilled wine, at least three times the size of its northern counterpart. The buildings were hewn from the same mountain-grey stone as the Fortress was, the houses painted even though the mountain had taken its toll and turned their once vibrant colours to faded blues, weather-worn reds, and sun-bleached yellows. Merchant signs creaked in the wind, and the occasional wisp of smoke from an early-lit forge drifted above the slate rooftops. Throughout their ride, Phillip couldn't shake what Elise had said about Arthur. He tried to quell his own disdain and study the man who was taking him through the mercenary camps.

'That one,' Arthur murmured, nodding towards one of the medium-sized mercenary companies. Their gear was serviceable, but nothing that made them stand out. 'Watch how their sergeant walks.'

Phillip observed the man's careful stride. 'He's favouring his right leg.'

'And?'

'If their sergeant is injured enough to limp but trying to hide it…'

'They're too proud or too desperate to admit weakness,' Arthur finished. 'Mark them down for second wall duty, not the gate.'

The casual insight struck Phillip like a physical blow. How many similar observations had he missed while judging the man's drinking habits? He watched as the First Templar commented on how a company's soldiers reacted to the presence of their captain, how well-maintained the weapons truly were beneath their surface polish, even which companies had been drilling together versus merely claiming to be a unified force. By the time they were done, Phillip had begun to wonder if his own guilt was projecting onto the man. Then, when Arthur suggested visiting another tavern, he realised his judgement hadn't been entirely inaccurate.

Phillip begged off, leaving the other Templar behind. He needed a place to clear his head.

Eventually he found himself at the practise yard, alone. The Light flowed through him as he executed a sequence of his forms. He would learn what he could from Arthur, but in the end he would find his own path towards serving the Light.

The enemy was coming, and ready or not, they would all face it together – drunks, warriors, charmers, and pious men and women alike.

CHAPTER SEVEN: THE COMING STORM

The sun had only just risen above the horizon when Arthur hauled himself into the stables, the familiar scents of hay and leather greeting him. Ezekiel was in the farthest stall, his brilliant white coat catching the morning light. He had been a gift from Arthur's wife years ago, her clever way of getting him out of the house so that he'd cease his constant fussing over their son. Beyond being his friend and companion, the horse reminded him of home.

Ezekiel stepped up to greet him, soft lips searching Arthur's pockets for treats. Arthur stroked his velvet nose before reaching behind the ear to scratch his powerful neck. The horse snorted, butting him with his head firmly enough to make Arthur step back. The reproach was clear.

'I know, I know I should be down here more,' Arthur said, pulling a bruised apple from his pocket. 'Been a busy week. But we might have time to stretch your legs today.'

The horse's ears pricked forward in interest while taking the apple in his mouth.

'We're going to parley with a demon army. Sounds like a grand old time, doesn't it?'

Ezekiel nickered, sounding almost enthusiastic. Not for the first time Arthur wondered how much the horse understood.

The enemy had arrived at the base of the mountain late yesterday. Today they would reach the Fortress, and Arthur had decided to meet them outside the walls.

Arthur inspected Ezekiel carefully. The stable boys were good, but the Templar still groomed him himself when he could. He began the routine that was as familiar as putting on his own boots. He worked the comb through the horse's coat, removing the loose dirt and hair while commenting on the preparations the fortress had made. More soldiers were arriving every day, their number getting close to twelve thousand, and they had enough arms and armour for another few thousand more. With a soft brush, he began to smooth down the coat until it gleamed like fresh snow. Ezekiel stood patiently, lifting each leg before Arthur even asked, letting him carefully pick out the packed dirt from his hooves and checking for any signs of thrush or loose shoes. Arthur's head pounded like a war drum, and his nausea urged him to seek a chamber pot. He pushed through it because this ritual grounded him more than any other, helping him keep from getting too deep in his cups on more than one occasion. This morning, he was doing it to soothe himself before he went to meet the demon army head on.

By the time he'd finished, the sun was peeking through the stable windows, and Ezekiel's coat glowed like moonlit silk. Arthur stepped back to admire his work, feeling more centred than he had all week. There was always more that they could have done, to groom Ezekiel and prepare the Fortress, but time had run out. The finality of it helped to calm him.

When he looked up, he realised he'd been so lost in his work that he'd missed the workers coming in to see to the other horses.

By the time he had Ezekiel saddled and out in the yard, Phillip was standing near his chestnut mare, the horse well-groomed but showing the same lean hunger as its rider – clear evidence of their months spent staying one step ahead of the enemy army.

Before Arthur could say anything, Elise led her dapple grey out of the adjacent stable blocks. On either side of the horse, several lance-sized javelins were attached to the saddle, like arrows in a quiver. Part of Arthur wondered how the creature would manoeuvre with those things strapped to it, but the horse looked at ease, maybe even a little bored.

Next to Elise was another female Templar. Tall for a woman, Rosamond wore her golden hair pulled back in a tight battle braid, revealing high cheekbones and clear blue eyes. A thin scar traced along her jaw, the only flaw in features that painters begged to capture. She wore her plate armour as naturally as a second skin, but its modest covering did little to deter potential suitors.

'Rose!' Arthur boomed, striding forward and embracing her in a bear hug. 'Wasn't sure you'd make it.'

'And miss all this? I wouldn't dream of it.' Her smile was bright as spring sunlight.

Ezekiel nudged her with his head, and she laughed, obliging Arthur's horse's need for attention by stroking his nose. Then Rose looked up, to see Phillip.

'You must be Phillip,' she said warmly, hitting him with a dazzling smile that rooted him in place. She strode forward, pulling the new Templar into an embrace. It took Phillip a moment to recover, but Arthur managed to check his laugh. The man would get used to how beautiful she was. They all did, eventually.

She pulled back, looking him up and down. 'Welcome to our family. It's been a while since we've all been together. We just need Oscar and all twelve will be here.'

'He's gathering all the recruits he can from the far reaches,' Arthur said. 'He's on his way.'

'Are things as bad as they say?'

'The Iron Gates have never been breached,' Arthur said. 'But I think there's a good chance they might be in the coming weeks.'

His admission left a silence hanging between them until Elise's banner caught the wind – Zadkiel's silver flame bright against white, a reminder of why they stood here.

'I missed your doom and gloom, Arthur,' Rose said. 'I want to head down to the walls, see this all unfold. And Arthur, try not to insult them too much. We may need to treat with them in the future.'

Arthur grunted as he grabbed hold of Ezekiel's pommel. Just before hauling himself up, he cheated a little and opened himself up to the Angel's Light, allowing it to compensate for the weight of his armour. Ezekiel, used to such treatment, braced and stepped accordingly so he didn't lose balance. Arthur turned to Phillip and Elise. 'I hope you two are ready to meet your destiny—' Arthur paused, '—or whatever hell-spawned shit this is.'

'We bear the Light's will,' Phillip said.

'Maybe it'll be enough to make the enemy back off,' Arthur said. Phillip's mouth thinned with disapproval, but Arthur ignored it. The man's awe of him had long since worn off. He shrugged, as he nudged Ezekiel forward, leading the three of them out of the Fortress stables and through the Iron Gates.

They rode through the northern city, where most of the citizens remained despite the looming threat. Soon, Arthur would have to order the soldiers to evacuate them by force. Though it would save their lives, the people would still curse his name for driving them from their homes.

When that was done, the northern city would become a war camp, Arthur thought. Yet as they rode through the streets, and he saw the large number of soldiers walking between the buildings, saluting as the Templars passed, Arthur realised it already was.

The stout oaken doors of the central northern gate stood open. Arthur slowed Ezekiel to a stop while he surveyed the battlements. Soldiers lined the walls almost to bursting. He frowned, before he realised the soldiers not on duty were only here to get a look at the enemy. Between them were barrels full of arrows, while pots of pitch were strategically placed along the parapets. The walls looked like a spotted gazelle, with fresh mortar to fill in all the gaps in the stone to make them stronger than before.

We've made our preparations, Arthur thought as he led the other Templars through the gate. They were as ready as they could be.

Stakes lined the walls, and trenches had been dug just beyond, while the rest of the pass had been cleared to create an effective killing ground for hundreds of metres beyond the wall.

The last of the scouts had returned the previous night, to relay the news that the enemy had camped out on the plains. They would likely march on the Fortress at daybreak. Arthur guessed they'd be here by midday.

'At least the preparation's over. The waiting is always the worst part,' Elise said, her breath misting in the morning air.

'You can say that again,' Arthur replied, reaching for his hip flask and sipping from it.

'It's been a week since you've been made a Templar,' Elise said conversationally to Phillip. 'How are you finding it?'

Phillip hesitated, glancing at Arthur.

'Go on,' Arthur said.

'A lot more drinking than I expected,' the Twelfth Templar answered.

Elise laughed. 'That's what happens with every task involving Arthur.'

'It's something small in the scheme of things, but people treat me differently. My brothers-in-arms, who've been through hell and high water with me, are now uncomfortable when I'm around. Whenever I visit, I can tell they're just counting down the seconds till I leave.'

Elise smiled sadly. 'Yes, I remember that happening to me, too. Though I still am friendly with my sister, my two brothers usually make excuses to leave if I turn up. It is a burden we must bear, and fortunately I have eleven Templars who are my new family.'

The woman's warm tone and motherly chatter had a calming effect on Phillip. Arthur had been so busy with the siege preparations that he'd barely gotten to know his protégé outside of the taproom. Yet now he saw the man opening up to Elise. They heard how Phillip had grown up in a military household, how his father had always pushed him to follow the Light.

Arthur waited until there was an appropriate lull in the conversation before he interposed.

'We might be here a while, so we should keep the horses warm,'

Arthur said as he nudged Ezekiel into a trot. The other two joined him as they exercised their horses along the length of the pass. The jolting of his mount's gait and the exercise of keeping his seat soon warmed him.

They were on their fourth lap when the sound reached them – a deep, rhythmic tremor that seemed to vibrate through the very bones of the mountain. The noise grew as thousands upon thousands of feet struck the earth in unison, complemented by the creak of wagon wheels, the jingle of armour and weapons, and the snorting and stamping of countless horses.

They took their positions at the centre of the pass, to meet the approaching enemy.

Their three horses consciously drew closer together in a defensive formation as the army's vanguard emerged. Sunlight glinted off forests of spear points and helmets, and black banners snapped in the wind like the wings of carrion birds. The front ranks consisted of elite temple guards, wearing polished black armour. Already they numbered in the thousands, and they were only the tip of the spear. Behind them, more regular soldiers entirely filled the pass. Their orderly lines showed at least some discipline, but even those already in the pass outnumbered the Fortress's defenders by at least ten thousand. The mountain pass became a funnel, concentrating the endless ranks into a river of steel and flesh that seemed to flow without end.

'You don't fully appreciate a hundred thousand until you see it in person,' Arthur said.

'Damn right,' Elise agreed.

They watched as dust rose in great clouds, caught by the wind and swirled upward along the mountain faces like pale ghosts. The enemy army's presence felt like a physical weight.

'I almost feel like running back inside the walls,' Elise said as the numbers continued to pour in, like an endless tide of black water through the mountain pass, each wave bringing more soldiers.

'It's times like these I'm glad my breeches are brown,' Arthur said.

'The Light will watch over us,' Phillip said quietly.

Several hundred yards from them, the enemy came to a stop. The commanders wore identifiable white plumes in their helmets while the Priests of Lucifer rode nearby, their robes as black as night.

Arthur glanced at Elise. 'They outside of our catapult range?'

'Well outside,' she said without hesitation. 'Mine too.'

Arthur gave an amused smile. They all practised with the Light to enhance their military prowess. Elise had the gift of throwing javelins that could sail hundreds of yards, hitting her target two out of three times.

'It's part of why I brought you – so you can get a good look at their hierarchy and know who to target,' Arthur said.

'I thought you just loved my conversation.'

Arthur paused. 'No, that's definitely not it.'

Elise laughed aloud.

'They're moving,' said Phillip.

Seven horsemen rode towards them, all wearing the black robes of Lucifer's priesthood and riding upon black horses.

'Embrace your power, young one,' Elise said, 'but do it subtly. If they strike with their magic, the Light will shield us.'

'They'd disrespect the banner of truce?'

'No point being unprepared,' Arthur said as he opened himself up to the Angel's Light. The power moved through him, banishing weariness and leaving him feeling as if he could lift a mountain.

The seven Priests approached like pieces of living shadow, their black robes absorbing the sunlight. Their leader's dreadlocks flowed behind him like dark serpents as he guided his midnight stallion forward. The skull-topped staff across his saddle seemed to watch them with its hollow eyes.

'Well met, Zadkiel's chosen,' he said, voice smooth as silk over steel. 'I am Guillamere, High Priest of Lucifer.'

'Great, now that you've introduced yourself can you turn around, head back to the north and just fuck off?' Arthur's crude response felt like a stone thrown at a glass wall.

Elise's quiet snort beside him carried more weight than laughter.

'There is no mistaking the First Templar's notorious sense of decorum.'

'Lot of big words in there.'

Guillamere ignored the barb, looking over towards Elise. 'The matron of the Templars. What an honour.'

'I will look for you on the battlefield,' Elise said.

If the threat had had any effect, the priest gave no sign as he addressed the last of their party. 'Which means you must be Phillip. Your actions in the northern kingdoms were quite a nuisance – at first I was surprised you were not killed for your crimes, but it only reminded me of the Light's hypocrisy. They like to condemn injustice and bemoan sin, but when it brings results,' he exclaimed with a wave of his hand, 'well, they promote you to the high station of Templar!'

'Word travels fast,' Arthur said. It had only been a week since the Twelfth Templar had been made and no traders had been permitted outside the gates, which made Arthur wonder how the Priest knew. It was a problem that required more thought. He focused back on Guillamere. 'What do you want?'

'My Lord Naberius wishes to journey south. Things would be much easier for you if you'd let us through.'

'I'm afraid I can't do that,' Arthur said.

The man gave a wide smile, as though explaining things to a child. 'It is not an option. This is a courtesy in case you wish to flee.'

'Why do you want to invade the south?'

'My lord wishes it. That is enough.'

'He's been moping around the northern kingdoms for the last few decades, trying to kill the chained bitch herself,' Arthur said. 'Why the change?'

'Maybe he wishes to visit the southern shores and see if they'll agree with his complexion,' Guillamere said with a wry smile before his face turned serious. 'But you insult me if you think I will give you the information so easily.'

'Are we not merely exchanging pleasantries?'

The High Priest looked bemused. 'The First Templar's reputation is such a curious mix, and I am pleased to see you live up to it. But I grow tired of these games – if you truly wish to stand against us, know that our numbers measure beyond counting.'

'And they will smash against our walls like water on a rock.'

Guillamere stared at Arthur for a long time before answering: 'An apt analogy. Rock crumbles to the continual pounding of the waves, which is exactly what will happen.' He looked at the Templars as a parent would an enthusiastic child. 'Treat the time you have left as a gift. The sun has set on the Citadel of Light.'

'You really think that we can't stop you?'

'Me?' Guillamere said. 'I am but a lowly servant. It is not I you should worry about. It is my master who should concern you,' Guillamere said, with a sweep of his hand.

While they were talking, Naberius had emerged around the pass. The demonic three-headed hound towered above his army, his massive form casting a shadow that seemed to rival that of a manor house. Muscles rippled beneath black fur that looked like spilled oil. Three heads rose from his shoulders, the faces scanning the rest of the army as all six of his blood-red eyes swept across the battlefield. The very air seemed to grow colder in his presence.

'Naberius was responsible for the fall of Michael,' Guillamere said, his outward calm unflappable. 'Now he seeks Zadkiel's wings to add to his hunting trophies.'

Phillip nudged his horse forward, anger clearly getting the better of him. Arthur held up a hand.

'Do not let him goad you. Naberius is a coward who will never take on a fair fight.'

'As much as I enjoy trading pleasantries,' Guillamere said, leaning forward in his saddle, 'the terms are simple. Vacate the Fortress and allow us to pass unfettered. If, in three days' time, the gates remain closed, know that we will be coming through regardless. Your answer merely determines the blood price.'

'Generous terms,' Arthur said.

'Considering your position, they are,' Guillamere smirked, wheeling his mount and leading the priests back towards their lines.

'We're not going to live through this one, are we?' Elise asked.

'Probably not,' Arthur said. 'But we can still do our most sacred task.'

Elise nodded thoughtfully.

'What's our most sacred task?' Phillip asked.

'We can't let Zadkiel's bleeding heart put him at risk,' Arthur said. 'We need to convince him to leave us here.'

CHAPTER EIGHT: ANGELS AND RAVENS

The Keep's courtyard was alive with activity when Arthur returned. Peter and Matthew were organising the latest arrivals, their voices carrying over the clashing of weapons being distributed and the stamping of the horses. Elise broke away to join them – all the Templars were gathering together on Arthur's orders. They needed to convince Zadkiel to leave, though none relished the task. The Fortress might fall, and men might die, but losing the last Archangel would doom them all.

'Arthur, you old dog!' a voice boomed from across the square. He turned to see a familiar face, though he couldn't quite place it. The man's braided hair and beard had once been a dark, lustrous mane, but they were now dominated by shades of grey. Despite his medium height, his powerful build strained against the buckles of his armour. The man strode towards him, a huge grin plastered on his face. 'Shit, you've gotten old.'

Such brash insolence stirred old memories to life.

'Cormac of the Wild Ravens,' Arthur said finally. 'I'm surprised you've lived this long with that mouth of yours.'

The man threw back his head and laughed loudly, and stepping forward, they clasped hands. 'Don't think you've met my son, Riordan.'

At his side stood his mirror image, carved twenty years younger, though where the father's braids had gone grey, the son's blazed like fresh copper.

'Templar,' Riordan said with a bow.

'Save the formality – Arthur and I have history. He still owes me for that mess at the Seraph.'

'As I recall,' Arthur said mildly, 'you broke ranks, destroyed a dam, and nearly drowned us all.'

'Didn't hear you complaining when the enemy reinforcements had to swim upstream.'

'No.' Arthur grinned. 'That part worked out rather well.' He frowned. 'I thought you'd sailed west years ago.'

'We've had our share of good fights over in the Empire, always plenty of rebellions to fight with or against,' Cormac allowed. 'But there's nothing like the home country. News of the dog's army reached us in the east; couldn't let you have all the glory down here.'

'The news has reached even there?' Arthur asked. There were always rumours of armies massing beyond their borders – south, west, and north – but something about this felt different. If Phillip's warning hadn't come when it did, they may have fallen before they could even muster their armies. But that thought would have to wait for another time. 'Sure you picked the right side?'

'Course I am.' Cormac's grin never faltered. 'Not from any sort of moral high ground. You guys pay your mercenaries, they don't.'

A grunt sounded from behind him. Arthur turned to find Phillip rigid with barely contained disdain.

'New Templar?' Cormac asked.

'He's still learning the role,' Arthur said, then addressed Phillip directly. 'Sometimes it means you have to deal with the scum of society – they come in handy sometimes.'

'Glad to be of service,' Cormac said with a mocking bow. 'You free for a drink tonight? Be good to catch up on old times.'

Phillip's contempt became almost tangible.

'He one of those righteous twats?'

'Father, by the Light,' Riordan said, scandalised, while Phillip was practically spluttering.

'Like I said, he's still learning,' Arthur said.

Before Cormac could respond, a hush fell over the square like a heavy blanket. All conversation died mid-word. Arthur followed the sudden silence to its source. Zadkiel was approaching, his commoner's dress and unassuming appearance at odds with the power that seemed to bend the very air around him. The Archangel's brow was creased as he strode directly towards Arthur.

'Archangel,' Arthur said.

Even Cormac looked momentarily stunned, giving him an earnest bow.

'I know what troubles you, but I will not allow you to stop me at the pass,' Zadkiel said, then touched his brow with a faint smile. 'Though perhaps I should choose my words more carefully.'

Arthur smiled briefly. 'Yes, we want you to leave – and you must do it.'

'You seek the counsel of the Templars to sway me,' Zadkiel said, 'but I will not be moved. The Darkness masses at our gates, and Light must answer shadow.'

'Their army is large enough to make ramparts out of dead bodies, and you are the last Archangel. If we lose you, then the war against the Darkness is lost.' He pointed at Zadkiel's chest. 'Your fight is not here.'

'If not here, then where? Every soul on the walls is pledged to the Light, and who would I be if I were to abandon them now?'

Though the Angel had not raised his voice, there was a determination in his tone. Arthur wished Peter were here; the man had the silver tongue to persuade him. He swallowed.

'It comes down to simple numbers: We need more. Your fight is out there,' Arthur said, waving to the south. 'With the power you have gifted the Templars we can fight in your stead, but you, more than any number of recruiters or conscriptors, can gather the troops we need to withstand them.'

Zadkiel was about to argue, but there was enough truth to Arthur's words to make him hesitate.

'Speaking of which,' Cormac said, cutting through the tension in the courtyard, 'my men and a couple of the Templars were just planning a trip into the mountains. Thought we might arrange a proper welcome for the enemy in the pass – nothing quite like a few thousand tons of snow and ice to greet an army.'

Zadkiel swung his gaze towards the man. 'You were?'

Arthur felt a beacon of hope at this outrageous lie, but he tried to school his face to indicate that it was the truth.

'Perfect timing, really,' Cormac said, his lies flowing smooth as honey. 'Spring thaw will weaken the ice up there. For a hundred gold pieces, the First Templar's buying himself an avalanche at a bargain.'

Zadkiel's eyes widened at the amount, then he glanced at Arthur, who nodded. 'That is quite a tidy sum.'

'We're quite the band,' Cormac said.

Zadkiel's eyes softened for a moment before he looked back at Arthur.

'Archangel, please,' Arthur said, 'I am begging you. We cannot fight at our best with our concern for you clouding our thoughts. Trust in us now. We will give you the time you need; make sure you use it so we can win.'

Arthur desperately hoped that the Angel wouldn't see through the lie.

Zadkiel stood in silence, his mortal form seeming to flicker as divine power roiled beneath the surface. His eyes swept across the courtyard, taking in each face turned toward him – soldiers, servants, and faithful all watching their Archangel.

'I will find you your army.' He spoke as if measuring each word. 'Though it pains me to leave these walls when darkness gathers.' His shoulders straightened, and for a moment his simple clothes seemed to shimmer with a ghostly armour. 'Begin the preparations; I would depart before my resolve weakens further.'

The Archangel soon moved away to wait while his escort gathered, leaving Arthur alone with Cormac, Riordan and Phillip. He looked at the leader of the Wild Ravens.

'That idea about the mountains was clever – is it actually possible?'

Cormac titled his hand in a side-to-side gesture. 'Never tried it before, but with a couple Templars backing us? We'll make it happen.'

Arthur considered, but then shook his head. 'I can't; I need all the Templars on the walls.'

'But there's twelve of you!'

'Eleven,' Arthur corrected grimly. 'Oscar's still delayed with the coastal cities' war.'

'Still, just one would—'

'I need them all on the walls,' Arthur said, cutting him off. 'If I had fifty Templars, I still wouldn't spare one.' The memory of that endless sea of soldiers made his voice heavy. 'The walls and the Templars are all that balance the scales against the horde at our gates.'

Cormac stared at him, his gaze incredulous. 'Time isn't on our side. I want to bring the mountain down *before* they breach the walls. I'm not sure I can do that without a Templar.'

Arthur grunted; the man had a point. 'Give me tonight to work on it, and I'll figure out a compromise.'

Cormac's eyes assessed him for a long moment before he shrugged. 'Alright, then I'd best get my men ready for some mountain climbing.'

'See Matthew, he can get you sorted with the right equipment.'

'He got my hundred gold, too?'

'You get two gold now, the rest when you get back,' Arthur said.

Cormac grinned. 'More than I was expecting – excellent.'

As the mercenary moved off, Phillip looked at First Templar with amazement.

'What?' Arthur said.

'You talked down an Angel and convinced a mercenary band to go on a mountain suicide mission for two gold pieces.'

'He might surprise you,' Arthur said, with an optimism he didn't feel. 'Come on, we need to find Zadkiel's master of the guard.'

'What for?'

'To ensure Zadkiel stays away.' Arthur didn't bother to elaborate. The Light Commander stood out even in the crowded courtyard – a giant wrapped in ornate armour that caught the sun like a beacon. Gold inlay traced sacred symbols across his breastplate, each piece carefully crafted to suggest the divine presence. It was elaborate misdirection, designed to draw assassins' blades from his true charge.

'First Templar,' he said easily.

'Light Commander,' Arthur said in reply. 'We need to talk.'

The man met his gaze, then quickly shouted orders at those nearby, ensuring preparations for their departure would continue in his absence.

'Yes, Phillip, you come too.'

Arthur led them into the shadow of the Fortress walls, where the space between buildings offered them some privacy. They drew close together, shoulders forming a barrier against prying eyes and curious ears.

'What I'm about to ask you borders on heresy,' Arthur said, his voice barely above a whisper. He met the commander's eyes. 'We must ensure Zadkiel never returns to these walls.'

The man paused, looking Arthur up and down. 'Okay, and how is that heresy?'

'Oscar marches from the coastal cities with his army. You'll meet him on the road,' Arthur said. 'Work with him and use whatever means necessary to keep Zadkiel away from here. Lie to him; deceive him. If your soul burns for it later, so be it.'

The commander looked at him for a long time, his eyes briefly glancing at Phillip before they turned back to Arthur.

'Are you so certain of defeat?'

'Look beyond the pass – their numbers blacken the land like locusts. They'll feed us to their war machine until our corpses choke these walls. Zadkiel might best Naberius in single combat, but the Hound will throw a thousand souls into the breach just to land one poisoned blade.' Arthur's jaw clenched. 'Convince Oscar and keep the Archangel away. This betrayal may damn us, but it will save him.'

'Will Oscar agree?'

'He won't like it, but he will understand.'

The man barely hesitated. 'I will do as you ask.'

Relief flooded through Arthur with such force that his knees nearly buckled. Each breath came easier, as if chains had fallen from his chest. The burden of protecting an Archangel from himself – at least that weight was lifted. He gave the commander a smile that held volumes of unspoken gratitude. 'Thank you.'

The man nodded, knowing the burden he had just taken, before moving off.

'You presume to manipulate the Archangel?' Phillip asked after he'd left.

'For his own good,' Arthur said, feeling the weight of the necessary betrayal settling deeper into his bones. 'First we drink, then we'll start on the mountain of work between us and this siege.'

CHAPTER NINE: DAWN'S DEPARTURE

$\mathcal{B}$oot steps crunching on frozen ground were all the warning Arthur had before his tent flaps burst open, sending a beam of Light directly onto his face.

'Argh,' Arthur shouted, trying to shield his eyes from the searing radiance. The tent flap closed, the light faded, and Arthur squinted as the tent slowly came into view. It held a measure of comfort – a worn but serviceable camp bed with woollen blankets, a solid oak table, and several locked chests containing maps and documents. It wasn't as lavish as Peter's quarters, but Arthur had made it his own, particularly with regard to the cabinet containing his collection of whiskey.

'It's time,' Phillip said brusquely.

A week ago the man had been timid whenever he woke Arthur, but now he did little to hide his annoyance.

'What happened last night?' Arthur asked, sitting up and immediately regretting it. His skull felt like it was being crushed in a vice, each heartbeat sending waves of nausea throughout his body. He held his head still, trying to make it stop spinning.

'You and that mercenary got into some sort of drinking competition, except neither of you really knew the rules. At one point you'd just laugh, point at each other and say *drink*.'

'That'd explain it,' Arthur said, shaking himself. He briefly opened himself up to the Light. The immediate feeling of being hung over retreated, until he felt somewhat human again. There were limitations to the Angel's gift, but it allowed him to get up to sit at his dining table, where his breakfast had been laid out. The mountain air had already chilled it. He took the jug of water and drank, a fair amount of liquid flowing over his beard and down his hairy chest. It made him feel better, but when he looked up he caught Phillip eyeing him with disdain.

'I'm a charming man, I know,' Arthur said, still holding onto the Light to aid him while he turned to the tray that contained his breakfast. Dark bread made that morning, hard mountain cheese, dried apples, and salted mutton. A pot of herb-steeped tea had gone cold, but Arthur was grateful for anything that might settle his stomach.

Phillip waited patiently while Arthur combed his hair, donned his plate mail and belted the mace around his waist. He ate between his preparations. By the time he stood up, he was ready. He shook himself like a dog, then slapped his face a few times to wake himself up.

Arthur then braced himself and released the Light.

The armour suddenly felt heavier; the tiredness had crept back into his eyes, but he felt considerably better than when he'd first woken up. He squared his shoulders and looked at Phillip.

'Now I'm feeling as fresh as a daisy,' Arthur said, striding out into the brisk mountain morning, the sun shining down brightly on the Fortress.

The courtyard was a blaze of light and motion as the Angel's contingent assembled. Banner-bearers held standards aloft depicting golden wings on fields of white, while white-cloaked guards with silver spears formed a protective ring around Zadkiel himself. Pack mules loaded with supplies and additional guards completed the procession.

Zadkiel sat atop his horse in the centre, dressed in inconspicuous white clothing. It was tastefully done, so that he looked slightly underdressed compared to his guard. He spotted Arthur coming towards him, and his smile was like the sun breaking through the clouds.

'I was worried you wouldn't make it,' the Archangel said.

'Wouldn't dream of missing it,' Arthur lied.

'Thank you, Phillip, for making sure he didn't.'

'Of course, my lord.' Though Phillip's tone was neutral, his disapproval was apparent.

'Keep an open mind, Phillip, and you will better serve the Light,' Zadkiel said, and the Twelfth Templar looked like he'd been slapped.

Arthur turned away to hide his smile. At the same time, he caught the commander's eye across the yard. Their glances met, and the man's subtle nod confirmed that their accord remained – at least Zadkiel would be safe.

The Archangel's voice rang clear as a bell as he addressed the Fortress courtyard. 'Keep the faith, hold on to your courage and wait for my return with a host large enough to banish the enemy.'

The response rippled through the courtyard like waves in a pond. Veterans stood straighter, their hands tight on their weapons, while the gathered civilians murmured prayers. The Archangel's gaze swept over them all, and though it obviously pained him, he turned his horse toward the southern gate.

The procession's departure echoed through the courtyard, each hoof strike on the cobblestones hammering against Arthur's temples. When the last horse had passed through the gates, he pressed his fingers against his throbbing head.

'Drank too much again?' Peter asked.

Arthur opened his eyes. The man stood before him, immaculate as ever – freshly bathed, perfectly groomed, his plate mail shining like a mirror.

'Not possible,' Arthur answered.

'I'm not so sure about that. I think I got drunk from the fumes alone when you stumbled into my tent last night.'

'I … what?' Arthur asked. He had no memory of that.

'You came in, babbling about a secret meeting – wanted me, Wilfred, Matthew, Elise, and Rose to gather after Zadkiel's departure.'

That felt vaguely familiar. 'Right. Well, make sure—'

Peter cut him off. 'Yes, the wall's covered. I made sure Paul thought we needed him up there, and even listened to Luke and James complain about it for ten minutes.'

The fog in his mind began to clear. He remembered bursting into Peter's tent, and something else.... 'Was there a young lady with you at the time?'

Peter laughed. 'There was, but truth be told, I think she found the whole thing exciting.'

Arthur stared at the man, then shrugged. 'When did I set the meeting?'

'In less than an hour.'

Arthur grunted. 'I might lie down until then.'

'No, you bloody won't,' another voice called. It was Cormac.

The man looked none the worse for wear. Considering Arthur's hangover, it felt dishonest somehow. 'How are you still upright?'

'Because waiting around is a luxury – the sooner we get up the mountain, the better we'll be. I spoke to that mute Templar.'

'Matthew,' Arthur amended.

'That's it. He uses words like a miser spends coins, so I didn't want to waste any on pleasantries. He gave me a map with the goat trails we've got to take to get into the southern ranges. Going up there during the spring thaw means we'll have to go slow. All I need is that Templar your promised me.'

'I, uh, what?'

'You promised me a Templar.'

'No, I didn't,' Arthur said. At least he was pretty sure he hadn't.

'You said if you couldn't find something to substitute what we needed, I'd get a Templar. If I get to pick, I'd like the pretty one.'

A curtain lifted in Arthur's mind; he really needed to ease off the cups. He remembered the discussion, but the solution stayed buried in the grog-enhanced fog.

'I believe I am to be your companion,' a man waiting under a nearby canvas shelter said. He was clad in a green robe, covered by a breastplate adorned with intricate floral patterns. His metal helmet boasted a collection of colourful feathers that could rival any peacock's. A mason's hammer hung from his belt. 'I have been paid in full and am ready to depart.'

'You?' Cormac asked incredulously. 'Him?' He said, turning to Arthur. 'He doesn't have the muscle to chop a twig.'

'It's alright,' Peter said, then whispered to Arthur. 'You barged in on Elise too last night. She followed your instructions just like I did.' He nodded toward where an anvil stood beside the lone mercenary.

Fragments of Arthur's memory were slowly piecing themselves together. There was something special about the man's hammer, which was why the anvil was there.

'I believe a demonstration is in order—' Arthur guessed at the name, '—Zahir, if you please?'

The man didn't correct him. The brightly armoured mercenary stepped up to the anvil and drew his mason's hammer. He paused, as if centring himself. Arthur felt as if the surrounding air were drawing breath, before the man slammed the hammer down onto the flat metal surface.

The sound echoed through the Fortress like a gong, causing soldiers to hesitate in their drills, while workers and merchants paused in their tasks to stand and stare. Even the Fortress cats, usually intent on their morning mouse hunt, stopped to observe the commotion.

The hammer fell again. This time the anvil cracked like a woodsman's log. Another strike would split it entirely.

'That's enough,' Arthur called out. 'No need to destroy the anvil.'

Zahir gave a sharp nod, replacing the hammer on his belt.

'Not a Templar, but someone with a magic hammer. Good enough,' Cormac grunted. 'We'll figure out a way to make this work. Come on Zahir, let's go.'

'I think not,' Zahir said. 'At least not yet. You are the commander of the Wild Ravens, are you not?'

'That's me,' Cormac said, holding out his hand. Zahir regarded it like a dead fish before giving it the briefest of shakes.

'But first, we must be clear: I carry my own gear and tend to my own needs. I serve at the Light's command – not yours.'

Cormac shot Arthur a sour look and whispered, 'I've got a feeling this'll be a long trip.' He sighed wearily before turning to Zahir. 'Fine, whatever you want. We leave within the hour.'

Zahir gestured at his pack behind him that looked already filled and ready.

'Right then, let's go,' Cormac said, then in an aside to Arthur, 'You'll owe me for this.'

Arthur watched the older captain rejoin his mercenaries. They were a hard-bitten lot, their armour a mix of stolen pieces and trophy gear, faces weathered by mountain winds and desert suns while most were marked with scars. Riordan, Cormac's son, caught his eye. The mirror image of his father, the younger man went to each mercenary, conversing easily while he checked his gear and needs. Arthur prayed they made it back. He needed more commanders like those two.

'The more you drink, the more schemes you hatch – and the worst part is, they work,' Peter said.

'It's my gift,' Arthur said. 'Can you get the others to join me in my tent when they arrive?'

'Sure.'

Arthur nodded his thanks and headed back inside his pavilion. Even that short outing had been a lot. He sat down, grabbing one of the bread rolls and tearing it open, pleasantly surprised to find it still slightly warm. He lathered it with butter and honey. By the time he was done, he resealed it and brought it to his mouth. Just as he was about to take a bite, Phillip appeared at the tent flaps.

'Come in,' Arthur said.

The Templar hesitated, looking much like had on that first day, timid and unsure of himself.

'What's on your mind, Templar?'

'I—' Phillip began, stepping inside and hesitating. 'I have forgiveness to ask of you.'

Arthur stared. Some of his hangover had retreated, but not quite enough to easily piece together what the man was asking.

'What?'

'I still think you drink too much,' Phillip said.

'That much has been obvious.'

'But I realise that I have been closing myself off to the results you've been achieving, regardless of your vices. You are my mentor, not the other way around. I think my own guilt has been manifesting and I projected it onto you.'

Arthur regretfully put the bread down. Whatever the man was about to say, he felt like it deserved his attention.

Phillip walked to the nightstand, where several bottles of whisky stood on display. He picked one up – Arthur's only bottle of Water-lord Whiskey. Arthur tensed, half-rising from his seat, fearing the Templar might destroy it in some misguided act of righteousness.

'When I became a Templar, I fervently believed it was my path towards expunging my sins. That my faith would cleanse my soul. But Zadkiel's words opened my eyes: He accepts you for who you are. Though I know I shouldn't, I still questioned it, because your excesses had blinded me. It is this morning, clearer than ever, that I see a strategic brilliance that I am only just beginning to grasp.'

'Take it easy on the compliments,' Arthur said. 'I'm just a functioning drunk.'

'No, you are more than that. You serve the Light in your own manner, and I was a fool not to see it. So please, I ask for your forgiveness.'

'Yeah, don't worry about it.'

Phillip stared.

Arthur took a deep breath, composing himself before he looked again at the younger Templar. 'You're not the first to judge me for drinking too much. I do it myself, but for the moment I have bigger problems,' Arthur said. Then on seeing that Phillip's expression was still dumbfounded: 'Look, if you want to make it up to me, join me for a drink tonight.'

Phillip, thankfully, put down the priceless bottle of whiskey. 'Alright then.'

Arthur reached over to pick up the bread roll again, just as Elise opened the tent flap and stepped inside. She eyed the rugs on the floor, then the other decor.

'This place really needs Sarah's touch.'

Arthur looked around at the furnishings. 'What's wrong with it?'

Before she could answer, Wilfred stepped inside, carrying his axes in his hands rather than in the loops on his belt or back. Peter and Matthew followed him in. The last to enter was Rose.

'Well, this is nice and cosy. I wish we could all get together more often,' Rose said as she took a seat at his table. The place was a little cramped for seven armed and armoured Templars.

Arthur took one last mournful look at the bread roll before putting it back on the table.

'Ladies, gentlemen, what I'm about to ask of you I want to stay between us alone. Questions or speculation must remain with those present.'

'What about the other Templars?' Elise asked.

'I fear the enemy has ears inside the keep, so if you tell them, make sure you're not overheard.'

They nodded. Arthur leaned forward.

'Matthew, are you sure of the integrity of the gates and walls?'

The man inclined his head, saying nothing.

'At some point today or tonight, I expect some sabotage, focusing on our defences. Let them do what they will, as long as it's easily repaired. Note what they do and where, then report back to me.'

Matthew frowned, but he eventually assented.

'Elise, I want the best marksmen on those walls tonight, but keep them quiet and out of sight.'

'You suspect a night attack?'

'Just being careful.'

'I'll see to it.'

'Wilfred, you ready for a fight?'

'Do bears shit in the woods?'

That caused Arthur to blink. 'Yes, good. I want you and your best War Priests at the ready. You know, the really crazy ones who would jump into a fight against two dozen Black Guards without hesitation.'

'All my Priests are like that.'

Arthur chuckled. 'Well, no need to leave anyone out.'

'And me?' Peter asked.

'I want you and Rose to assist the others, help them keep it discreet. I don't want anyone not directly involved to know anything about it.'

'That'll be hard.'

'I've got faith in you,' Arthur said.

'You know that doesn't make it possible, right? It's not a magic sentence.'

'Just act like you're sneaking one of your mistresses around,' Arthur said.

Peter's face soured.

'We'll see it done,' Rose said with a laugh.

'What's this all about?' Matthew asked.

That caused everyone to stop and stare. It was the most they had heard Matthew say in a long time. Arthur had forgotten how surprisingly deep his voice was.

'Could be nothing, but I've got a hunch that I want to see played out.'

He was grateful that they all trusted him, that this explanation was enough.

'If there's no more questions,' Arthur said, and when no one spoke, he tapped his hands on the table. 'Alright, Templars. You have your tasks. Let's see it done.'

They filed out, leaving only Phillip and Arthur in the tent.

'What are we going to do?' Phillip asked.

'Regardless of what happens tonight, our walls will soon be tested, and there's at least a dozen things that still need doing. We'll accomplish what we can, then there's a taproom near the northern walls that has a spectacular view of the gates.'

CHAPTER TEN: THE OWL'S CALL

Dusk had already settled over the Fortress as Phillip followed Arthur through the streets. Despite the late hour, the northern city bustled with nervous energy – the citizens unable to rest with the enemy army camped outside their walls. All but the most stubborn residents had been evacuated south of the keep, their homes now occupied by soldiers, transforming the northern city into a makeshift war camp.

A mountain chill was sweeping through the streets, and Phillip tugged his cloak closer to him. They'd traded their distinctive plate mail for common leather armour at Arthur's insistence – a choice that allowed Phillip to carry his preferred weapon without drawing attention, as spears were common among the rank and file.

Near the northern gates stood an inn, its grey stone walls weathered with age-worn cracks. Arthur led them inside and straight to the rooftop staircase. The roof itself was arranged with water barrels lining the edges, the chimney stack encircled by racks of drying herbs, while two fur-laden chairs sat in one corner.

'Can you tell me what we're doing here now?' Phillip asked.

'Acting on a hunch,' Arthur said, his low voice carrying through the wind. He threw a blanket at Phillip. 'No fire, and no use of the Light. We don't want to draw any attention.'

Phillip settled into one chair, wrapping the blanket around himself against the chill. From this vantage point, he could see how the buildings nearest the walls had been systematically demolished and cleared away, creating both a mustering ground for defenders and a killing field if they were forced to retreat. The tactical significance of their position was just sinking in when Arthur rematerialised beside him, offering a mug of frothy ale.

Phillip took the proffered mug, his eyes moving from the drink to the nearby cask as he pieced together Arthur's intentions for the evening.

'Don't you think that we should, you know—' Phillip hesitated; he was trying to keep an open mind, '—stay sober in case the attack starts tomorrow?'

'Not sure I can think of anything worse.'

Phillip bit back the first reply that came to mind. Instead, he took the mug and considered it.

'You're not going to get off my back about the drinking, are you?' Arthur said. Then, when Phillip remained silent, he sighed. 'I know it's not the most noble of pastimes.'

'So why do you do it?'

Arthur stared into his mug, his eyes growing so distant that Phillip began to doubt that he would answer. When he finally looked up, all traces of his usual mirth had vanished.

'We are the vanguard of the Light, always first into the fight, always at the heart of the battle. The horrors we witness ... they crack something inside you, piece by piece. I've seen it consume soldiers – their nights shattered by screams, their sleep poisoned by memories of what they've done. There are people like Wilfred, who revel in battle, and those like Elise, who are unflappable no matter what they see. But for the rest of us, we are affected. I can already see it beginning with you, and—' Arthur hesitated, a faint look of disgust crossing his face, '—what you did in the north. Now, given the chance, would you go back and change what you did?'

The sudden gravity of Arthur's question caught Phillip off-guard, leaving him silent as he wrestled with his answer. Finally, he shook his head. 'I would. There were other ways to achieve the same results.'

Arthur inclined his head knowingly. 'We are not omnipotent, and often we must stain our souls with evil deeds so that Light can prevail. There is no retirement for people like us, so we must find a way to cope. I deal with it by drinking, in the same way silence works for Matthew and womanising distracts Peter.'

Phillip was beginning to see the logic in the man's choices. 'Doesn't it make it worse in the long run?'

'Do you know what I see at night when I go to sleep?' Arthur asked, ignoring the question. 'I dream of a river. On the other side are all the people who have died because of me. Those I've killed stand next to those who have died on my orders, and...' he hesitated, '... those who have died because of my incompetence.' The man paused, glancing up at the stars that blanketed the sky. He studied them for a long moment before he returned his attention to Phillip. 'And now I've got the lives of our entire nation resting on my shoulders, on my decisions.'

The words between them felt as heavy as stone. Phillip looked for something to say, but Arthur continued before any words could come.

'When I see my son's face, bright with mischief, or feel Sarah's warm embrace ... for a moment, the demons grow quiet. Without those...' Arthur trailed off, before taking a long drink from his mug, draining almost half of it. 'Drinking is one of my few refuges, which grants me a few hours of sleep. It helps remind me there is some joy in this world.'

Phillip took a long look at his mug before drinking from it, too.

'You could pass command off to someone else.'

Arthur smiled wanly. 'None of the other Templars want it, and I don't trust anyone beyond them.'

'There are generals here.'

'None worth their salt.'

'I thought General Wolfhaven pulled off that bait and strike manoeuvre against the coastal cities' armies,' Phillip offered.

'Aye, he'll make the history books for that one. Here's what the history books don't tell you: Those "brilliant" manoeuvres are the gambles that paid off. They might report on other the gambles that didn't fare so well, but it's rare. I will not have some vainglorious arsehole who wants to create his own legend take control here. I'll never gamble with people's lives unless I absolutely have to. For me, a good commander makes solid decisions that let his soldiers go home to their families.'

Phillip considered Arthur's words, searching for another objection, but finding none. He realised no one else possessed that rare combination of sound judgment and natural authority that Arthur carried so effortlessly. He had a way of inspiring both confidence and camaraderie, making you believe he would listen to you while never surrendering command. For a brief moment, Phillip glimpsed the man beneath the mantle of leadership, but then Arthur drained his mug and smiled, the mask settling back into place as naturally as breathing.

Despite Phillip's attempts to draw him out again, Arthur deflected each probe with a quick jest. Eventually, Phillip surrendered to the silence, nursing just two cups of ale over the next few hours while Arthur made his way through half a dozen.

The night around them was rarely still as patrolmen moved between houses or relieved those on the walls. Arthur seemed particularly interested in this current relief. Phillip followed his gaze and realised the gate was manned by only ten soldiers. There should have been fifty, at least. He frowned.

Before Phillip could question what was happening, he saw Arthur signalling him and pointing.

Down the road, figures moved like oil on water, their robes and cloaks blending with the shadows. Furtive glances darted left and right from beneath hooded cowls as they crept towards the gate. In the centre, Commander Ashworth's bulk was unmistakable, his borrowed stealth making him look like a bear trying to tiptoe. Around him, his men carried heavy hammers and crowbars that glinted dully in the starlight.

Arthur cupped his hands to his lips and released a low whistle – a perfect imitation of a mountain owl's call. The sound drifted through the night air, causing the approaching figures to freeze, their hooded heads turning sharply as they searched the shadows.

'What was that?' one of them hissed into the night.

Arthur repeated the call, and Phillip looked at him in alarm.

'Nothing,' another said. 'It was just an owl.'

'In the mountains?'

'An owl of death,' Wilfred said in his deep voice from the end of the alley. He appeared then, twin battle axes held as though they weighed nothing. He had embraced the Light enough to glow.

'We're discovered,' one man shouted, drawing his sword.

From the neighbouring alleys emerged Peter, Elise, Matthew, and Rose – armed, armoured, and glowing with light – blocking every escape route. Wilfred gave a war cry, his twin axes blurring as he charged. His first strike hit the man's raised sword, whipping it out of the way. The second axe cleaved down on his shoulder. His opponent died before he could scream. Wilfred ripped his axe out, already advancing on the next man. The sudden brutality froze the traitors until the other Templars descended on them. Any thought of mounting a defence crumbled as they smashed into the traitors.

'I need him alive!' Arthur shouted, pointing at the fort commander as the melee turned into a slaughter. For a moment he wasn't sure anyone had heard him, until Matthew slipped around the fat man's clumsy sword swipe and clobbered him with the hilt of his dagger.

Wilfred carved through the other traitors like a scythe through wheat, leaving nothing but death in his wake. Phillip stared down at the carnage, his eyes finally finding Arthur, who wore a predator's grin. 'Let's see what we've caught.'

Still numb from the swift brutality, Phillip followed Arthur downstairs to find Matthew had already subdued Lord Ashworth, the commander's bulk draped over his shoulder like a trussed pig.

'How did you know?' Phillip asked, glancing from the unconscious fort commander to Arthur.

'I would like to know, too,' Elise said.

'Combination of things,' Arthur said. 'Word of the invasion had reached across the dividing sea but not south of the mountains – that made the foul play obvious. And Guillamere knew Phillip was a Templar despite us cutting all communications.'

Phillip stared at him, waiting for more, but Arthur offered nothing further.

'And from only that, you figured they'd try to sabotage the gates?'

'Like I said, it was just a hunch.'

'Hell of a hunch,' Peter said.

Arthur shrugged. 'You feel up to interrogating him, Peter? I want to warm up by the fire for a bit.'

'Sure,' Peter said. 'Wilfred, wait a moment – I want you to look dangerous.' The big Templar had been wiping blood off his face, but quickly grasped what Peter wanted and grinned.

'Oh yeah, that's appropriately terrifying,' Peter said. 'Matthew, heat up some pokers. Phillip, you'd be good too – stand right over there. When he wakes, say something about how you want to torture him for throwing you into that dungeon.'

'I, uh, sure … I guess.'

'Be more confident and bloodthirsty, like our mountain-born brute.'

'You dandy. You scream when mud splatters on you,' Wilfred retorted.

Peter only smiled, his attire still looking remarkably clean despite him just having been in a fight. As he rearranged his cloak, he looked more like a man about to step out and have a fine dinner. The Templar spun a chair around to face the unconscious prisoner.

'Rose,' Peter said. She turned to him. 'Do what you do best, look pretty and smile as though he might have a way out.'

She grimaced. 'If you torture him, I'm probably going to throw up.'

Phillip stared at the woman. She'd been cutting through the enemy with that great claymore of hers a moment ago, and now she was squeamish?

'Don't worry, the man's a coward at heart. I doubt it'll come to that.' Peter looked around. 'Everyone ready?' When no one objected, he reached out with his index finger, his skin glowing to show he had embraced the Light. He lightly tapped the commander on the nose, transferring some of the Light into the man. The commander blinked, slowly opening his eyes as he looked around. His eyes bulged as he took in the surrounding Templars.

'What is the meaning of this?' Ashworth said. 'Why did you kill my men?'

Peter smiled. 'Come now, Commander, there's no need to play games. We know you're in league with Naberius's army. The last thing we like is traitors to the Light.'

'Me, in league with the Darkness? You have some nerve!'

'We caught your men sneaking towards the wall with weapons in hand to destroy the gate. Plus, Matthew caught a couple trying to sabotage the Iron Gates. Didn't you, Matthew?'

The silent Templar nodded, not taking his attention from the fire.

Ashworth's mask of innocence dropped, and he sneered. 'Fine, throw me in the dungeons. It won't be long until they overwhelm this Fortress and set me free.'

'Now Commander, don't be so naïve. You won't survive that long, unless you cooperate.'

Ashworth's face paled.

'I'd like a go at him,' Wilfred growled, his voice a guttural rumble. The firelight danced across his blood-rimed face, casting grotesque shadows that transformed his grin into something bestial. 'I'll start with his fingers, one knuckle at a time.'

The commander looked between Peter and Wilfred as if the former might save him.

'My apologies, Wilfred,' Peter said. 'But I promised Phillip he would go first.'

Every eye turned towards Phillip, making him shrink inwardly. For a moment he floundered, caught between his natural hesitation and the role he needed to play. Then he swallowed hard and forced himself to step forward. 'Did you think betraying the Light would go unpunished? What I did to the villagers in the north is nothing compared to what I will do you,' he said, his voice dropping into a deep tone that didn't quite feel like his own. 'I will string you up and use you as a practice dummy for my spear.'

The vehemence in his voice caught everyone by surprise and they all stopped and stared.

'I'm not sure we need to go that far,' Rose said.

'But if we do,' Peter said, 'Matthew is heating some irons to cauterise those wounds, so there's no danger of you bleeding out.'

Ashworth's eyes darted towards the quiet Templar as he held up a glowing poker, frowned, then put it deeper into the fire.

'Things will go more smoothly if you just cooperate,' Peter said mildly.

The commander's eyes bulged as words spilled from his trembling lips. Peter played his role perfectly – a sympathetic ear at just the right moments, and a gentle prompt when the confession faltered. Slowly the story of Ashworth's corruption emerged: It had started small, a few coins here, a blind eye there, each bribe seemingly innocent enough on its own. But with each compromise, Ashworth had found himself deeper enthralled, until it eventually ended in plotting against the very city he'd sworn to protect.

As Peter skilfully drew out every detail, the commander revealed his co-conspirators, his voice growing hollow as he named the men whose bodies now lay cooling in the street outside. The names poured forth like poison from a lanced wound, each confession making Ashworth seem to shrink further into himself.

'And the plan tonight?' Peter asked.

'Sabotage the gates,' the commander said, 'hold them open and send the signal.'

'Which was?'

'You have to understand, I didn't mean for it to go this far.'

Peter's voice softened. 'I do; it's an easy slope for anyone to fall down. The Light offers forgiveness to those who truly repent.'

'I do,' the commander said, leaning forward earnestly. 'I swear I do!'

'Then what was the signal?'

'We'd wave a torch in an arc above the gate four times, then repeat it ten minutes later.'

'And what would happen then?'

'They'd send a force to hold the gates until the army could get through.'

Peter glanced up at Arthur. 'Do we need anything else?'

'I think that's about it,' the First Templar said.

'I want to be at the front of the fight,' Wilfred interjected.

'…from Ashworth,' Peter said pointedly.

Wilfred looked slightly abashed.

'What?' The man's face drained of colour as realisation dawned.

Peter looked at each of the other Templars. One by one, they shook their heads.

'Take him outside and kill him,' Arthur said flatly.

'No!' The commander thrashed against his bindings. 'Wait—'

But Matthew struck him across the face, stunning him. The Templar then dragged him outside. Less than a minute later, there was a small scream that was quickly silenced.

'You're not thinking of springing the trap?' Elise asked.

'Of course we are,' Arthur said. 'It's a chance to have a good crack at their best soldiers while we're still fresh; this will be our first blow against them. If we are to take down this giant, it must be one cut at a time. Let's make the first one count, by hitting them right at their heart.'

CHAPTER ELEVEN: FIRST BLOOD

The soldiers gathered beneath the northern wall's towering gate, their breath forming ghostly clouds in the bitter mountain air. Wilfred's War Priests prowled the shadows with barely contained energy, dressed in the black cloaks of Ashworth's men. Behind them, Elise's marksmen stood quietly, quivers full and bows strung. Peter and Rose's hand-picked soldiers formed the centre ranks, armour muffled with cloth, weapons held close and ready. The Templars stood as silent sentinels before them all. Even without their shining plate armour, the aura of their presence could be felt.

'Listen up,' Arthur called quietly, and the men turned to face him, their murmured conversations falling away. 'I see that hunger in your eyes – the same one I feel in my gut. These bastards think they've outsmarted us, that their numbers will overwhelm our walls tonight.'

A ripple of knowing laughter spread through the ranks.

'It takes more than courage to spring a trap like this; they need to think they've won. That, more than anything, will test your nerve. Let them creep close – then we'll show them what happens to rats in a cage.'

The soldiers' eyes gleamed in the darkness, a few grim chuckles echoing off the stone walls.

'You know your roles. Hold your positions until my signal,' Arthur said, his grin turning wolfish. 'Then we paint these streets red.'

The men's mirth faded as Arthur nodded to Matthew. The silent Templar raised his torch on the wall. Four times he swept it through the darkness, the flame carving bright arcs against the night sky.

'We have ten minutes. Trust in the Light and we will prevail!' Arthur said as the soldiers took their respective positions.

'I don't enjoy being so far back,' Wilfred said. 'I think I should be inside the inn, ready to charge out.'

'I've got to give the others a chance to bloody their weapons,' Arthur said, then clapped him on the shoulder. 'I'm holding you back in case things get out of hand. If they break through our lines, I need you ready to contain them. You are my only safety measure and there's no one I trust more.'

Wilfred looked serious. 'Very well, I will do this task for you.'

The man stalked off while the others were taking their positions. The archers were playing dead on the walls, while the War Priests stood in their borrowed enemy clothing.

Arthur turned to see Phillip regarding him, his expression difficult to discern.

'I think I liked you better when you disdained me,' Arthur said.

Phillip smiled. 'And I think I am beginning to understand you.'

'At least someone is,' Arthur said. 'Now get to your position and don't fuck it up.'

'Yes, First Templar,' Phillip said, gripping his spear as he headed for the inn where the other spearmen waited. If the cavalry made it through the gate, their wall of steel would be the first to meet them. Arthur followed him inside but continued up to the roof, where his chair offered a perfect vantage point over the killing field below.

On the opposite side, Peter was standing with his own cadre of spearmen. They would funnel any enemy soldiers towards Rose and her squad, with Wilfred waiting in reserve.

Arthur settled back into his blanketed chair. His own soldiers waited nearby, cramped on the rooftop, taking a knee to avoid being seen and huddling together for warmth. He could see Elise and Matthew walking amongst all the 'dead' soldiers on the parapets.

Ten minutes were up and again Matthew waved the torch, the flame leaving a trace through the air. One, two, three, four times. Then they waited.

Arthur drew just enough Light to sharpen his hearing, but even that heightened sense caught only whispers through the howling mountain winds.

'They're coming,' Peter hissed from the walls.

Minutes passed slowly before Arthur heard the first sounds of leather creaking and mail clinking as shadows slipped through the gates. They moved like cats testing unfamiliar ground, but with each unchallenged step their confidence swelled, until they flowed into the streets like dark water.

Eventually the first black-clad figure emerged from the darkness. This was no robed priest – the man wore fitted leather armour that seemed to drink in what little light reached him, the silver symbol of Lucifer gleaming at his throat like an eye. Two more clergy materialised beside him, their soldiers following behind like a dark tide.

Arthur's fingers tightened on his weapon as his heart hammered against his ribs. Every instinct screamed at him to give the signal, to spring the trap now – but no, not yet. He forced himself to stay still, to count the shadows that slipped through his gates. Thirty. Forty. Fifty. Still he waited, even as his city filled with enemies.

Peter, much to his own chagrin, had messed up his hair and outfit, so that he looked like a disreputable defector.

'Where's Ashworth?' the Priest asked.

'Dead,' Peter said. 'The Templars caught him, but we slipped something into his food to kill him off before he revealed too much.'

'And who are you?'

'The guy who got the job done,' Peter said. 'And who will get Ashworth's share of the reward.'

The Priest grunted with amusement as his soldiers continued to explore the streets, while several went to inspect the gates.

Arthur's grip tightened as he watched them look over the gate.

One wrong move, one overeager scout with a torch, and their entire plan would collapse as surely as those unhooked hinges. He forced a slow breath through clenched teeth. The gate was a calculated risk – but then, wasn't this whole night balanced on a blade's edge? Sometimes you had to let the enemy think they'd won before you could truly defeat them.

One soldier came up to the Priest. 'Besides the dead, the streets are empty. We're setting up defences,' he said. The man had broad shoulders but moved with a fluid grace despite his bulk.

'The gate?'

'Off its hinges. It can't close.'

'I'd like my money now,' Peter said.

'Patience,' the Priest replied, going up the stairs to the parapets. He took the torch from Matthew's hand while he grasped the symbol of Lucifer with his other. For a moment, nothing happened.

Then darkness pushed in around the torch, flooding it with an inky blackness, turning the flame darker than night. Yet it still illuminated the surrounding area. The Priest waved it back and forth across the walls.

That was it, Arthur thought.

'Now!' Arthur shouted.

The Priest's head snapped toward Arthur's position, his eyes widening – but too late. Peter's dagger found his heart in one fluid motion, and his shocked cry cut through the night as Peter kicked him from the parapet. His body hit the ground with a dull thud, which was quickly drowned out by the chaos erupting around them. The remaining Priests had no time to react before Matthew's massive arrow and Elise's javelin struck them down simultaneously, the force of the impacts throwing them backwards like ragdolls.

All around them, sounds of fighting erupted as the Light-illuminated Templars emerged from their hiding places to attack those who had entered the fray.

The archers surged to their feet along the walls, arrows already nocked as they shed their disguises as fallen soldiers. Their bowstrings sang in harmony, sending the first deadly volley into the confused enemy ranks below. In the narrow street behind the gate, Arthur heard Wilfred's familiar battle cry – a sound of pure, terrifying joy that still made him flinch involuntarily. The savage Templar burst from his hiding place like a demon unleashed, his massive battle axes trailing golden Light as he crashed into the enemy. Screams of panic replaced the shocked silence as his War Priests followed in his wake, their weapons carving paths of divine retribution through the trapped soldiers of the Dark.

The clash of steel on steel and screams of dying men echoed off the stone walls, but beneath the chaos, Arthur felt it first – a deep vibration in the bones of the earth. His stomach dropped as the trembling grew stronger, and understanding dawned with cold clarity. Not an earthquake, but rather hundreds of hooves thundering toward their gate, the enemy cavalry bearing down on them like a storm.

Arthur's stomach twisted as he surveyed the battlefield. Inside the walls, the enemy fought with desperate fury to keep the Templars from reaching the gate. Every second lost to this skirmish brought the cavalry closer. If they couldn't secure those hinges in time, they'd be gifting the northern city to the enemy on a gilded platter.

No choice left but to get my hands dirty, Arthur thought, drawing the Light into himself. Power surged through his veins like liquid fire, burning away his fatigue as the divine radiance spilled from his skin. With strength enough to shatter mountains coursing through him, he launched himself from the inn's roof. What should have been a bone-crushing fall felt no more taxing than stepping off a curb stone.

The enemy soldiers gaped at his sudden appearance, frozen for one critical moment. By the time they'd reached for their weapons, Arthur was among them. His mace carved deadly arcs through their ranks, each blow sending men flying like leaves in a storm. Bones shattered and bodies crumpled beneath his onslaught, the Light lending terrible force to every swing.

Arthur's assault had given Phillip's men the opening they needed, and they surged forward to cut down the remaining soldiers with brutal efficiency.

When Arthur reached the gate, his blood ran cold. Moonlight

painted the approaching army in silver, their mass flowing across the open ground towards him like a tide of steel. Shouts of alarm rippled along the walls as archers scrambled into position, and somewhere in the night, a bell tolled – deep and sonorous, its warning echoing through the streets of the northern city.

The massive gate lay twisted off its hinges like a felled oak. Arthur seized it, drawing deeper on the Light as he strained against the weight. His stomach churned, protesting the combination of ale and divine power, but he pushed through the discomfort. Even with the Light singing in his veins, the wooden behemoth barely moved, groaning under his hold.

The city's warning bells were answered by deep-throated war horns that made his blood freeze. Against his better judgment, Arthur turned to look at the enemy. The cavalry was bearing down on him like an avalanche of steel and flesh, their weapons catching the moonlight as they charged. Close enough now that he could see their faces, twisted with bloodlust beneath their helms.

Arthur's muscles screamed as he tried again, but the gate refused to budge. 'Hell's fire,' he spat through gritted teeth.

A shadow fell across him as Rose materialised on his right, and Phillip appeared on his left. The three of them heaved together, and finally the massive door began to rise. But it swayed treacherously as they manoeuvred it toward the hinges, each wobble threatening to tear it from their grasp.

'Leave it!' Wilfred's battle-hungry roar cut through the chaos. 'Let us face them head on!'

Rose and Phillip, like Arthur, kept their focus on the gate, deaf to the other Templar's battle cry.

The thunder of hooves grew louder, accompanied by the metallic song of drawn steel and the deep-throated war cries of the charging horsemen. Arthur could smell horse sweat and kicked-up earth on the wind, while moonlight glinted off their raised weapons. The gate creaked in his hands.

The door slammed home just as the thunder of hooves reached a deafening height. He dove clear as Rose heaved the gate shut, and arrows thudded into the wood as he threw himself against it, shoulders braced for impact.

Phillip appeared with the crossbeam, sliding it home just as soldiers rushed forward with wooden bracings. The sound of mallets striking wood echoed off the walls like war drums as they secured their defences.

Arthur sagged back against the wood, his chest heaving. Another few heartbeats and they'd have been overrun. The Light slipped from his grasp, and mortality crashed back into him like a wave, leaving his limbs trembling and heavy.

'Loose!' Elise called.

The sound of bows twanging heralded the air being filled with arrows.

The screams of men and horses suddenly overtook the noise of the charge, though the wind and war horns quickly swept it away as the enemy army continued to advance.

Arthur and pulled the flask from his hip with trembling fingers. The whiskey burned a familiar path down his throat, and he let out a long breath as warmth spread through his chest. For a moment he stayed there, eyes closed, feeling his heartbeat slowly steadying as the sounds of battle gave way to the groaning of the wounded and the continued thunder of the enemy cavalry. The mountain wind cut through his sweat-soaked clothes. Taking one last steadying breath, he pushed himself upright and climbed the stairs to join the other Templars on the parapets, his legs still unsteady from channelling so much of the Light.

'You tied that one up nicely,' Peter said. 'Though what would you have done if Naberius had been the one leading the charge?'

'Shit my pants, probably,' Arthur said.

Peter laughed.

'I didn't even think about Naberius attacking,' Phillip said.

'A calculated risk,' Arthur said, his hands steadier now. 'That dog will rarely join anything resembling a fair fight and tonight there was too much that was unknown.'

'Catapults!' Elise called.

Wood moaned and ropes snapped as the catapults unleashed their loads. Boulders arced through the moonlit sky like falling meteors, then crashed into the enemy ranks with devastating force. The stones didn't stop after impact – they bounded through the mass of soldiers and horses, leaving broken bodies in their wake. Screams cut through the night, only to be suddenly silenced as more projectiles found their marks.

'That one!' Arthur pointed, yelling to Elise.

The other Templar followed his finger and spotted the target: A commander who'd realised what had happened and was hastily trying to order a retreat.

'Seen,' Elise called, hefting a javelin that dwarfed a knight's lance. She took three quick strides and unleashed it with fluid grace, the massive spear cutting through the night like a diving hawk. The shaft sprouted directly from the commander's chest, tearing him from his saddle.

Across the battlefield, other commanders fell to precisely aimed arrows, their deaths spreading chaos through the enemy ranks. But the adversary's army was already melting away into the darkness, disappearing before the catapults could loose another volley.

'How many do you think we killed?' Phillip asked, as he watched their retreat.

'Tough to say,' Arthur answered, eyes scanning the battlefield. 'You think over a few hundred, Matthew?'

The quiet Templar raised his hand in a higher gesture.

'Five or six?'

The man gave a silent nod.

'Did we lose anyone?' Arthur asked.

'Couple of the soldiers got scratched, but they're still good to fight,' Peter said.

Arthur watched the enemy retreating into the darkness, their torches fading like dying stars. Though they had won tonight, it was just the opening move.

'Well, least our first fight was a success,' Arthur said, feeling the tension of this gamble leaking from his shoulders. 'Elise, you good to take tonight's watch?' At her nod, he smiled. 'Great. I'm going to have a drink and a bath. Call me if you need anything, but I don't expect them to attack until morning at the earliest.'

'You think they won't hold off after this defeat?' Peter asked.

'They might, but we need to be ready for when the actual bloodshed starts.'

'I am ready,' Wilfred said stoutly.

'I think even your aptitude for battle will be sated before the end,' Arthur said.

CHAPTER TWELVE: DARK COUNSEL

Guillamere's fingers traced over the ornate silver clasps of his black robes. The demon skull atop his staff seemed to be watching him with its hollow eyes. Naberius had summoned him to account for their failure at the gates. The pavilion loomed before him like a monument to darkness, vast enough to house a platoon yet serving as quarters for the demon hound alone. With a steadying breath that did little to calm his racing heart, he stepped through the tent flaps.

Inside, shadows pooled in the corners, despite the many braziers of burning incense. The air held a cloying sweetness that failed to mask the underlying taint of burning sulphur. Three massive cushions dominated the space, each large enough to cradle one of Naberius's mighty heads, arranged in a semicircle around an immaculately clean rug. Rich carpets layered the floor. A war table dominated one side of the tent, its surface covered with maps of the Fortress.

Guillamere's eyes were drawn to the trophy stand where Naberius kept the divine relics; on an obsidian pedestal sat the Burning Crown – Michael's corrupted halo. Even unadorned, it radiated waves of heat that distorted the air around it, its surface flickering with a hellfire that never dimmed. Beside it, inside its own hardwood case, lay the Mirror of Jasper, its gilded frame etched with symbols. Its surface reflected deep truths on whoever gazed on it. And there, on a stand of blackened bone, lay the Black Scroll, Beelzebub's original contract with the demon princes. Its angelic script glowed faintly, like dying embers beneath a layer of ash.

A nervous attendant led in a fat mountain goat for the evening meal, its hooves clicking against a raised feeding platform. The creature's eyes rolled white with terror when it caught Naberius's scent. The attendant's hands trembled as they quickly secured the animal, then they retreated to the shadows, desperate to avoid notice.

'Mountain goat again?' the right-most head sighed, his ears flattening in displeasure. 'The meat's always too gamey.'

'It's perfect,' the left-side head said, its tongue lolling between knife-like teeth. 'The mountain grazing gives it the ideal seasoning.'

'You eat it then,' the right head said, lip curling. 'I've had enough of goat.'

The middle head remained focused on Guillamere, though one ear twitched toward the developing argument. 'Your assault has failed.' Its voice sounded like a cascade of basalt rumbling down a mountainside, vibrating through Guillamere like thunder. But with the focus of only one head on him, Guillamere allowed himself to relax slightly.

'It would have been nice if it had worked, but Ashworth's capture was hardly surprising. He wasn't the most competent of servants.'

'Such disloyalty ensures a temporary life in our ranks,' the right head said.

'He can answer for his failure in hell,' the left head said.

Guillamere waited until there was a lull before continuing: 'The siege will begin tomorrow, regardless.'

The middle head paused, its head tilting slightly as if it could smell Guillamere's terror. 'You should not fear me so. We will not punish you for things outside of your control – you are a worthy servant and have long since have earned Lucifer's favour,' the main head said.

'You were but a young pup when we found you,' the left head drawled.

'Now a worthy addition to the pack,' the right head added, its voice quick and sharp.

Guillamere remembered their first meeting all too well: the devastation left in the wake of Lucifer and Michael's battle; the Archangel eventually slaying the ruler of hell; and how horribly wounded he'd been from the ordeal. Little over ten years old and only an acolyte, Guillamere had called out to the hound. Despite his fear of both Naberius and Michael, he had led the hound to the wounded angel, where the demon had slowly and painfully killed his weakened adversary.

Since then, Naberius had kept him close, eventually raising him to the rank of High Priest.

'As you wish, milord,' Guillamere said, feeling some of the tension leaving him.

'Good.' The middle head said. 'How long until the Fortress is taken?'

The three heads watched as Guillamere carefully considered his words. 'The Templars complicate things. Without them, we could have taken it within a few days through sheer numbers, but while they are strong and able—' Guillamere shrugged, '—a month, maybe more.'

The left head cackled, a sound like breaking glass that sent chills down Guillamere's spine. 'Do not seek to manipulate us; we see through it.'

'We will not risk ourselves needlessly,' the right head said through a toothy grin. 'Lucifer's final wish rests with me.'

'My master's will stands above all,' the middle head said.

Guillamere suppressed a sigh, watching as the massive demon hound's muscles tensed beneath its dark fur, which rippled like liquid shadow. He had harboured faint hopes that Naberius might join the siege, but those hopes were fading.

'With the Templars scattered along the walls, risk to your person would be minimal,' Guillamere said. 'Our armies can isolate them for you, while you rain hellfire on the defenders until nothing remains.' He looked up to find all six eyes fixed upon him, and his voice faltered as the right head bared its gleaming teeth. Too close to commanding, he realised, and shifted his approach. 'Of course, we will take the Fortress however you order us to, but with your might behind us, we could achieve it in days rather than weeks. The sooner we break through, the sooner we can pursue Lucifer's true mission.'

'We shall ... consider it,' the middle head rumbled.

'Though your suggestion borders on presumption,' the right head added, 'it has merit.'

'And watching Templars burn is always entertaining,' the left head grinned, the strand of drool hanging from its lips snapping and landing on the carpet.

Guillamere kept his expression neutral, though inwardly he savoured the small victory. Rarely did all three heads agree on anything, let alone with him.

'Have you considered what we will do once we've taken the Fortress?' Guillamere asked, moving closer to the war table. His shadow fell across the mapped territories of the southern nations.

'What we discussed,' the right-side head said curtly.

The main head lifted himself higher than its companions, shadows deepening the hollows of its eyes until they seemed like bottomless pools. 'Lucifer's final will – we will find a way to kill Astaroth for defying him. There is untamed power to the south, a wild magic near the Ancient forest. We will claim it for our own.'

'Oh, he has something to suggest,' the left-most head said, its tongue lolling out in amusement. The goat bleated nervously as all three heads shifted their full attention to Guillamere, six red eyes burning like coals in the gloom.

'I do,' Guillamere admitted, tracing the edge of the map with one finger. 'Astaroth, despite all her vaunted power, is trapped in her stronghold.'

The right head's ears flattened in irritation. The massive paws shifted on the carpets, their claws catching in the worn fabric with sounds like daggers being drawn.

'We know how she earned her prison – how the last Ancients died to seal her there,' the middle head admitted.

'She claimed some of the ancient magic for herself,' Guillamere said, watching as the incense smoke curled between them like serpents. 'But it took decades, if not centuries, to gain that control.'

The middle head nodded. 'Your point?'

'Such mastery may take you years, and we cannot let our enemies regain their strength while you pursue this power.'

The middle head's brows furrowed into a deep frown, while the left head tilted with curiosity, its earlier mirth fading. The goat stamped nervously on its platform as the tension in the tent grew thick enough to choke on.

'I suggest that after we take the Fortress,' Guillamere said, his voice steady despite his racing heart, 'we march on the Citadel to end Zadkiel and his kingdom of Light.'

Silence hung heavy in the air, with even the goat keeping silent at the weight of the proposal.

'Dead Angels cannot meddle in our affairs,' the left head said at last.

'And the Templar gnats will finally be crushed,' the right head exulted.

The main head considered, then the great hound eased himself onto the carpets with unsettling grace, paws crossed beneath it. The cushions creaked as the heads turned – the right in thought, left in excitement, and middle in doubt.

Guillamere waited, knowing not to interrupt his master's thought processes.

'It will detract from our mission.' There was a note of uncertainty in the main head's gravelly voice.

'The reward is worth the delay. Zadkiel lives only to devise our downfall.'

'And when we bring Lucifer the heads of both Astaroth and the Archangel?' The left head's eyes shone.

The main head's frown gradually smoothed, like storm clouds parting. The massive body shifted, and the carpets moved and tore with him.

'Very well. After you have taken the Fortress, we march on the Citadel of the Light to kill the last Archangel.'

'Very good, milord.' Guillamere bowed slightly, the demon skull on his staff catching the light.

'Now go and do our bidding,' the left-most head said, turning back to the forgotten goat with renewed interest.

'Do not fail us,' the right head added.

'Remember, Guillamere—' the middle head's voice rumbled like distant thunder, '—do not become distracted by the future. You must first take the Fortress. Thick walls and stout defenders stand between us and victory.'

Guillamere breathed a sigh of relief. The interrogation had gone better than he'd hoped; he didn't pretend to understand all the politics of the battle between heaven and hell, or why they picked this world for a battlefield, but he knew his place. He was a servant of Naberius and would do the hound's bidding for as long as he was able.

'We will be south of the mountains within a month,' Guillamere said with quiet confidence, turning to leave. As he reached the tent flaps, the sound of tearing flesh and cracking bones followed him out into the night, accompanied by the disparate opinions of Naberius's heads regarding the taste of mountain goat.

CHAPTER THIRTEEN: MOUNTAIN RAVENS

Riordan's ice-encrusted braids clicked together as he pulled himself over the ledge, stars dancing in his vision. Ten days since he'd left the Fortress, and the air up here still felt like breathing through wet wool. He lay where he was, not bothering to retrieve his axe, its pick point still dug into the ice while he caught his breath. After a few minutes, he reluctantly got up.

Dressed mostly in white, he nevertheless found his red hair stuck out like a bonfire on the peaks. He pulled up his hood, not wanting to give away their position. Despite the chill mountain air that swirled around him, Riordan felt quite warm. He'd have to thank Templar Matthew when they got back; the thin layers of fine wool clothing were the same thickness as a good woollen cloak, while still being incredibly warm.

Riordan scanned the surrounding area and felt a brief sense of elation. There was a gentle decline, then a traverse through a valley, then a ridgeline all the way to Mount Moriah. The monstrous peak was their destination; stunted, wind-twisted trees blew on the exposed face, while tall pines grew in the shelter of the mountain. The massif itself was bloated with snow and ice.

They'd found their path, and it was there that they would try to bring the whole weight of the mountainside down on the enemy.

Riordan scanned the rock ledge for a suitable anchor point. An ice-covered rock feature caught his eye, and he retrieved his axe before hacking at the frost. Though every swing felt natural, he had to take a few seconds after every blow to recover. With steady work, the blade chipped away the ice until he'd created a groove for the rope. He circled the rock twice before tying it off and tossing the looped end over the edge, the rope's length uncoiling all the way down until it reached his father and the remaining Wild Ravens. They'd make the same climb up the treacherous path and small ice wall as he had, but they would have the rope to guide them.

Riordan sat on the edge to look down upon the Fortress. Today the view was clear of mist or fog, and from these heights, the enemy camp and the Fortress itself looked so tiny. The encampment was like a forest of weeds that dominated every spare space inside the pass, trailing backwards and out of sight. They were gathering for another assault at the front of the dead zone between the camp and the walls. Two hundred yards of open ground, where enough people had died to fill a few graveyards.

Riordan reached for his pack and pulled out some rations. At these heights, he didn't feel hungry, but even so he forced himself to eat. He'd liked the flavour of the salted beef before they'd started, but the altitude had destroyed his appetite. With each bite, he had to focus on swallowing and not losing his stomach. He chewed on the meat while he stared at their adversary. It felt surreal as he watched the enemy army swarm towards the walls while the defenders scurried to meet them. It was like two colonies of ants desperately fighting over a rock. Several beacons of Light flared up, signalling that the Templars had engaged in battle.

Grunting from the direction of the cliff face drew Riordan to his feet. At the edge, he found Cormac ascending the rope at a steep angle, his braids whipping in the mountain wind. When his father came within reach, Riordan extended his hand. Their grips locked, and he hauled Cormac onto the ledge.

Like Riordan before him, his father collapsed to the ground to catch his breath.

'Getting too old for this shit?' Riordan asked. It was one of his father's favourite lines.

Cormac, conserving his breath, gave him a rude salute.

Riordan grinned. He moved back to the edge and helped the next person up. There were only about forty of them left. More than half their number had succumbed to the altitude and retreated down the mountain, their bodies unable to cope with the thinning air. One by one, he helped the Wild Ravens until there was only Zahir left.

The man declined Riordan's offer of support, pulling himself up without assistance, though the effort cost him visibly. He was forced to stand panting, hands on his knees, to recover. While he was crouched over, the hammer on his belt gleamed. Riordan stared at it. No frost or scratches marred it, and instead strange markings had appeared on its surface, almost as if it had been tattooed.

'It will not work for you.'

Riordan looked up to see Zahir giving him a hard stare. 'What?'

'The hammer. You are not the first to covet it. Should you get your hands on it, it will not work for you.'

'I wasn't going to steal it,' Riordan said indignantly.

'It would go poorly for you if you did.'

Cormac interrupted. 'No one wants your bloody hammer.'

'I am merely—'

'No one gives a shit. We've got a job to do.'

'Let it go,' Riordan said to Zahir. 'Please.' The lone mercenary looked highly affronted, but remained silent. His father and Zahir had taken an instant dislike to each other, and ten days of close proximity, tiring work, and limited rations had worn all their patience paper-thin. Zahir sniffed and, still winded, pushed on after the others as they descended toward the final valley before Mount Moriah.

'I really want to introduce that man to the sharp end of my sword,' Cormac said.

'Keep your voice down,' Riordan snapped. 'We need him.'

'I'm not sure we need him *that* much.'

'Father!'

Cormac took one sharp look at Riordan. 'Fine. I'll keep my sword to myself.'

'I swear you pout like a child sometimes.'

Cormac dramatically raised a hand to his forehead. 'It's the burden of leadership.'

Riordan couldn't help but smile as they joined the others on the path. At the edge's traverse, the Fortress came into view again, and his smile vanished.

Eleven beacons of Light were converging on a single point. It took him only a moment to spot it. Even at this distance, he could see the Demon Hound Naberius with its three heads as it assaulted one part of the wall. While the Templars were occupied, other sections of the wall faltered, the defenders buckling without extra support.

'Come on lad, the faster we get this job done, the faster we can aid them,' Cormac said.

Riordan nodded mutely, feeling helpless up here while he trudged onwards, his feet crunching in the snow. The Fortress disappeared again from sight. After the sixth step, he had to remind himself to slow down, as he was already beginning to lose his breath. 'Do you really think we can do this?'

'There's a small chance,' Cormac said, 'but by the nine hells, it's enough.'

A small hope it would have to be, Riordan thought.

They caught up to Conner at the head of their line, where he was probing the ground ahead with his unstrung bow. Their progress was slow but caution was necessary – the path forward twisted like a serpent's trail.

An hour's careful trudging had gained them just a few hundred yards to the ridgeline. From there, the Fortress spread below them once more. Beacons of Light dotted the walls again, while cavalry patrols swept through the northern city's streets, routing pockets of attackers who had breached the defences. The major enemy force had retreated to their camp in the pass.

'Looks like they've bought another day,' Cormac said. 'We'd best make use of it.'

Riordan breathed a sigh of relief; his father was right. He hiked on. They should be nearly at the valley where they'd camp for the night. Then they'd figure out how to bring Mount Moriah down on the enemy.

A shout up ahead shattered his reverie. Conner had vanished into the snow, but the rope tied around his chest gave the others something to grab. They heaved him up, his form caked in frost, while he spluttered and his comrades brushed him clean.

'These types of journeys are hard on the body, and the—'

'—mind,' Riordan finished. It had been his father's mantra for half the trip, ever since part of their company had descended the mountain. 'You're getting too predictable, Father.'

A moment later, a snowball sailed through the air, striking Riordan on the chest. The whole thing broke apart on impact, but when he looked up, he saw his grey-haired father grinning at him like a little boy.

'How's that for being predictable?'

'I am continually astounded that your men willingly follow you,' Zahir said from one side.

'Just like I'm astounded someone hasn't knocked your brains out yet,' Cormac retorted.

A whistle cut through the air. Cormac and Zahir's eyes shot forward as Conner beckoned them ahead. All forty Wild Ravens advanced to the edge, where their planned campsite lay in full view – and already occupied. Dozens of tents were sprawled haphazardly across the space. Men emerged from them, shouting and pointing at the Ravens' approach. Riordan made a quick count: Somewhere between one hundred and fifty to two hundred.

'Some of the local mountain tribes?' Riordan asked.

'Doubtful,' Cormac said, then raised his voice. 'Men, drop your packs! Spread along the ridgeline and mind your footing. We'll use the height against them – let them come to us and see how many the mountain claims.'

The Wild Ravens were quick to respond. Those at the front pulled their weapons free and lined up, while Conner and the other archers strung their bows. Riordan dropped his own pack, feeling the immediate relief in his shoulders while he retrieved his axe and shield.

Even at their higher vantage point, forty against two hundred seemed like long odds to Riordan. Still, the Ravens never hesitated as they lined up, ready to meet the enemy.

'Draw them in; I will smash them with ice and snow,' Zahir said.

Cormac stared at the man, then at the soft snow around them. 'You heard him, hold the line and Zahir will take them out. Even if he can't, they'll be well fucking tired by the time they reach us.' He looked over at the archers. 'How many arrows we got?'

Conner looked over his own quiver, pulling out and testing an arrow's fletching. The frozen feathers snapped under the pressure. 'Ones that will fly true? Hard to say.'

'Be conservative with them, unless I say otherwise,' Cormac said.

'Aye, captain.'

Below, an officer with a plumed helmet arranged his lines. After having surveyed the Ravens' numbers, he barked the order to advance. His men, emboldened by the small opposition, eagerly surged forward.

'That was stupid,' Riordan said.

'The numbers make them overconfident, but you're right. Hey, Conner!' Cormac said.

'What?' the man shouted back, as he was testing the string on his bow.

'See their commander? Don't kill him until I say so.'

The archer, still partially covered in snow, glanced down at the opposing commander, then grinned. 'Right you are, captain.'

The enemy began their ascent toward the ridgeline. Though only a few hundred yards distant, they struggled through the deep snow-drifts. Riordan's hand twitched at the sight of their weapons glinting in the mountain sun – part of him yearned to charge down and meet them. Instead, he occupied himself with whatever preparations he could. Starting with his belt knife, he began to work it free of its frozen sheath.

'Steady, men,' Riordan said, still fighting his own urge to charge. Around him, the other Ravens shifted restlessly, but he caught Cormac's approving nod.

The enemy's advance slowed further on the steepening slope. Their commander bellowed for greater speed, but his men were already gasping for breath. Riordan fixed on one soldier directly ahead – an olive-skinned northerner, face flushed with exertion. The man's next step met empty air, his expression frozen in shock as he plunged into the snow. His comrades scrambled to help, abandoning their advance.

'Three arrows each; pick your targets,' Cormac called. 'But not the commander.'

The six archers nocked their arrows, each waiting for the wind to calm before they drew their string and loosed. The arrows flew surprisingly true, drawing screams from a few enemy soldiers. The next volley brought down more and the enemy hastened to close the distance between them.

More soldiers vanished into the snow as they advanced, but the arrows and their commander's shouts drove the rest onward. Holes and collapsed crevices marked the treacherous footing their comrades had discovered the hard way.

'Zahir, how long do you need?' Cormac asked.

'A few hammer falls at most. Shall I begin?'

Cormac looked around, his eyes taking in the sloping landscape.

'Men, three steps back, Zahir is going to take the mountain down around us!' Cormac turned back to the northern mercenary. 'If you would be so kind?'

The man stepped forward and slammed his hammer down on the snow. There was the same odd pulse as from the courtyard, but instead of the devastating force they'd witnessed on the anvil, the snow merely crumbled and compressed beneath the blow. He struck again, harder, but the impact only drove the snow into forming a dense, icy plate.

By now, the enemy was trailing up to them, like the rivers of a delta funnelling towards a lake.

'Knew it wouldn't be that easy,' Cormac said. 'Men, hold the line. We'll cut them down the old-fashioned way.'

His men held firm. Their calm readiness made Riordan fiercely proud to be counted amongst their number.

They waited as the enemy laboured upward through the snow, their clumsy advance almost comical if not for the deadly glint of steel against the white. The first to reach them charged straight for Zahir, who met the attack with his hammer. The weapon's impact shattered the soldier's axe into fragments, leaving him staring dumbfounded at the broken haft in his hands. Before he could recover, Zahir's second strike caught him square in the chest. The blow launched him backward like a stone from a sling, his tumbling body bowling over his comrades before disappearing over the edge into one of the mountain's hidden caverns.

Two more attackers surged forward to replace their fallen comrade. Already drained by the thin air, Zahir struggled to deflect an incoming blow from the first. The second spearman approached from the flank, where Cormac moved to meet him. His blade opened the attacker's shoulder in a spray of crimson across the snow. Riordan caught the spear of the first opponent on his shield and countered with his axe. The man's scream was short-lived as he tumbled backwards, but the effort left Riordan gasping, unsure if he could face another adversary.

The Ravens quickly fell into a rhythm of fighting together to protect each other when they could, with the ease of long practice.

'Thank you for saving my life,' Zahir said to Cormac. 'Rest assured, I would have done the same for you.'

'You'll get the chance in a moment!'

What followed was the most bizarre fight Riordan had ever experienced. The enemy, already spent from their climb, staggered upward as Conner's archers picked off the stragglers. Though the hidden caverns created perfect choke points for defence, even a single strike left Riordan winded. Nevertheless the attackers pressed on. His vision dimmed more than once as they rotated with fresh Ravens, conserving what little strength remained. The entire clash lasted barely twenty minutes, but in the crush of battle and the desperate struggle for air, it stretched into an eternity.

'Conner, kill their commander,' Cormac called.

The archer nodded and drew a steadying breath, sighting on the plumed officer. His first arrow sailed wide, caught by the mountain winds. Three more followed, depleting his quiver, before the fifth struck true. The officer stared down at the shaft that had barely pierced his armour. Even at this distance, fear radiated from his rigid posture. He turned and ran, and like a breaking dam, his men poured after him.

Though Riordan stayed standing, many Ravens dropped to their knees, gasping for breath. A few lay motionless in the bloodied snow, but even with those fallen, they'd weathered the assault better than he'd expected. Cormac allowed them a brief respite.

'Alright lads, let's get moving. Take it slow, but we need to clear the valley.'

Under his father's steady command, they approached the encampment with measured steps. At their advance, a few enemy stragglers fled, triggering an avalanche of retreat as the remaining forces scattered into the twisted trees and mountain wilderness. Cormac had his followers methodically clear the poorly-placed tents that dotted the flat ground. Though ill-suited for mountain weather, the enemy's abandoned provisions far exceeded their own meagre supplies.

'We all clear?' Cormac called.

'Aye, looks like it,' Conner replied.

'Well done, men. Be glad they can't fight worth a damn in the snow. Take a load off and be merry; we'll sleep well tonight.'

'Here?' Riordan asked. 'Won't that be dangerous?'

'We'll set trip wires, post watches,' Cormac said. 'But the enemy's long gone – the wilderness will claim them before nightfall.'

Riordan grunted.

'Cheer up, tomorrow we get to bring down the mountain!'

CHAPTER FOURTEEN:
SIEGES TOLL

The trebuchets towered amid the sea of enemy forces. A red flag went up; there was a collective groan as the latches on the siege engines were released. They pivoted in unison, swinging in a hypnotic curve and flinging the projectiles high.

The men guarding the walls ducked behind the battlements. Arthur stood alone amongst them, watching as the boulders reached the top of their arc and slowly descended. They slammed into the stonework, booming like thunder. One boulder flew high, sailing over the wall and crashing into a two-story house. It smashed through the roof, the floor, and out the back wall. The building was in limbo, as though it might still stand. But then the foundations faltered, causing the entire edifice to come crashing down and sending up a cloud of dust.

Arthur stared down at the crumbled building huddled inside the curtain wall. He turned to scan the rest of the parapets. After a moment of silence, when it was clear no one had been injured, he let loose a breath of relief.

There was a collective cheer from the defenders.

'Which house was that one?' Arthur called out.

'Rum, First Templar!'

'Two-story house, so two barrels it is!' He pulled out his hip flask and took a sip. "It's whiskey, but consider it an advance." He passed it to a soldier with a blood-stained bandage wrapped around his head. Despite almost half their number being injured but still forced to fight, the prospect of rum had made the defenders cheer. Arthur turned back to the enemy lines where, two hundred yards away and safely beyond their catapult range, infantry stood waiting, while the siege weapons reloaded.

Turning on his heel, Arthur continued along the parapet. He took the flask from the last soldier and went to take a sip, but there was only enough left to wet his lips. He sighed, already regretting his generosity as he continued along the walkway.

The bulwark had been stained red with blood, and scorch marks marred the upper battlements. Men rose and saluted him as he passed. A couple grinned while one man stepped up to hold out a hand.

Arthur recognised his face, but by the Archangel, he couldn't recall his name.

'You bloody rascal, still alive?' Arthur asked, clasping his hand.

'Just long enough to get me some rum.'

'Save me a cup,' Arthur laughed, as he continued on.

He spared another look over the walls at the waiting enemy forces – they were getting quicker at reloading their trebuchets. Yesterday had been a bloodbath, but they had broken the enemy's assault. The charred remains of siege towers and scaling ladders at the base of the walls stood testament to that victory. Hundreds of faces flashed through his memory, thousands of bodies, yet when he looked at the horde spread across the mountain pass, their numbers seemed endless, stretching back until they vanished from sight. Arthur tried to remember how long the siege had lasted.

Light, has it been only two weeks? Arthur thought, reaching for his hip flask, then cursing when he realised it was empty. Two weeks and no word from Cormac and his scheme to bring the mountain down on the enemy. Arthur lifted his hand to shade his eyes, searching the snow-covered mountains as if Cormac might suddenly materialize on their slopes. It was a gambler's hope, but it was better than Zadkiel returning to the slaughter.

'Light watch over them and keep them safe.'

When his eyes turned back to the sea of enemy forces, he caught sight of the demonic hound himself. The three-headed beast, wider than a grizzly bear and taller than a draft horse, had a mercurial liquid darkness flowing where his fur should be. Standing head and shoulders above even the tallest man, his three heads scanned the walls through his red eyes, searching for signs of weakness. Arthur repressed a shiver. Whenever it attacked the walls, it took the combined strength of all the Templars to resist it. But without the Templars spread out along the defences, their army had suffered heavy losses.

Whatever cheer the men had felt at the announcement of rum rations vanished at the sight of Naberius.

'You think he's coming to surrender?' Arthur asked loudly, trying to break the gloom that had settled over them.

Some looked at him incredulously while others broke out in light chuckles. His comment had lifted the dark mood, if only for a moment.

He continued along the parapets. Soon the enemy's red flag rose again. A moment later, the groan of the trebuchets could be heard as they loosed their projectiles. Though it absolutely terrified him every time, he stayed upright as the air was filled with flying boulders that crashed into the masonry, filling the air with dust. He tried not to cough, then wondered at his actions. Did this reckless display of courage inspire the others? He hoped so.

Once the attack had finished, he continued his rounds, stopping to chat idly with ranker soldiers as he walked. Most knew who he was, while he couldn't for the life of him remember a single name. As he was nearing the end of the wall, his stomach grumbled. Grateful that his shift was almost over, he could … his thoughts froze as his eyes caught on something outside the walls.

Beneath the burnt husks of a siege tower, a shadow caught his eye. It was too dark, too irregular.

'Captain,' Arthur called.

'Sir?' the man answered. Though when Arthur looked at the youth's acne-covered face and inexpert shaving cuts, recognition flickered. The name suddenly sprang to mind. 'Hadrick!'

'Sir?' the man said, alarmed at his sudden shout. Arthur didn't want to admit he'd just been excited to remember someone's name. He calmed himself.

'Weren't you the gate corporal a few weeks ago?' Arthur asked, looking at his epaulettes.

'Only found out I was a captain an hour ago, Templar.'

'Good to have a captain who knows these walls. Wish we had more men like you,' Arthur said. Though the words felt empty, he could see the boy captain straighten his back. 'But I was wondering if there's been anything unusual about that tower?'

Hadrick looked down at the burnt-out husk of a tower and hesitated. 'One man thought he saw something, but no one else saw anything, even in the daylight.'

Arthur grunted. His mind immediately thought of sappers – how far had they come? He didn't know, but there was an easy fix to it. Along every section of the wall they had burning pitch, the thick black liquid bubbling away over a fire.

He reached for his empty flask and cursed again.

'That's the last time I'm going to be generous,' Arthur muttered.

'Sir?'

'Don't worry about it,' Arthur said, clenching his armoured gauntlets. He opened himself up to the Angel's gift, and the power of the Light flooded him. His weariness vanished, and he felt strong enough that he could have flung a boulder further than the trebuchets.

'Get the archers ready, captain.' The man hesitated only a moment before springing into action, ordering the archers to the walls. 'And grab me a fire brand.'

The pitch bubbling in his ears, and the smell of tar filling his nostrils, Arthur stepped forward and grasped the two side handles of the cauldron. He hauled it up as though it weighed nothing. He ignored the shocked gasps of the surrounding soldiers. The heat of the handles was already seeping through his gauntlets while he paused at the wall, judging the distance. When he was ready, he hefted the cauldron and threw the contents as easily as you'd throw water from a bucket.

The pitch flew true, smashing into the shadow, and the black canvas crumpled and disappeared to reveal a hole. Screams erupted as the boiling pitch found human flesh. Arthur grabbed the firebrand from the captain and flung the flickering flame towards the cavern.

The fire left a glowing trail as it sailed down into the hole. The whoosh drowned out the screams as the pitch caught alight.

It was like manufactured hellfire.

A wave of nausea threatened to overwhelm Arthur, but he forced himself to watch. More than one man burst from the hole, trying to quench the flames. A sickening cocktail of burning flesh and dying screams filled the atmosphere. Arthur swallowed the bile rising in his throat.

'Tell your archers to put them out of their misery.'

Soon, arrows were flying, slamming into the men and cutting off their harrowing cries.

'Keep your archers at the ready. There will be more in the hole, but the smoke will force them out. In one hour, send some men down on ropes. I want that tunnel collapsed.'

'Yes, sir.' The boy captain saluted.

Unable to stand the sight any longer, Arthur left Hadrick and descended the spiral staircase. The palms of his hands tingled; woodenly, he took off his gauntlets. There were circular pink burns on his palms from when he'd lifted the cauldron. He'd known when he released the Angel's light that the pain would come.

Away from watching eyes, Arthur sagged against the stone wall, letting his mask slip. Exhaustion hit him like a physical blow. The screams of the men he'd burned would join those already in his nightmares. At least the thick stone spared him from seeing the endless horde beyond their gates – they bloodied the enemy with each passing day, but he wondered how long they could hold on.

CHAPTER FIFTEEN: BEHIND THE WALLS

*A*rthur's brief rest was interrupted as another volley from the trebuchets sent cracks through the stone, the sound rippling like thunder down the narrow staircase.

'Ah, for the Light's sake!' Arthur clapped his hands over his ears, his voice echoing off the walls, as though he were trapped inside a beating drum. After the stone had stopped rumbling and his head no longer rattled, he continued down the last of the spiralling staircase and out into the streets.

The northern city's ruins stretched before him, a maze of crumbling walls and fallen stone. Near the outer wall, only skeletal buildings remained standing, their wounds inflicted by the siege laid bare. Arthur stepped over scattered shards of clay pottery, his boots finding familiar paths through the rubble. These broken streets had become as ordinary to him now as the worn forest trails around his home.

Halfway up the road, a platoon of men moved past him in two uniform lines, marching with efficiency. They were heading for the inner walls before the next bombardment.

'Templar,' the captain said. The men saluted as they passed.

Arthur followed them towards the Keep. He always looked at the inner walls that rose high enough to rival the surrounding mountains, as it was one of the few things that filled him with hope. Then there was the entrance itself. The Iron Gates stood before them, their dark metal surfaces seeming to drink in the light. These monstrous doors, crafted by the Archangel Jophiel herself, were a testament to forgotten arts – impossibly massive yet swinging as easily as a garden gate, while strong enough to shrug off any battering ram.

Arthur walked between them to see the courtyard, which had been transformed into their army's kitchen made largely from the debris of the northern city. Large pots full of stew stood steaming throughout, while soldiers sat eating at tables and chairs under canvas shelters. Though it was quiet, he could see several of them smiling and joking with each other, something becoming increasingly rare amongst the men. The smell of the cooking pots made his stomach rumble. He hadn't eaten since he'd woken up from another drunken debauch this morning.

Arthur joined the queue for a bowl. The man in front immediately stepped aside to let him through.

'Don't be daft. We're all brothers on the wall,' Arthur said.

The soldier's smile revealed a couple of missing teeth. His broken grin reminded Arthur of his son, Richard. When he'd left, the boy had lost a tooth that made him whistle when he spoke, and his smile had been even more infectious.

The memory occupied Arthur while the line moved steadily forward, until it was his turn. His bowl was ladled with a thick stew filled with beef, beans, and potatoes. The smell of it made his stomach clench. Before the merchants had stopped coming to the Fortress, Arthur had secured a store of high-quality provisions that would last several weeks before they ran out. He tried not to think about what would happen when they did, as he breathed in the meaty aroma of the stew.

Before he could find an empty seat, he saw a healer coming out of the Keep. The man's white priestly robes were splattered with a combination of blood and dirt, his shoulders were slumped and his feet were dragging.

Arthur recognised him, but again, the name of the man escaped him.

'Are you alright?' Arthur asked.

The man looked up, his eyes taking a while to focus. His tired eye sockets resembled bruises.

'The triage is hard. We don't have enough strength left to keep everyone alive. I need to conserve what little Light I have left for those who most need it.'

Arthur looked the man up and down. He was only in his twenties, but these few weeks had aged him terribly. His smile, which had once been as clear and bright as the sun, was growing clouded.

'Give me your hand.'

'No.' His eyes showed some steel.

'Don't try to be noble.' Arthur grabbed his hand, and opened himself to the Angel's Light. He felt the power flow into him, alleviating the burns on his palms. Enough Light was flowing in him that his skin emitted a luminescent glow, and he pushed that power through their physical connection. For a moment, the two of them glowed noticeably; people around them paused, their faces illuminated by the power.

'You shouldn't have,' the healer said, though his heart wasn't in it. 'But thank you.' He turned and headed back up into the Keep and to his patients.

'Wait,' Arthur said, and pressed the bowl of stew into the healer's hands. 'I'll get another, you go.'

Arthur was already walking away before the man could try to protest. The Priest looked torn, before he took a bite and turned back towards the Keep.

'Now I'm the one being stupidly noble,' Arthur said, annoyed that he'd have to wait in line again, but before he could rejoin the queue he saw Templar Phillip come out of a nearby queue holding two bowls.

'I could kiss you,' Arthur said.

'I think once was enough,' Phillip said.

Arthur laughed, remembering the night after Ashworth's execution. They'd pinned Phillip to the ground, planting exaggerated kisses on his cheeks – though Phillip's protests had died quickly enough when Rose had joined the revelry. The memory faded as Arthur caught sight of his companion's eyes, seeing a new hollowness there that stopped the teasing words in his throat.

'I feel like a quiet meal. Let's go to my tent,' Arthur said.

Phillip hesitated for a moment before he nodded his acceptance. Arthur led the man around the back of the Keep, where the Templars' tents had been set up. The table with the map of the battlefield had largely been removed; there was no need for constant reminders. Instead, he moved to his nightstand, where he'd left the silver medallion with his family's portraits. He picked it up, running his thumb over the worn surfaces. After almost losing it in battle a week in, he'd begun leaving it here during his shifts. He traced Sarah's likeness with his gaze, drinking in her untameable curls and that smile that still warmed him even in silver. On the other side was Richard, forever captured in that restless age between child and boy – the same boy who'd never met a puddle he wouldn't splash. A wave of homesickness washed over Arthur as he set the medallion back on its stand.

With a grim smile, Arthur focused on the present and indicated Phillip take the seat across from him. He waited, hoping the man would come out with what was bothering him, but instead he just pushed his stew around with his spoon. Arthur gave the other Templar time and took a bite of his own dinner. The beef was little over salted, but the potatoes crumbled delightfully in his mouth. He'd had several mouthfuls before he looked up to see Phillip still hadn't touched his food.

'Alright, out with it.'

Phillip looked up, startled that he wasn't alone.

'You've been moping around like some lovelorn teenager. What's wrong?'

The new Templar sighed, staring down at his bowl. 'I just keep wondering if Zadkiel made a mistake when promoting me to Templar.'

'Yeah, that doesn't go away,' Arthur said. Phillip's eyebrows shot up in surprise. 'It's a reminder to prove you are worthy of it.'

Phillip went quiet for a long time, before he whispered, almost too softly to hear: 'That's just it. I don't think I will ever be worthy.'

Arthur weighed his words carefully. Phillip's deeds in the northern kingdoms still disgusted him, but time had dulled the edge of his revulsion just enough for him to see the man beneath the sins. 'Were you honest with Zadkiel?'

Phillip blinked. 'Of course I was.'

'Did you know Peter became a Templar because he killed a Priest?'

'He what?'

'It's true,' Arthur said. 'He was an orphan, and one of the local women took him in, gave him food and shelter. But the local clergy would demand favours from her for the privilege of helping orphans.'

'What sort of favours—' Peter began then stopped, his mouth forming an O.

'Exactly. When Peter found out, he crushed the Priest's skull with a chunk of rubble, simple as that. The other Priests would have burned him for it too, but when Zadkiel came, Peter stood proud and declared what he'd done and why. And Zadkiel saw something in the boy that was worth saving.'

The words seemed to mollify Phillip somewhat.

'Is that why he dresses the way he does, cause he grew up poor?'

'Could be part of it. Now he's chasing after every woman who wouldn't have given him a second glance before. Making up for lost time, I guess.'

It brought the ghost of a smile to Phillip's lips. 'What about you?'

'Me what?'

'How did you get made a Templar?'

'Oh,' Arthur said, a grim smile tugging at the corners of his mouth. 'Got into an argument with the Primate himself.'

'You what?'

'Aye. I was only a lowly sergeant then, arguing with the actual head of our church. Been at that rank for years – didn't have the silver tongue or deep pockets to climb higher, but I was content enough. Then my captain retired and we got some rich tit who couldn't tell his arse from his nose. The fool volunteered us to hunt bandits in the woods. I warned him about ambushes, but he just kept spouting nonsense about how "the Light will protect us." And me, being the good soldier I was, followed his orders.' Arthur's voice darkened. 'Half the unit died, but we got those bandits in the end. And for that brilliant victory, they gave us commendations at the altar of the Light.'

'Is that when you started drinking?'

'Of course not. I've always loved drinking,' Arthur said easily. 'But I still wonder if those lads would be alive if I'd fought harder against those orders.' He took a breath. 'I might have had a bit too much before the ceremony. When they started praising the brilliance of my new captain, I couldn't hold my tongue. Stood up right there in front of the primate and told them exactly how incompetent the man was. Caused quite the scandal, but that's what caught Zadkiel's eye. We had a long talk after, and next thing I knew, I was a Templar.'

'Just like that?'

'No, but I assume it was something similar to what happened to you.'

Understanding flew across Phillip's face as he nodded. 'What about the other Templars?'

'Less exciting. Elise won a javelin contest. Wilfred got noticed during one of his battle rages, of course. Matthew for tracking bandits through impossible terrain. And Rose?' Arthur's expression darkened. 'She put a noble in his place when he wouldn't take no for an answer. Broke his jaw and his pride.' He leaned forward. 'Point is, Zadkiel sees something in each of us that makes us worthy of his gift. Our job now is to prove him right.'

'I have a lot of redemption to earn before that can be possible.'

'Luckily, we have plenty of opportunities around here. Just think – if you kill Naberius, that will probably do it.'

Though Phillip did not respond, he took a bite of his stew, and Arthur counted that as a victory. They finished their meal in companionable silence before Phillip got up to leave.

'Let me help you with that armour,' Phillip said, already moving to assist before Arthur could protest. Too bemused to argue, he allowed the other man to help him remove his vambraces, then his breastplate, before he worked his way down to the metal-clad boots. Each piece of plate mail came away with practiced care, and it was placed on the armour stand. Arthur rolled his shoulders, feeling suddenly weightless without his steel shell.

'Sure you don't want a drink?' Arthur said, moving to his alcohol cabinet. Someone had restocked it – the lone bottle of Waterlord whiskey stood in the centre like a promise. He left that one untouched. That was for after their victory, if it came at all.

'Not tonight. I think I want to contemplate what you said.'

'Suit yourself,' Arthur said, pouring a generous portion of regular whiskey into a tumbler. 'No lectures tonight about my drinking?'

'I wouldn't dream of it, First Templar.'

Arthur paused mid-sip. 'Was that ... a joke?' Then he threw back his head and laughed, the sound filling his tent like warmth. 'By the Light, we'll make a Templar of you yet.'

He took another sip, allowing the whiskey to burn away the day's weight. It felt like the first real breath he'd taken since morning – or maybe since the siege began. The alcohol couldn't wash away the siege or the responsibility, but it could dull their edges just enough to make sleep possible.

Tomorrow would bring more battles, more decisions, more weight. But for now, in this quiet moment, with empty bowls and honest words between them, Arthur could almost believe they'd make it through.

CHAPTER SIXTEEN: MORIAH'S WRATH

*A*rthur floated in the blackness of sleep before the images appeared. Awareness seeped in: He could feel the gentle press of a linen shirt and plain brown breeches, and his bare feet sank into the soft riverbank. The wind bent the reeds and sent gooseflesh over his skin, while his eyes wandered across the fast-moving body of water. On the opposite shore was a sea of people. They stood, shoulder to shoulder, their eyes following his every move.

He recognised them – they were memories he had tried to block out. They were the faces of the dead. He tried meeting their gazes, the stares of the men, women and children who looked back at him. They were the ones he had failed because he hadn't been fast enough, smart enough, or strong enough.

Calling out to them was fruitless. They never answered, but the weight of their expressions felt heavier than a mountain. The guilt of his duty and how he hadn't measured up weighed on him. There were fresh faces in the crowd, those from the siege. Both men he had killed, and those who had fought alongside him.

Though not every soul he'd killed or failed waited for him on the other side, the faces that greeted him were in the hundreds. Light, how he just wanted to wake up, and find another bottle of whiskey to drown out the pressure of their stares. He tried closing his eyes, but it just made the feeling worse.

A loud thunderclap rolled through the dream, shattering it like shards of glass.

He woke with a start as the thunder continued, shaking the very ground. Storms were common enough in the mountains, but this was different. The rumbling was growing in size and intensity. Still coming to terms with his surroundings, he thought it was an earthquake, his first thought being of how it might destroy the walls.

Then he realised what it really was and leapt to his feet. He tripped over his bedding and fell hard on the floor.

'For the Light's sake,' he cursed, feeling the effects of his hangover. He disentangled himself from the covers and got to the entrance, ripping the flaps open. Immediately the mountain air kissed all along his exposed skin, raising gooseflesh at the cold. He ignored it, his eyes fixed on Mount Moriah.

The massif loomed before him, its immense bulk making even the Fortress's highest towers seem like children's toys. The mountain commanded the pass, forcing it to bend around its ancient stone like a river around a giant's knee. From the outer walls, its base stretched over a thousand yards away, but its presence felt much closer as its peak unleashed hell. A wall of white death was cascading down its slopes – a churning mass of rock, snow, and splintered trees that devoured everything in its path. The roar of it thundered through the Keep in rolling waves, drowning out everything else. The sheer volume of ice and snow pouring down seemed impossible, as if the mountain itself were collapsing to seal the pass like nature's cork in a bottle.

Snow continued down the hill in a never-ending landslide. The sheer ferocity of it made him tremble with fear. He glanced up at the peaks on either side of the Fortress, but they were solid rock. Very little ice or snow adorned their summits.

The rumbling slowed, the thundering died down as clouds of dust and snow floated through the air, blanketing the entire pass in an eerie silence. The devastation it must have caused to the enemy....

'They did it!'

Arthur snapped out of his reverie. Peter was outside too, pointing at the avalanche and laughing. Taut, naked, lean muscles completely exposed to the brisk mountain air, he danced a merry jig. 'Those hell-born bastards did it!'

The amount of people who had died, the way the snow would have destroyed the pass and all those in it. A spark of hope kindled inside Arthur's chest. Shame quickly followed it over all the death it had caused. He tried to reason that he hadn't started this war, and it helped. A little.

Peter glanced at him, his smile never faltering. 'Morning Arthur, it's a damn fine morning – isn't it?'

It was hard not to get caught up in Peter's air of revelry.

'My lord?'

A woman, clothed in a Templar's robes, stepped out from inside Peter's tent. She had the blonde hair of the mountain women, with fine curves that would turn half the heads in the army. The woman looked over and saw Arthur, and her cheeks immediately went bright red.

'I am sorry, my lord.'

'It's alright, Bonnie,' Arthur said.

'Ah,' Peter said quickly. 'This is Sheena.'

'Thought she looked different,' Arthur said, feeling a smile tug at the corners of his mouth. He enjoyed seeing Peter squirm.

Sheena crossed her arms and her glare might well have been enough to halt a demon in its tracks. The Templar stepped forward and reached for her hands, and though reluctant, she allowed him to hold them.

'Sheena, even though Bonnie was special to me, she did not have the love you hold for your brother, Aran. I could see that when you came to me to ask me to protect him. Nor does she have your sweet singing voice, something you shouldn't keep hidden from the world. Your warm smile is as bright as the sunrise, and you are my joy in these dark times.' Some of Sheena's outrage softened, and Peter smiled a brilliant smile. 'Can you forgive me?'

Sheena hesitated. 'I don't know.'

Peter laughed again. He pulled her in, sweeping her up and around in a circle. A smile quickly spread across her lips, devolving into laughter. When she landed, her cheeks were flushed, but Peter held her up so she didn't lose her balance. Sheena's smile was bright and her eyes were dancing.

Arthur coughed loudly, gesturing at the avalanche.

Peter looked at him, completely unabashed at his own nakedness or the public show of affection. 'It will take them hours to sort out that mess, and the army can survive without me a little longer. Don't worry, I'll meet you at the walls soon,' Peter said, sweeping Sheena up again. 'But not too soon.'

Arthur smiled, feeling a spark of hope that maybe the war would be over. He knew he shouldn't entertain it, but he couldn't help himself. He looked back as the avalanche's dust cloud settled. Their own troops would need reassurance and direction, but Peter had spoken the truth: It would take some time for the enemy to reorganise, but when they did, he wanted to be battle-ready.

Arthur retreated inside his tent and methodically donned his armour. The soldiers would be shaken from the avalanche and he would need to be a pillar of strength. The task took far longer than he would have liked, his fingers itching with impatience as he tightened every strap. Yet by the time he emerged, dust still floated in the air.

He proceeded down through the Keep, passing lines of men marching towards the bulwarks, their lines sweeping up from inside the southern town all the way to the besieged part of the northern walls.

Matthew joined Arthur as they headed for the battlements. The quiet Templar nodded in greeting, his face hidden by his long strands of stringy black hair. His bow was already strung, quiver at his belt. Together they continued towards the parapet, where every platoon was moving along the walls. The captains were trying to get their platoons into formation under the colonel's watchful eyes.

Phillip was a bright beacon of Light moving amongst the troops on the walkway.

'I'm going to check with the colonel. Can you get onto the walls and assess the situation?'

Matthew lifted his bow in a silent salute and moved towards the parapet.

Arthur moved towards the formations. He recognised the colonel; the man had grown a ghost-white beard that emphasised his strong jawline. Arthur had seen the man take an arrow to the leg, refuse infusions of Light, and rebuff all attempts to get him to leave the defences. Yet despite this vivid memory, he couldn't remember the man's name. Was it Edward? Joseph? Or Robert?

'Colonel.'

'First Templar.' The colonel saluted him and looked over at the gathering regiment. Several thousand men were manoeuvring on and around the fallen buildings. 'I ordered the men mustered for whatever need may arise.'

'Good thinking,' Arthur said. 'I want all our horses saddled and ready to go, particularly the heavy horse.'

The colonel's eyes widened at the implications. 'Yes, Templar.' He saluted, turning to his men, and was already shouting orders.

Arthur turned back towards the ramparts, joining the others – Phillip, Wilfred, Matthew, and Rose – on the walls.

Earlier, it had been nothing but a writhing sea of enemy forces, but now broken trees, smashed boulders and a mixture of snow and dirt had buried where the enemy had been hours before. As he looked around at the pass, it resembled an impassable labyrinth of snow, ice, rocks, and trees. The siege engines had vanished, and there were hundreds of men and women on the surface of the snowy debris, desperately digging to rescue buried comrades and loved ones. A disorganised chaos reigned over the enemy.

'Matthew, you have a better eye for this sort of thing,' Arthur said. 'Are they trapped in there?'

The quiet Templar looked up at the sky, scanning the surrounding mountains, his eagle eyes searching the debris field. He sniffed the air before slowly shaking his head.

Arthur felt his heart sink. 'You mean the army on the other side can still get through?'

'Difficult maybe, but yes.'

Arthur felt a coldness grip his heart. He knew what he needed to do, but the sickness threatened to overwhelm him.

Before he could steel himself to do it, he heard exclamations and shouts from the Keep. On the main road was Peter, shining like a bonfire and moving as swiftly as a horse. Sprinting in full plate mail with his slender blade and long dagger strapped to his belt, the man didn't slow as he charged toward their position. Soldiers paused to watch him as he rushed at the walls, and then at the last second he crouched and sprang upwards. The leap launched him high into the air, allowing him to arc over and land on the battlements in an awesome display of power and agility.

There was a ragged cheer from the men as they saw him do it.

'Good entrance,' Rose said.

'You like that? Been practising it for a while,' Peter said.

'It's very *you.*'

Peter frowned, as if debating whether he should take that as an insult. Before he could comment, Arthur spoke.

'Templars, as hard as it is to say, the battle is not yet won.' The Templars turned to him. 'So we must take the advantage while it presents itself. We are to ride out to meet them. The heavy horse are being mustered, and I want them led by the Angel's chosen.'

Peter eyes shifted from him to the others. 'This is a joke, right? They're beaten and bloody. If we strike now, we will—'

'They still outnumber us,' Phillip interrupted him. 'Even now, their numbers are in the tens of thousands.'

'What of Naberius? We cannot face him in the open.'

'He is nowhere in sight,' Arthur said. It was true, and it had been the first thing he'd looked for, but the enemy's camp was in shambles. Some on the opposite side of the pass had been spared the avalanche's wrath, but while the enemy horde was wounded, it wasn't beaten. 'I hope he is crushed beneath those rocks, but even if we're not that lucky, I am still ordering the assault.'

Colour drained from Peter's face.

'Matthew, I want you on the walls. You will have full command.'

The Templar nodded.

'The rest of you, gather down there. Get your men and standard bearers ready. We ride as soon as we are able,' Arthur continued, hardening his heart. 'With the Light to guide us, and all the luck in the nine hells, the siege ends today. Now move.'

'Yes,' Wilfred said with such relish that it struck at Arthur's confidence. He looked out at the destroyed enemy camp and recoiled at the thought of slaughtering the helpless. He tried to reassure himself that he hadn't started this. It didn't help.

CHAPTER SEVENTEEN: THE RECKONING

The outer walls had hidden their movements from the enemy. Over a thousand horsemen were mustered within the ruins of the city, almost two hundred heavily armoured, ready to break the enemy ranks, while the rest would sweep in behind, killing the enemy as they came.

A stableboy held Ezekiel. The white stallion was covered in plate and chain mail, and as the destrier moved, his armour shifted and clinked.

'Easy, Ezekiel. Soon,' Arthur ran his gauntleted hand along the horse's neck, finding the gaps between the plates of armour. The destrier pawed at the ground, steel-shod hooves gouging the earth, his impatience matching the tension in the air. A smile crossed Arthur's face as he saw his mount's eagerness – then froze as movement caught his eye. Luke and James, the Templar cousins, were striding toward him with matching scowls beneath their formidable moustaches. Though both shared the same stocky build of career soldiers, Luke towered over his shorter kinsman like an oak over a stunted pine.

'Templars,' Arthur said cautiously.

'Why are we babysitting Wilfred again?' Luke said without preamble.

'You know how he gets – the battle lust makes him bloody crazy, and we can't afford to let him go full Wilfred on them,' Arthur said. 'You two are not only skilled fighters, but you work better in tandem than any of the other Templars.' The praise wasn't entirely false, but for all their skill, the cousins' endless complaints made them about as pleasant as an empty whisky bottle.

'I hate being dependable,' James said.

'We're going to be in the thick of the fighting too,' Luke continued.

'I'll make it up to you.'

They breathed identical heavy sighs, then looked at each other and came to a silent conclusion.

'Alright, we will shadow him and pull him out if we need to retreat,' James said.

'Thank you,' Arthur said, thinking he'd just adverted another crisis, yet before the two of them had ridden off, he saw Peter coming towards him, his brow creased with determination.

Bracing mentally, Arthur prepared himself. He'd been expecting him sooner.

'Arthur, my friend,' Peter said, his voice unusually sombre. 'The enemy is broken. They're scattered and leaderless. The siege is done. With Naberius buried, those who were our enemies are just lost in a war they never chose. These aren't demons we're facing, but farmers' sons and merchants' daughters. Surely we can show them there's a better path than more bloodshed.'

Arthur had been having the same doubts about his actions. He didn't want to kill helpless people and endanger his own troops needlessly. Light, he needed a drink.

'Though the snow has temporarily blocked the pass, they still outnumber us at least five to one,' Phillip said loudly behind him. 'They will spit on our offer of mercy, then once they take this Fortress, they will conscript whoever they can and butcher the rest. Naberius may be buried but I doubt we have seen the last of him. Now is the time to attack.'

'We don't all have your penchant for killing the weak,' Peter snapped.

'I fought against their army, delaying them long enough so we could prepare while you were off sleeping with someone else's wife!'

'Templars!' Arthur shouted. 'If you have a problem with each other then sort it out in the yard tonight. But for now, we are brothers. Apologise, both of you. Now!'

'I'm sorry Peter, that was uncalled for.'

Peter still looked furious, but he muttered, 'As was my comment.'

Arthur moved up next to Peter. 'I know this is hard for you, but they are our enemy. Naberius will force them to fight us again, whether it is in a day or a week. This is our best chance to end the attack once and for all.'

'And what of honour?' Peter asked bitterly.

'It is for the story books and when it's convenient. I won't let our lands fall because we feared to stain our hands. And I won't let harm come to Zadkiel.' Arthur rested a hand on his shoulder. 'When this is over, we'll make amends. Together.'

Peter's dark eyes searched Arthur's, as if looking for something. 'You will carry their deaths on your conscience until the day you die. No, don't answer. I will fight, but I don't like it.' He then gave Arthur a bitter smile. 'There will be a reckoning for what we do here today.'

The words enlarged the cracks in Arthur's confidence. He tried to shake them, but they rattled around inside his head. He tried to distract himself by grabbing Ezekiel's pommel and pulling himself up into the saddle. Adjusting his seat, he glanced over at Captain Hadrick and nodded. The boy captain, holding the standard of Zadkiel aloft, waved the banner back and forth.

Other Bannermen copied the signal up and down the walls. Wooden mallets were used to slam back the drawbars; the wood creaked, the dust shifting as they were pulled out of their place, unlocking the gates. Hinges groaned as the heavy oak doors swung open for the first time in weeks.

Ezekiel tugged and snatched at the reins. Arthur gave the horse his head, and he took the lead. They were the first through the gates and onto the killing fields, the stench of burnt siege towers and decaying bodies hanging like a haze. The cawing of scavenger crows echoed as they took flight.

Only two hundred yards from the walls, the enemy camp began with an orderly display of military might – rows of tents still stood in precise formations, their banners hanging limp in the morning air. But beyond this thin veneer of order lay devastation. Like a tide waterline marking nature's wrath, the avalanche had transformed the thousand-yard-wide pass into a ruined patchwork quilt of destruction that extended for leagues into the distance. Brightly coloured tents lay flattened and torn, their remains twisted with splintered supply wagons and broken standards. The rolling earth had churned everything together: rich pavilions, common soldiers' shelters, the banners of a dozen armies, all ground down like grain beneath a millstone.

Against the stark backdrop of the rocky mountainsides, thousands of dazed survivors picked through the wreckage like ants on a disturbed hill. Some frantically dug through the debris, searching for comrades. Others sat or lay in eerie silence, shock having rendered them as still as the stones that had brought about their destruction. Here and there, makeshift paths had been carved through the chaos, winding between massive boulders that had rolled down with the snow and earth. The few standing tents looked like islands in a sea of ruin, while the cries of the wounded echoed off the valley walls, competing with the cawing of the feasting crows above.

The devastating power of the avalanche was evident in how it had reshaped the valley floor – the neat rows of the surviving camp giving way to haphazard mounds of snow-mixed earth and debris, creating an uneven field that had once been an almost flat path.

'If any of the Archangels are listening, will you keep an eye on this lot? Save me the trouble in this life and the next,' Arthur muttered. It was the only mercy he'd show them this day.

The horsemen were fanning out, sitting shoulder to shoulder, knight alongside commoner across the length of the walls. Lances stood in rawhide loops tied to the men's saddles, their metal tips glinting in the sunlight.

Now was the time. Arthur reached for his necklace of Sarah and Richard, seeking its familiar reminder of why he fought. He realised he'd left it on the bloody nightstand. His hand fell away. Instead, he opened himself up to the Light, and power flooded through him – his weariness, thirst, and hunger vanished as his senses sharpened and his armour turned featherlight. He lifted his lance and channelled power into his voice. His men would need to act without hesitation.

'Men of the Light!' The sound echoed through the pass, amplified as it bounced off the mountains. Those eager for battle picked up the call with their war cries. 'For weeks we have been fighting and bleeding, because of Naberius and his army of Darkness. Today we strike back!'

Arthur paused, allowing the roar and the battle vigour to infect them all. 'Today, we pluck at the strings of destiny! Here we have the chance to burn so brightly that we can banish the Darkness back to the bowels of hell!' His voice rode over the mountains, drowning out the cheers, silencing the crows, quietening the wind itself. When the echoes had faded, the horsemen lifted their spears as one, and their clamour rose again to a monstrous roar. The Templars added their own Light-enhanced voices to the battle cry. Whatever trepidation that still lingered was suffocated by the battle lust of their comrades.

'Let our actions echo across eternity.' Arthur spun Ezekiel to face the enemy. 'Men of the Light, forward!'

Ezekiel reared, adding his own cry to that of the men. He landed hard on the ground, hooves churning the earth as they pounded forward. Arthur worried he'd have to rein the beast in, but his fellow horsemen were spurring their mounts onwards to keep the line steady as they surged across the field like an advancing tide. The bones of the dead rattled at their passing.

The enemy camp erupted into chaos at the sight of the charging cavalry. Those nearest the intact portion of the camp tried to gather in formation, but the ordered lines dissolved as panic spread through their ranks like wildfire. In the avalanche-ravaged areas, the scene descended into pure mayhem. Men and women scrambled in every direction, some desperately trying to climb the treacherous slopes of fallen earth, while others fled blindly through the debris field. They stumbled over half-buried supply carts and collapsed tents, their feet tangling in torn banners and abandoned cloaks. The uneven ground betrayed every hurried step – soldiers slipping on loose scree or sinking knee-deep into pockets of wet snow and mud.

Their commanders' voices cracked with desperation as they tried to rally their forces. Orders echoed off the valley walls – calls to form ranks, to stand fast, to present spears – but each command only added to the confusion. Some soldiers tried to obey, turning to face the charge even as others fled past them. Though their numbers still reached the tens of thousands, their formation resembled a shattered mirror.

Arthur let go of Ezekiel's reins, allowing the horse to leap to the fore.

I will take first blood.

Using his knees, he steered his mount directly towards one pocket of gathering pikemen. Lowering his lance, he aimed for the first man, who stood with shaking hands and an unsteady spear. Letting loose a roar, Arthur spurred Ezekiel onwards. The lance took the man in the chest, piercing through cloth and flesh. Its point carried so far through him that it propped him up when the tip dug into the ground. The soldier stared down at his impaled chest in disbelief.

The force of the charge continued forwards, and Ezekiel ran over the second man in the line, crushing him like a sack of oats. Screams and battle cries echoed around Arthur as the line of heavy horse thundered into the enemy formation. Arthur pulled his heavy war mace loose. Using his enhanced strength, he struck left and right, crushing through shield and bone.

The initial charge had made the pocket falter, the unsteady line fracture further. The horsemen had smashed into the enemy like a wave, crashing and crushing them beneath their charge. Men shrieked, skewered and flattened by the horsemen's onslaught. Like a breaking dam the pocket fled, first in a trickle and then a flood. They had stood their ground for less than a minute.

Arthur wheeled his horse while his squad reformed. The breaking enemy group ran to other nearby pockets of men and pikes, their numbers compacting up against the walls of the valley. Many tried to scramble over the hills, though the unsteady nature of the avalanche's fallen earth made the climb treacherous. Captains ordered different squads to sweep over the retreating forces, running them down beneath lances and hooves.

Arthur surveyed the field. The other Templars had led their own men in the charge. All across the lines they had squashed the enemy's resistance, but the foe was scrambling like ants, surging out of fallen tents and breaking out of their stupor and rallying to the scattered formations. Commanders and Priests of Lucifer were gathering pockets of resistance, their hell-born powers launching spears of pure Darkness to skewer the horsemen of the Light.

Rage built up inside Arthur as he looked at these enemy commanders. They were carriers of the demon's will, true perpetrators of death and misery. Filling himself with the entirety of the Angel's Light, he rode directly for them.

He could hear Hadrick shouting behind him for the men to form up and follow the First Templar into battle, but Arthur wasn't waiting on them, and he urged Ezekiel into a gallop.

The Priests of Lucifer shot their dark lances at him, but they shattered like broken glass when pitted against his glowing aura. The force of their strikes was absorbed so that they carried all the stopping power of a tuft of grass.

The brightness of his presence caused the enemy lines to shield their eyes from his Light. It also caused their spears to bounce off Ezekiel's armour as Arthur laid into them with his mace. His first blow caved in the skull of a man with a sickening squelch. Already swinging his mace around to the next opponent, he felt Ezekiel trampling the first foe beneath his iron-shod hooves.

A courageous enemy soldier leapt forward, spear aimed at Ezekiel. The horse screamed in pain as the blade cut across his foreleg. He tilted, and sent Arthur sprawling forward in a somersault, directly into the centre of the enemy forces.

The surprise of his fall was the only thing that saved him. A semicircle of faces stared down at him in shock; still brimming with Light, Arthur leapt to his feet despite the weight of his armour. His supernatural power and strength allowed him to move like a whirlwind, sending bodies flying like seeds blown from a dandelion.

Despite his tenacity, hundreds still surrounded him. A war hammer slammed into his back, and though his armour saved him, still he stumbled forward. He swung around behind him, crushing two people together with a single blow. A spear glanced off his breastplate. He swung and swung, so deep in his bloodlust that he didn't know if any blows had penetrated his armour.

He almost slammed his mace into Captain Hadrick, before suddenly recognising him. The horsemen had followed him in, blowing open the enemy lines and killing the foe with swords and axes, their lances spent. Chaos reigned as the horsemen fought the enemy foot soldiers.

Arthur looked around for the Dark clergy, but Phillip and his cohort had hit that pocket from behind. The Templar's spear was a blur as he carved his way through them.

It took Arthur a moment to collect himself. He looked at the blood and carnage he had left in his wake, and the red mist was the only thing keeping him from being sick. He looked down, checking himself all over. His plate was dented and bent, and his undercoat of mail had been pierced in half a dozen places, but none were serious wounds.

Despite the battle raging around him, he spun, looking for his mount. Maybe Ezekiel still lived. He ran back to where he'd been unhorsed, weaving through the maze of the dead and dying, slipping in the blood-soaked mud.

The stallion was lying on the ground, his white hair marred with black and red. He looked up, and Arthur felt his heart go still with relief. Miraculously, the stallion still lived, though blood flowed from his leg.

It would be better to end him than let him be captured by the enemy – but when Arthur gripped his mace, sticky with gore and bone shards, he knew he couldn't do it. He dropped the weapon and pulled a bandage from his belt. Ignoring the clashing of steel behind him, he stepped close, resting a hand on the horse's head.

Ezekiel laid his head down, allowing himself to be treated. Carefully, Arthur wrapped the bandage around his horse's leg. The first few layers were quickly stained red. His movements were efficient and firm, tying it off at the end, and when he'd finished, he channelled Light into the horse, giving him part of the Angel's strength. He coaxed Ezekiel to his feet. The destrier tentatively put pressure on the injured leg, but with the power of the Light coursing through him, it could hold his weight.

'Go, back to the Keep.'

The horse looked at him reproachfully.

'Go,' he commanded, slapping it on the rear.

With a last glance, the stallion trotted away from the battle.

CHAPTER EIGHTEEN: THE PRICE PAID

The ground trembled beneath Arthur's feet as he retrieved his war mace, likely an aftershock from the avalanche.

All around him the enemy formation was breaking up, his men riding down those who were fleeing. Phillip shouted orders for his men to regroup. Battle standards lay crushed under churned earth and fallen soldiers; the screams and cries of the dying were a chorus sung to the systematic slaughter of the enemy. The metallic tang of blood was mingled with the rust of swords and armour to hang heavy in the air.

Phillip stood over a downed member of the black clergy – the Priestess raised a pale, pleading hand – but the Templar paid it no mind as he slammed his spear through her chest and into the ground. Her body went limp.

Arthur felt the bile rising in his throat as he looked further afield. His eyes travelled over the avalanche that had transformed the pass into a treacherous hill of wood, snow and dirt. Pockets of pikemen were forming up at the base of the switchbacks, where men and women were climbing up to escape the carnage caused by the horsemen. Amongst their number was the High Priest of Lucifer, his dark dreadlocks a rallying point as he raised his staff with a demonic skull on the end. Guillamere's presence was the calm after the storm, causing the enemy's panic to recede.

Another tremor moved through the ground. Arthur looked around, thinking they would need to get away if more of the mountain was going to come down. His men had won every single skirmish, resulting in the deaths of thousands, but their foes were regrouping. Soon they'd be in position to swarm the attackers. Phillip came to stand next to him, following his gaze.

'I think we may have lost our edge,' Arthur said. 'If we push any further, the ground will become too treacherous for our mounts.'

'Time to retreat?'

'An orderly one,' Arthur agreed. Then, infusing his voice with Light, he called: 'Captain Hadrick. Send the signal for withdrawal – back to the walls.'

Hadrick brought a horn to his lips, his boyish face pale, but he held steady as he blew three quick blasts. Bannermen turned to him, awaiting confirmation before waving their flags. Each of the squadrons recognised the signals. James and Luke were busy encircling Wilfred's battle cohort, creating a living wall as they convinced the battle hungry Templar to withdraw. The others were more orderly, getting their men to disengage and withdraw, while more enemy soldiers gathered around Guillamere.

'Peter is locked in battle at the moment,' Phillip said.

'I think a moment or two more … and there we go, they're breaking,' Arthur said as the first of the enemy group Peter had engaged began to run. He motioned for Hadrick to leave. The captain sent the wounded, and those who had lost their mounts, back towards the walls. Those still mounted and able formed up around him.

Together they watched as Peter used his slender sword and dagger to lay waste around him.

Then the ground shook again, harder than before.

For a panicked second, Arthur looked up at the mountains, but they were still. The rumbling was coming from nearby. Arthur's eyes trailed down the path of destruction left by the avalanche. A feeling of dread crept down his spine, and the glowing Light around him flickered.

A sudden quake shook the landslide, rocks and fallen trees shifting. They stilled and then burst apart like a volcano erupting as a geyser of hellfire shot into the sky. The flame was darker than the night, drawing in the surrounding light, and Arthur shielded his face as the heat blasted him like a furnace.

Not enough whiskey in the world for this, he thought. *Naberius is free— of bloody course he is.*

As though erupting from the very bowels of hell, the three-headed hound appeared. He muscled apart the earth, snow and debris, shaking off the remnants of the avalanche like a mortal dog would water. His liquid black fur reflected the sunlight as the beast stood to his full height, his size and weight rivalling that of one of the largest wagons. He was taller than Arthur when he sat on horseback and looked as clean and unharmed as though he had just stepped off a mural.

Three pairs of red eyes scanned the battlefield.

Peter's squad was still reforming when the hound's eyes fell on them. The Templar did not hesitate, ordering his men back into formation.

'Go, go!' Arthur shouted, already running, reaching for the Angel's Light. It was like a dying fire, and there was not enough warmth to fill him. He knew Peter would likely be worse off, as the man was always too free in gifting the Light to others.

'Light, give him strength to withstand the hellfire,' Arthur said in a quick prayer as he charged towards Peter.

Phillip was by his side, while Hadrick was ordering the horsemen with him to charge.

It's a rescue mission. We just need to buy him enough time to escape, Arthur thought.

The three heads of Naberius howled as one. When they stopped, the beast growled like thunder and moved like a fox.

Arthur was at least a thousand paces away. He tried to force his protesting muscles to move faster.

Peter held his twin weapons in front of him, ready to meet the beast head on. Mounted troops and those on foot rushed to stand beside him.

The hound loped onward, his lead head drawing in a deep breath. Hellfire erupted from its maw, engulfing Peter and his men in a searing wave that turned the air itself into an inferno. Men screamed as they were roasted alive from inside their armour, their shrieks quickly cutting off as the smell of burnt flesh filled the air. Yet from amidst the flame, Peter leapt forward with his blade extended as he dove at Naberius. Faster than Arthur would have believed possible, the lead head ducked out of the way, while its right paw batted Peter off like a gnat. Slammed backwards, Peter crunched into the ground with his leg bent the wrong way.

Beside Arthur, a blazing blur passed him by as Phillip sped towards Naberius, but even so, they were both too slow. The left head picked Peter up before they could close the distance. He shook him like a rag doll, its teeth puncturing armour and skin. The man didn't even have time to scream.

'*No!*' Arthur shouted. He watched the entire thing unfold, his heart stilling in disbelief as Peter was flung to the earth, torn flesh and gore splattering on the ground around him. He never stopped running, rage adding more fuel to his limbs as he sought vengeance on Peter's killer.

Naberius saw the two other Templars coming, then the three heads growled, spittle flicking from their mouths as he bared his sword-like fangs. Phillip's speed caught it by surprise as it reared back, the lead head sucking in air to unleash its hellfire. The Templar's aura of Light grew brighter just as the hellfire struck it.

Arthur dodged the left-most head as it snapped at him. He swung his mace, but the head moved like quicksilver, rising out of its path. However, the move had opened the way to its body. Arthur continued his forward momentum, stepping inside the demon creature's guard. He swung his mace with all the fury of the Light behind it. The steel club cracked against Naberius's foreleg with an audible crunch.

The hellfire ceased as the hound leapt back with a howl of pain.

The liquid darkness on his skin was moving like warm honey, encompassing and shielding its injured limb. He hobbled back on three legs, the two side-most heads snapping while the lead head looked ready to breathe fire on anyone who would dare come close. Yet Phillip continued to harass it, spear moving like a hummingbird as it floated faster than Arthur could follow.

Hadrick had wheeled his mounted troops to rush over past their flanks, stopping any of the enemy forces from interfering.

'Shields up!' Hadrick called.

Arrows, casting shadows like a flock of ravens, arced above them. Arthur raised his armoured arms to protect his head and body as the arrows rained down. Most of the shafts bounced off their plate armour, but the squeals of horses and men alike meant some had found their mark.

Arthur stood there, watching the demon carefully, as it now rested his injured paw on the ground. In a matter of minutes, he would be fully mobile again.

'Back! Everyone fall back!' Arthur called.

Hadrick pulled up beside him with two riderless horses. Phillip struggled with Peter's body, his hands trembling as he tried to secure his fallen brother to the horse. Arthur reached him, and together they bound the dead Templar to the horse.

Arthur stared hard at Naberius. The beast felt so close, almost as though he could take revenge for Peter now. He could feel the three pairs of eyes watching and waiting. Yet more and more enemy soldiers were crowding around the demon, making any attempt on him complete suicide.

Arthur released a low growl of frustration, knowing vengeance would have to wait. He swung into the saddle and wheeled his mount in a circle, the whisper of approaching arrows urging him into motion.

Not one of their enemies pursued them; Arthur half wished they would. But as he rode back towards the city, he could see archers lining the walls, Matthew's stoic figure among them. As he pulled in front of the gate, he looked back at their adversary. Despite thousands having been killed in their charge, their numbers seemed undiminished as they rose from the chaos like weeds after a spring rain.

In the centre stood Naberius himself, the beast's hulking form easily identifiable amongst his army.

The siege will continue, he thought in frustration as they retreated inside the walls. What had he gained today, besides more death? Worse, he had forced a friend to his grave; he pondered it as he watched men and women rushing to pull the fallen Templar off his horse.

'I have failed you,' Arthur whispered, his mind flitting to Sheena, Peter's most recent lover. He closed his eyes, holding back a grimace – knowing he would have to be the one to break the news to her. And to all the others who would come. He would have to hold it together until things were in place, then only after that could he grieve. Forcing a grim smile, he empowered his voice to congratulate the soldiers on their successful sortie, to tell them they had dealt a serious blow to the enemy. Arthur didn't believe his own words, and he wasn't sure they did either. But there were enough cheers to drown out their doubts. Beneath his veneer, he felt a growing numbness, one that he wasn't sure alcohol could fix. But he knew he was going to try.

CHAPTER NINETEEN: WAKES AND DREAMS

The flames of the funeral pyre rose in the Fortress courtyard, the fire consuming what remained of their friend and brother. The heat pressed against Arthur's face, but he couldn't step back – didn't deserve to look away. Peter's warrior band stood vigil beneath the dancing lights of their commander's funeral fire, their bandaged wounds and haunted eyes a testament to the fight they had put up.

A chorus of soft sobbing rose from the gathered women. Arthur watched them – Sheena with her summer-sky eyes, Bonnie's raven hair catching the firelight, and so many others. They'd all known about each other, about Peter's wandering heart, yet they all bore the weight of their shared grief. The man had touched so many lives, left so many hearts behind, both warmed and broken. Now those hearts broke one last time.

When the embers began to die down, it was Wilfred who stepped up. He looked out over the waiting masses, his face unusually sombre. He spoke, and his usual gruff voice cracked. 'And so does his body return to the Light.'

Elise and Matthew went up to comfort the big man, who seemed to have taken the loss of Peter the hardest. Phillip stepped up behind him and place a hand on his shoulder.

Arthur left the funeral pyre, holding back the grief as he made for his tent. They were holding a more private wake there.

When inside, and alone, he swallowed, feeling tears threaten to spill out. By some miracle, he held them back, not wanting to show how much Peter's death had affected him. To distract himself, he began pouring the dark mountain ale – thick stuff brewed with pine needles and honey, strong enough to warm even the coldest nights on the peaks. The rich aroma filled the tent as the other Templars arrived. Two Templars were keeping watch on the wall, but the rest were here.

They dutifully took a mug each and sat down around the table. The eight of them remained in sombre silence, taking silent sips of their mugs. The weight of the stillness felt as heavy as an anchor.

'I suppose we should go around the table and say something nice about Peter?' Elise suggested as she was the last to take a seat. Arthur avoided meeting her eyes, as did the other men. He took a drink, not wanting to go first.

Rose stood. It took a moment for Arthur to realise what was wrong. In the past, he'd seen her wrestle with Wilfred in the sparing arena, coming up still looking beautiful despite the dirt and sweat. Yet today, though she looked perfect, she was like a covered lantern. Her usual radiance was muted, and her red-rimmed eyes took them all in. 'Though the man never stopped inviting me to his bed, I knew he was a friend I could count on in the worst of situations. He made me feel safe. I never thought I'd meet someone like that, nor do I think I ever will again.'

She raised her cup and drank. They all followed suit.

Phillip went next. 'I didn't know him that long, but he was always kind, trying to help me navigate the political intrigue that surrounds being a Templar. He had a way of smoothing things over that I don't think will ever be matched.'

Arthur thought about their argument this morning and felt

incredulous laughter burst through his grief. The sound made every eye fall on him.

'He had plenty of practice smoothing things over.' Then at people's confused look, he glanced around. Luke and James's twin moustaches looked ready to bristle with indignation. 'Let's save the rose petals for the history books. I want to remember the real Peter,' Arthur said, then clenched his fists, realising he was struggling to find the right words. 'Like that time he got every Templar banned from Lord Ester's estate.'

'And the fine table he set,' James added.

'I remember that!' Wilfred exclaimed. 'He was caught with the eldest daughter. What was her name again?'

'Elizabeth,' Elise answered, a laugh breaking through her grief. 'He came running out stark naked, glowing like a beacon!'

The memory snapped into focus: Peter running out of the house, an enraged Lord Ester behind him, swinging a sword that was far too big for him. All the while yelling for his men at arms to hunt Peter down. Laugher bubbled out of him like an overcooked pot, he couldn't help it. He wiped tears from his eyes, unsure whether they stemmed from laughter or sorrow. 'The look on Ester's face!'

'Peter nearly outran his own Light trying to escape,' Elise added, and the tent erupted in the laughter that comes when joy and pain collide. Even Wilfred's massive frame shook with it, though his eyes remained wet with unshed tears.

'Well, at least we can return to Lord Ester's estate,' Luke said. The comment deflated them like a punctured waterskin. They all immediately sobered up.

Elise's smile persisted. 'The man was many things, but he was not great at commitment. I cannot remember him being with a woman for more than a week or two.'

'There was that mountain woman,' Arthur said. 'You remember her. She was huge, almost as tall as Wilfred.'

'I forgot about her,' Elise said. 'She bested me in wrestling in three straight rounds.'

'Me too,' Rose said.

Arthur didn't want to admit she'd gotten him as well.

'That was a fine woman,' Wilfred said, stroking his beard.

'It was one of his longest relationships,' Arthur said. 'Mostly because he was too terrified to end things with her.'

The others started laughing.

'How did things eventually break it off?' Phillip asked.

'Paid my cousin to marry her,' Luke said.

'He did not,' Phillip said, choking on his beer.

'My cousin was not well off,' James said. 'It was his way to a better life and her way to children.'

'And Peter's way out of his longest relationship,' Arthur said, a smile breaking out. 'Of four or five weeks.'

'An eternity,' Rose said.

'To courting for an eternity,' Arthur said, raising his cup. The others did the same.

The cheer mingled with sorrow continued as they told stories about Peter. Arthur was soon refilling their mugs; when he went for the third refill, James begged off.

'We had better go relieve the others,' James said. Luke nodded and the two Templars stood up to leave. It heralded the others leaving as well, with Matthew exiting soon after, followed by Phillip, Rose and Elise.

Soon it was only him and Wilfred left.

They sat, taking quiet sips but not engaging in conversation. They finished their entire mugs in complete silence, barely even making eye contact. Arthur got up to refill them again, but before he did so he caught Wilfred's eyes unusually intense as they stared at him.

'I see you are carrying the weight of the dead, but you already carry the living. Do not second guess yourself – the assault was right. It had to be done.'

'Peter said I shouldn't have ordered the assault,' Arthur said. 'If I had listened…'

'If there is blame it should be placed at my feet,' Wilfred said. 'I knew he wasn't the best fighter amongst us. A fine duelist, but not great in battle. If I had not been so battle-hungry, I, or Luke or James, could have saved him.' Wilfred said. 'No, I will not have you blame yourself. You are a good commander, do not forget it.'

'I wish I could believe that.'

'Do not believe it, know it,' Wilfred said, pointing his finger towards Arthur's chest. 'In there. Like we all know it.'

Arthur forced a smile. 'Thank you.'

Wilfred drew in a shuddering breath. 'I will extract a high blood price from Naberius.' For the first time Arthur had known him, he did not sound enthusiastic about battle. Wilfred stood, and Arthur made no attempt to stop him as he left the tent with a nod of farewell.

Arthur was alone, and emptiness crept into the tent. He reached for the bottle, then thought better of it. He stripped off his funeral finery, leaving it crumpled on the floor, and collapsed onto his cot. The fire's flames dwindled to glowing coals as he lay there, staring into nothing. When sleep finally came, it was a mercy born of exhaustion, grief, and ale.

The dreamscape river stretched before him, black water moving like oil between muddy banks. His white shirt, now stained crimson, clung to his skin. And there, across the dark water, the waiting crowd had grown. Peter stood at the forefront, his once-vibrant face now still in death.

Arthur tried to shut his eyes against the vision.

When he opened them, he could see a familiar farmstead, with its small wooden house and vegetable garden out the back.

It was his home.

A low rock wall surrounded the place. He stepped through the gate, and into the wildflower garden, full of yellow, red and purple flowers. His wife loved to be amongst them, cultivating them. She stood nearby, watching Richard playing with a wooden sword. His blond hair was filled with grass and dirt.

They both turned at his approach.

But their faces ... Sarah's warm smile had turned to winter, and Richard's innocent eyes held a hurt that pierced Arthur's soul.

'Why did you let Uncle Peter die?' Richard asked.

Arthur gaped, feeling the weight of those words. 'I tried to save him.'

'Not hard enough.' Sarah's voice cut like mountain ice.

The words pierced his heart.

Then they turned away from him. He tried to call out to them, but he could feel them fade, their backs a wall against his pleas. Arthur tried to run towards them, but they continued to fade into the distance.

Jerking bolt upright, Arthur's eyes snapped open. The ghosts of the dream lingered, Peter's broken body flashing before Sarah's accusing eyes. The familiar gloom of his canvas shelter helped reassure him of reality, though his mind had accepted the fact it was only a nightmare more readily than his body.

Arthur threw off the blanket and swung his legs over the side of the cot. The cold canvas floor reminded him of the mountains, but the memory of the dirt beneath his feet and the warm summer breeze lingered in his mind. Absentmindedly, he scratched at his bare chest and recently stitched wounds. He guessed it was only midnight, and he'd been asleep for less than an hour.

He rose and went to where the silver medallion of his wife and son hung. He clutched it like a lifeline for his soul, trying to conjure Sarah's tangled hair and bright smile as she stood on their porch, and Richard with his blond hair flying as he climbed the nearby tree. But the nightmare's images would not be undone; their accusations lingered because he believed them. He set the medallion down, and then, finding that insufficient, threw his cloak over it.

He went to his liquor cabinet, pulled the door open harder than necessary, splintering the wood. He grabbed one of the whiskey bottles and tore off the cap. Then he chugged it, the contents spilling over his beard in his haste to drink it down. He only stopped when he coughed, spluttering even more onto the ground. It wasn't enough to drown out Peter's final moments replaying in his mind. The bottle slipped from his numb fingers, dark liquid pooling on the canvas floor like spilled blood.

Maybe he deserved his wife's scorn.

Maybe he deserved worse.

CHAPTER TWENTY: THE MIRROR'S TRUTH

*A*rthur awoke in a pool of his own vomit. He'd fallen out of bed at some point, or maybe he'd never made it there. Instead, he was curled up on the floor, with half the rug wrapped over him. He shivered, realising the tent flap was open.

Matthew stood in the doorway, scrutinising Arthur's almost naked body. The man didn't say a word as he knelt next to Arthur and helped him to his feet. Then he made sure he could reach the nearby washstand, and wet a cloth before handing it over.

Arthur took the cloth gratefully, his throat raw as desert sand. The cool dampness against his face was a mercy, momentarily dulling the throb of his hangover. As he cleaned his beard, his fingers traced the patchwork of stitches and healing wounds that scored half his body. By some miracle, none of them had torn. He reached for a shirt and eased it over his shoulders, each movement careful against the threading. Peter would have joked about him looking like a tailor's failed experiment. But instead of happiness, Arthur felt hollow at the realisation that the man would never speak again.

'Peter?' Matthew asked quietly.

Arthur shrugged, and Matthew nodded in understanding. He pulled a small vial from his tunic – a rare herbal remedy Arthur knew very well. The mixture settled both mind and stomach, dulling the worst of any hangover. If Matthew offered it now, there must be urgent need.

'What happened?' Arthur asked.

'White flag.'

'Them?' Arthur asked, instantly more alert. 'Are they surrendering?'

Matthew shrugged.

'How long have they been there? Who's there?'

'Better if you see.' With that, Matthew stepped outside the tent.

Arthur wanted more information, but the man barely spoke on a good day, so Arthur held his tongue. He downed the vial's contents – tasting of a foul mixture of mud weed and bile – and chased it with a swift pull of whiskey. Settling onto a stool, he let the remedy work through him. Once his head had cleared, he dressed in his battle armour with practiced care, secured his mace, and walked out into the morning air.

Matthew and Phillip were both waiting for him. The three of them started off towards the outer walls. None of them spoke as they made the trek through the ruined northern city and up to the battlements.

Luke and James stood watch, their attention fixed out onto the killing fields. Arthur clapped Luke on the shoulder as he joined them on the parapet.

Where chaos had reigned the day before, a brutal order had emerged. The fallen earth that had crushed them now served as terraced walls, with the standards of the armies of the Dark fluttering from crude poles.

Across the thousand-yard width of the pass stretched a fresh ditch, with fresh stakes behind it. The palisade rose as an amalgam of broken siege equipment and wagon parts, lashed together with salvaged rope and chain. Archers crowded the higher ground with strung bows, while rows of pikemen stood behind the stakes, their weapons forming a forest of steel points.

Arthur's eyes swept the battlefield, from the jagged mountain walls to the killing field before their fortifications. Despite their losses, the enemy host still numbered in the tens of thousands – a sea of armour and weapons that filled the pass. Somewhere in that mass of humanity lurked their true adversary, but the three-headed hound was not visible among the troops. Its absence felt more threatening, like the silence before a storm.

Their situation had improved from certain death to almost certain death.

Right in the centre of the killing grounds, halfway between the walls and the enemy camp, a small canopy had been set up. Next to it, a large pole had been dug into the ground and attached to it there was a ruined white bed sheet. The makeshift white flag was unmistakable as it flapped in the wind.

In the shade, there was a small polished table. Arthur had no idea where they had found it, but he recognised the Priest with the dreadlocks sitting behind it.

'How long has he been there?'

'An hour, give or take,' Luke said.

'Any word?'

'I think they're waiting for us.'

Arthur nodded. 'Matthew, get the archers up and ready. Luke, James, I want enough men ready to provide a guard in case there's a trap. We don't need everyone, but enough. I'll go out to meet them – Phillip, you'll be with me.'

'Why me?'

'Because you're lethal with that spear but have more control than Wilfred.'

Luke and James shouted orders to their respective captains and soon the wall was a bustling hive. In less than ten minutes the battlements were lined with Matthew's archers, and Luke and James had their warriors formed up at the base of the wall, along with Hadrick and several hundred soldiers.

The sound of the wooden mallets hammering against the beams filled his ears. Hinges groaned as the gates opened, and Arthur stared out again at the open fields. The bodies had been cleared away, but there were battle crows perched on the burnt-out siege towers –

entire flocks of them were on the ground, creating moving blankets of shadow.

Arthur pushed aside his thoughts of nightmares and fallen friends. He held his head high, strolling out past the gates and into the brisk mountain air. The dark Priest was hundreds of paces away, but it felt like several leagues. Every eye from both armies was on him, the onlookers weighing him down with their expectations.

Guillamere rose when they grew close, his loose dreadlocks draping down over his dark robes. The silver emblem of Lucifer dangled from a chain around his neck. The man leaned against his long black staff, the skull of a horned demon adorning its top.

'Thank you for meeting with me,' Guillamere said with wide open arms.

'What do you want?'

'To discuss terms.'

'Do you really think we will treat with you now?' Phillip demanded.

'I hope you've got something bloody good to offer if you want us to accept your surrender,' Arthur said.

Guillamere smiled ruefully. 'We are not surrendering.'

'Then why are we here?' Phillip said loudly.

'Because we do not wish more bloodshed.'

Arthur felt his own anger rising. 'You mean you have lost so many men that you cannot afford to lose any more?'

Guillamere inclined his head. 'Your defence has been most robust. You are right, we would like to travel south with the rest of our army still intact.'

Phillip laughed derisively. 'And you think we're just going to up and leave?'

The High Priest gave the same smile one would offer an unruly child. 'You are reaching your end; so many of your men have fallen. Your numbers and, more importantly, your morale, are dwindling. Do you really think you can stand against the might of Naberius? We have more than enough strength to take the Fortress.'

'Do you want to test it?' Arthur asked before Phillip could respond.

'What we are offering you is a mercy.'

Arthur almost spluttered at the audacity of that, but Guillamere continued: 'Think of all the lives that you would save. If you let us pass, this will be the end of the bloodshed. Naberius will not trouble you or yours unless provoked for a hundred years. All you have to do is open the gates and let us through, untroubled.'

'Why do you want to come south?' Arthur asked.

The High Priest's dark eyes searched his. Then he inclined his head. 'My Master seeks a way to bring down Astaroth.'

'Then you're going the wrong way,' Arthur said, pointing to the north. 'She's over there, somewhere.'

'We are aware of her location. Her prison makes it difficult for her to hide. But his current strength cannot match hers and my master wishes her downfall, a goal that Zadkiel also shares.'

'We would never work with you,' Phillip snapped.

'Why?' Arthur asked. 'Why does he want to kill Astaroth? I thought you were both on the same side.'

Guillamere looked affronted. 'I will not share the mechanisms of my master's mind.'

'What's in the south that makes it possible?'

'I am afraid that is all the information that I will provide.' Guillamere raised his staff, and darkness burst from it like water from a leaky bucket.

Arthur immediately opened himself to the Light, expecting treachery. Phillip, likewise, had done the same beside him.

The Darkness above them swirled and spun, forming into a symbol that floated in the air for a moment before disappearing entirely under the bright sun. The High Priest offered no further explanation as dozens of men came out from the enemy camp, carrying chests and trunks. Behind them came a train of women.

As they grew closer, the men formed a semicircle, laying their caskets on the ground. At Guillamere's signal, they opened the trunks to reveal jewels that glittered like stars. Gold coins, bearing the stamp of northern kingdoms, spilled out like a river of molten sunshine. Behind them stood a procession of young women, loose dark hair cascading over their colourful northern kingdom style of dress, which exposed their slender stomachs and narrow shoulders.

'You seek to tempt me with wealth and flesh?' Arthur asked. He knew Peter would have loved such a display. The thought only hardened him against what this man might offer.

Guillamere smiled and signalled to one of the young women, who offered a small box. Her dark eyes flitted towards the two Templars for a moment, before she glanced away, a shy smile coming to her full lips. She opened the box to reveal an ornate gilded mirror with a large X drawn on it.

'The mirror of Jasper,' Arthur whispered.

'Yes – one of the last artefacts of Gabriel left in this world,' Guillamere concurred. 'It represents the mysteries of the Light and provides wisdom, does it not?'

Arthur reached out to take it. Then stopped.

'You may hold it,' Guillamere said.

Arthur stared at the mirror of Jasper. The woman held it like an offering, and the bone-deep exhaustion in him – the part that yearned for Sarah's touch and Richard's laughter instead of endless bloodshed – whispered to just take it, to end this. His conscience screamed against the temptation, but his fingers moved of their own accord. The ivory handle felt cool against his calloused palm, and as he turned it, the flawless surface revealed a man he barely recognized. Deep worry lines carved valleys in his weathered face, dark hollows beneath his eyes spoke of too many sleepless nights with only whiskey for company. But it was his own gaze that struck him hardest – the desperate longing of a commander who'd led too many good soldiers to their deaths, who secretly wished to trade his duty for one more peaceful morning with his family.

Then the mirror's surface rippled like disturbed water, showing him the price of this devil's bargain: The Citadel standing proud and untouched, but at its feet were lying mountains of blackened bones – all that remained of the cities he'd sacrificed. The darkness crept south like a plague, devouring everything in its path, while he watched from safety, knowing he'd traded thousands of souls for a few years of borrowed peace. The truth of his temptation struck him like a mace to the gut. He dropped the mirror as if it burned, his hands trembling from the horror of what might have been.

The woman made no comment as she retrieved the mirror from the dirt, cleaning it off and returning it to its case.

'Before you answer,' Guillamere continued, 'consider this: If we are forced to fight, we will win. Astaroth is far from escaping her prison and, if angered, Naberius will focus on you. Remember, he is the one who slew the Archangel Michael. Even together, you and your ilk do not have that kind of power. The hound of Lucifer will prevail, but if you stand in his way, his new target will be the Citadel. When your army fails, there will be nothing to stop him. Your city of Light will fall and Naberius will be most thorough in his—' the High Priest paused, '—revenge.'

Arthur imagined all those people on the other side of the dream river. They were filling his thoughts. How many more faces would fill those banks if he ordered them to continue to fight? He felt his resolve waver.

'If you accept, then our soldiers will live,' the High Priest continued. 'And so will yours. Let them go home to their families. Your heroic defence has forced us to offer this bargain. But should you refuse, know that every village between here and the Citadel will feel Naberius's wrath. There will be no mercy for women, children, dogs or horses. All will burn.'

Arthur's stomach cramped, and he felt the bile rising in his throat. He looked to Phillip for support, but the other Templar was staring at the mirror of Jasper. There was deep longing in his gaze. Arthur swallowed.

Can I let them through? Let the other nations fight this fight? Arthur thought. Zadkiel would be safe, as would Sarah and Richard, his family in front of their farmstead, who flashed in his mind. *The only good thing that can be said about the Dark is that they honour a bargain, regardless of the cost, if you can get them to agree. I just need* the right wording. Would his defiance of them even stop the vision he saw in the mirror?

Arthur wavered, almost saying yes.

'No.' Arthur had barely realised he'd said the word, but as he met the High Priest's gaze, the words felt more true. 'I know my faults and they are many, but that does not mean I will let others deal with the crimes of Naberius. You will not gain another foothold in our land. You will break on our walls. We will stop him here and now.'

'Do not make a decision without consulting the others.'

Those words struck at Arthur's resolution. Before the siege, his confidence never would have faltered, but now…

'Know that this offer will stand until the next sun rises,' Guillamere said. 'After that, not even your prayers will save you.'

Arthur met the man's dark eyes and held them. 'On the battlefield, I will look for you.'

Guillamere smiled, nodded politely to them, and with a signal, the men and women were closing their treasure caskets and joining him as he walked back to the enemy lines.

'Let's go,' Arthur said.

* * *

CHAPTER TWENTY-ONE: TERMS OF LIGHT

Arthur's mace thumped against his thigh while he walked, each step echoing off the stone walls as he strode through the Keep's corridors. The war room's heavy oak door stood ajar, torchlight spilling out to reveal the gathered Templars within. Though spacious, the chamber felt cramped with the surviving chosen of Zadkiel present.

Wilfred stood near the hearth, holding one axe, while the other rested against the wall. Matthew occupied his own corner, face hidden behind his stringy black hair. Rose and Elise studied maps spread across the oak table, while Luke and James conferred quietly nearby. Phillip maintained his rigid posture, though shadows had gathered under his eyes. Paul and Bartholomew's armour still bore the dents and scratches of recent fighting. Arthur looked at the two with a moment of regret. He never got to spend as much time with them as the others, and didn't know them half as well as he should.

Arthur closed the door behind him, the hinges groaning as wood scraped against stone. The others took their seats without prompting, and the weight of what was to come hung heavy in the air.

'What terms did the black Priest offer?' Elise asked, her voice cutting through the silence.

Arthur's hand twitched toward his empty hip flask. 'They'll spare the Fortress if we let them pass south unmolested.' He met each of their eyes in turn. 'Guillamere claims Naberius seeks a weapon there – something to help him kill Astaroth.'

'Why would one servant of darkness want to slay another?' Rose asked, leaning forward, her braid falling onto the table.

'Perhaps hell has its own civil wars,' Elise mused. 'Though more likely it's another deception.'

'Since Michael's fall,' Arthur said, 'three powers remain in this world – Zadkiel, Naberius, and Astaroth. If she were freed from her prison...' He let the implications hang in the air. 'The question before us is whether we can afford to reject these terms.'

'And if Naberius gains this weapon?' Matthew's deep voice resonated through the chamber. 'What then?'

Arthur hadn't considered that. The silence that followed was heavy with the implications.

'We cannot simply step aside,' Elise said quietly. 'Whatever Naberius seeks in the south, Zadkiel would bear the consequences of our choice.'

'We've received a message from Oscar. He has convinced Zadkiel to go through the southern reaches. It will take them three weeks, even if they march swiftly. But I expect Oscar will delay him further,' Phillip added. 'We stand alone in this.'

Arthur felt that it was a mixed blessing. His hand strayed to where his flask was. The weight of command had never felt heavier. 'Perhaps...' He faltered, drawing every eye in the room. 'Perhaps we should consider their terms. I do not want my decision alone to be heard when so many lives hang in the balance.'

'Since when does the First Templar doubt?' Wilfred's voice carried no judgment, only curiosity.

'Since I watched Peter die.' Arthur's words came out harder than intended.

'You're not alone in bearing this weight,' Rose said softly. 'We all chose to stand here.'

'Did we?' Arthur laughed bitterly. 'Or did you simply follow my lead, like sheep to slaughter?'

'If you think any of us are sheep,' Wilfred growled, 'then you've forgotten who we are.' He beat his chest with a fist. 'We're Templars. The Light chose us all.'

Elise reached across the table, her hand finding Arthur's arm. 'Every one of us could walk away right now. We stay because we believe – not only in the Light, but in each other.'

'We are ready to die,' Bartholomew said, his baritone echoing in the chamber. 'Better that than live with the knowledge we cleared the path for whatever darkness Naberius seeks to unleash.'

Arthur looked around the table at these warriors he'd fought beside for so long. The Light had chosen them all, bound them together as a family. Now it would bind them in death as well. Their faith in him, despite his doubts, steadied him.

'We hold the walls until our end, or theirs,' Arthur said. 'Peter gave his life defending this pass. You are right; we would dishonour his sacrifice if we did any less.'

One by one, they nodded. For a moment, Arthur could almost feel Peter's presence among them, could imagine his friend's knowing smile. The Templars would face this together. Their support made Arthur straighten – it was only then he realised he'd been slouching. He smiled grimly as together they rose and filed out into the night air, where the wind howled through the mountain pass like the moans of the dead. The decision had been made. All that remained was to see it through.

CHAPTER TWENTY-TWO: THE BREAKING POINT

*P*eter had only been the first Templar to fall.

In the days of fighting since the avalanche, Bartholomew had fallen to Naberius's surprise attack. The next day, Luke had caught an unlucky arrow to the throat, where not even his Templar's light could save him. James, driven into a rage, had charged into the enemy, eventually falling beneath the sheer mass of their numbers.

Their faces had joined those in the dream, watching Arthur from the other side of the river. The rage at that hound grew inside him, his hand twitching towards his mace. Now he stood on the wall, ready to face the enemy again.

The adversary's lines stretched across the pass as the army marched on the outer walls. The front ranks carried tower shields, while the trailing afterguard held bucklers raised above their heads. War drums echoed through the mountain peaks, the rhythm matching the soldiers' pace. Long ladders were being carried aloft by the enemy as they advanced on the bulwarks. Three large battering rams, with attached shelters, were lumbering towards the three northern gates.

'Which one do you think Naberius is hiding under?' Phillip asked.

'Knowing our luck, probably whichever one I'm not looking at,' Arthur said, staring at the battering rams and trying to find the demon hound. 'Though I wouldn't mind if he showed himself – getting tired of this cat-and-mouse nonsense.'

'We'll repel him today, just like we have on the other days.'

'I want more,' Arthur said. 'I want him to die.'

Phillip's face frowned with concern, but Arthur ignored it. There was a lot of that being directed his way. Whether it was charging into battle without thought for his own safety, or the drunken stupors it now took for him to get to sleep.

'The Light will prevail,' Phillip said.

Arthur looked down at their curtain walls. The grey stone had been stained with blood and fire. The smell of death hung heavy in the air, but the soldiers were used to it now. He looked at one of the ruined towers and remembered their last fight with Naberius.

'We are ready this time,' Phillip said.

'How many are still out there?' Arthur asked.

The man's eyes darted over the enemy's lines and their bulging ranks.

'Twenty thousand? Maybe thirty.'

Arthur barked out a laugh that made Phillip jump. 'Five thousand against thirty? Better than some odds I've had in tavern brawls.' He sobered slightly, looking at their wounded manning the walls. 'Though I'll admit our lads have had better days.'

'We are down to seven Templars. It is the same number as the Archangels. There is significance in that number,' Phillip said.

'Damn right. Today, the seven of us will banish Lucifer's hound back to hell,' Arthur said. His eyes swept to the eastern gate where Wilfred's huge form stood next to Paul, the man with the gold inlay armour. Then he swung his gaze to the western gate, where Rose and Elise stood watch. His eyes moved forward, as he watched the enemy ranks advancing to the beat of the drums, his eyes moving over the killing ground where many of the dead still lay. The enemy had been relentless in their assaults, offering no further parley or quarter. There had been no cooperative truce to retrieve the dead. His eyes moved from the remnants of the siege towers to their own battlements. Their men stood, watching the advancing foe. Their cheeks had grown hollow, their eyes distant as they stood waiting.

Only the Templars are keeping the lines steady, but if we cannot stop Naberius, the Fortress will fall, Arthur thought.

Between Arthur at the central gate and the Templars at the western gate, Matthew stood with his archers at the longest stretch of the wall. He raised a hand; the nearby Bannerman raised the blue flag. A moment later arrows were being nocked, and together the bowmen raised their weapons, followed by the loud echoing twang as hundreds of bows released their shafts all at once.

The arrows darkened the sky as they rose in a graceful arc, before they began their deadly descent. The enemy soldiers crouched, raising their shields to block the rain of death. A scattering of screams rose from their ranks as the projectiles found their targets. Yet once the bombardment had finished, the enemy arose and continued their inexorable march.

'Ready to do it again?' Phillip asked.

Arthur took out his hip flask, taking one long draught. The sensation burned pleasantly down his throat. He stoppered it, knowing this was likely his last chance. 'I am now.'

Matthew raised another hand. The red flag went up.

Thwaps could be heard at regular intervals as the catapults slung their payloads, clay pots filled with a combustible liquid and a burning rag at the mouth of each. They sailed through the air like shooting stars before landing amongst the enemy. The pots shattered on impact, splattering the burning pitch, flowing between and around the shields. Men fell shrieking as they burned alive. The lines wavered, then broke as those unaffected tried to smother the flames of their comrades.

Matthew raised his hand, and the blue flag waved again. The twanging of bows echoed down the wall, the arrows striking at the exposed soldiers. The burning enemy and their would-be rescuers were felled alike by the feathered shafts.

The exchange continued as Matthew alternated between arrows and firebombs, causing the enemy advance to falter.

'There's a brutal genius to that,' Phillip said. 'Your idea?'

'Funny how war makes monsters of us all,' Arthur said, watching another cluster of soldiers disappearing in the flames. Sarah's face flickered through his mind – that understanding smile she always wore when he explained why duty called. He could almost hear her gentle voice: 'Just make sure you come home to us.' He pushed the thought away with a grimace. Richard would ask about the fighting when he returned, but how could he explain this? He tried to shut out the thought. There'd be time for guilt later, assuming they survived. For now, he'd add these deaths to his tab – just another debt to settle when he crossed that river himself.

The advance of Naberius's army had slowed, but their numbers were great enough to absorb the losses. The scaling ladders were raised, while the battering rams continued to roll towards the gates. Arthur stood with Phillip, looking down at the nearest battering ram. A large tree had been carved to a blunt point, suspended from ropes, and it hung between the wooden pillars that rose from the base to create a mobile structure with heavy roofing and wet ox-hide shields to protect it from arrows, flame, rocks and sight.

Is Naberius under there? Arthur wondered. He hoped so.

The ram stopped before the gate. Men hammered wooden chucks beneath the wheels. Through a complicated system of ropes, pulleys and counterweights, the enemy turned several wheels and the suspended ram was pulled back on its ropes. Then it was released – the ram was propelled forward, slamming against the gates with a solid thud. The huge wooden doors groaned but held. The enemy soldiers reset it as the other rams began their assault, the sound interrupting the steady beat of the war drums.

Climbers were moving up the ladders, thrusting spears and longswords at defenders on the parapet. Enemy bowmen shot arrows at the battlements, felling men on the walls. Arthur could see it: One section of the wall was faltering. Phillip was edging towards them.

'Hold,' Arthur commanded. The Templar looked pained, but stood his ground. The Templars were spaced together down the walls, ready to intervene where they were needed. He hoped the men would rally; he had to give them the time. But when he saw the ropes being thrown down from the battlements, allowing a steady stream of soldiers to make it to the parapet, he knew it was done.

Phillip paced back and forth. 'He's waiting for us to commit.'

'I know, but if we wait, we will lose anyway. Go, clear that section of the wall.'

'You sure?'

'Yes,' Arthur lied.

Phillip needed no further encouragement. Light erupted around him as though he'd been doused in lamp oil and set ablaze. He sped down the wall, his long spear at his side, plate mail clanking as he ran faster than an ordinary man could sprint.

The battering ram had broken through the western gate, and the enemy was pouring through. A line of the church's soldiers was there to meet them, with Rose at the forefront. At the same time, the green flag had gone up and their calvary were charging to reinforce them. Yet amongst the enemy soldiers were the High Priest Guillamere's unmistakable dreadlocks. He raised his demon-skull staff, darkness pouring out of it and streaming into an enormous globe of black above him. Their numbers were forcing Rose and her soldiers back, while Elise rallied those on the wall to repel the invaders.

'Naberius!' someone screamed.

Arthur spotted one of his slingers, terror painted on his face. Following the man's gaze, he saw the demon, his black shadow racing through the enemy lines. Those too slow to get out of his way were crushed under his claws.

'Black flag,' Arthur shouted, already running. He reached for the Angel's light and his strength and speed dramatically increased, the light around him growing almost painfully bright. A shout raced ahead of him and the church soldiers quickly cleared a path along the battlements.

Yet even now he could see that Naberius was heading straight for Matthew. The Templar watched the approaching demon before calmly raising his oversized bow. Its arrows were large enough to arm a small ballista. Glowing with light, the Templar pulled on the steel wire he used as a bowstring and released.

With a growl, Naberius leapt back with an impressive display of speed and agility. The arrow slammed into the space he had just vacated, sending up a spray of dirt.

Matthew drew another quarrel just as Naberius resumed his charge.

Arthur was still so far away, but he couldn't see the other Templars. Had they seen the black flag? Arthur's heart thundered in his chest. On the city side of the walls, the church soldiers were forming up, trying desperately to hold the enemy at the broken gates, but Guillamere now had a large orb of darkness floating above his head. The globe shot black bolts like javelins that skewered church soldiers one after another. It was enough to send Rose staggering back while they tried desperately to hold. The foe was pushing further into the city, almost to where their men could force their way up onto the walls and trap the defenders on the parapets.

Arthur could see it now. They weren't waiting for the Templars to commit; Matthew was already isolated and Guillamere and his men would cut off any immediate reinforcements.

As Naberius was almost upon the walls, Matthew loosed another arrow. The quarrel flew true, striking the hound on the shoulder and causing the creature to careen to the ground, crushing several of the enemy soldiers. But he was back on his feet in an instant. One head wrestled the arrow, mangling the wound, before removing the bolt. His coat of liquid darkness poured into the hole, healing and covering it over. But Matthew had already drawn another arrow. Naberius growled and leapt at the wall. His claws dug into the stone as though it were clay, and he scrambled up the walls like a deranged monkey. In a matter of seconds, the demon was hauling himself over the top.

Matthew was waiting, bowstring taut. But before he could release it, a gigantic bolt of Darkness struck him from behind. He staggered, loosing the arrow wildly off target. Guillamere had shot the Darkness bolt at him, and the Templar's light flickered one more time as a second bolt of Darkness shattered against his protective aura. The impact robbed Matthew of the chance to nock another arrow.

Hold on, you quiet bastard, Arthur thought as he closed in on them.

Matthew threw down his bow, drawing the short sword and dagger from his belt. With a loud war cry, he charged Naberius. Simultaneously, the Hound leapt forward. The two crashed together, but Naberius's superior mass carried them backwards and onto the Fortress side of the walls. During the fall, Naberius yelped and whined while Matthew repeatedly stabbed the beast.

Somehow, Matthew avoided the jaws and claws of Naberius, but when they at last hit the ground, the mass of the enormous beast landed on the Templar.

'No!' Arthur screamed. But he felt a moment of hope as Naberius clambered backwards, black blood pouring from half a dozen wounds across its torso. Matthew rolled away, getting to his feet. The surrounding light flickered and dimmed. The Templar tried to stand tall, but his Light was almost spent.

To reach him on time, Arthur would have to jump. Only the landing would determine if he was brilliant or demon-shit insane. Arthur leapt, sailing through the air, hefting the heavy mace in his hands. He swung hard. The steel club slammed down onto Naberius's ribs.

Several bones snapped under the impact as the force sent Naberius sprawling to the ground. The three heads yelped in pain as he got to his paws, then one head whimpered while the other two snapped and growled, revealing fangs as large as carving knives.

The lead head sucked in a breath, and Arthur knew he had only moments. He ran, jumping between the hound and Matthew, as at the same time hellfire spewed forth. Arthur reached for all the Light available to him. Flame rained down on him, darkness engulfing him like the ocean, drowning out light and sound. The blast of heat made his steel armour feel like a cooking pot. The Angel's light was the only thing keeping the vortex of flame at bay.

As suddenly as it began, it was over: The hound had stopped breathing fire and Arthur looked up. He was whimpering, his broken ribs clearly troubling him. Arthur felt a glimmer of hope. If the beast didn't retreat soon, then they might actually have the chance to finish him.

Naberius pushed forward, trying to move past Arthur and get to Matthew. The quiet archer had found a fallen spear and held it in front of him, though he swayed with exhaustion. His aura of Light was like a dying coal.

The enemy at the gate was being pushed back; Phillip had cleared the wall and had joined in the counterattack. He was being the catalyst in breaking the enemy's advance. Though part of Arthur grimaced – he hadn't seen the black flag. *Even wounded, I can't take him alone*, Arthur thought. But then he saw his salvation. From the other end of the walls, Wilfred was charging towards him, his twin axes gleaming with Light. Arthur felt a wave of relief. It gave him confidence to engage Naberius. He rushed forward, his mace raised as much to distract the creature as to attack him.

Yet the three snapping sets of jaws were effective at keeping him back. It felt like a duel, as Arthur waved his mace, threatening anytime the beast tried to get around him to Matthew, but it still hamstrung him and neither could gain advantage.

Before Wilfred could reach them, the enemy's horns sounded the retreat, echoing across the battlefield.

The ears on Naberius's three heads perked forward, his red eyes looking beyond Arthur. He grinned savagely before turning and leaping back at the walls. His injuries made him clumsy, but he muscled his way to the top of the barrier and over the battlements.

Arthur spun. The Dark orb above Guillamere shattered into a thousand pieces. Every single shard hovered for a moment before shooting forward, straight towards Matthew. Powerless to intervene, Arthur watched it all in slow motion. The man's Light absorbed a few before disappearing completely, then the shards were striking his armour. It held for a heartbeat before the shards broke through and tore into the man's flesh. The Templar stood there as though frozen in time. Then he smiled. An impossible hope filled Arthur, before blood came spilling from Matthew's mouth and he crumpled to the ground.

Arthur rushed to his side, cupping his hand as he tried to push Light into the man.

Yet there was no soul to receive it.

Matthew was already dead.

CHAPTER TWENTY-THREE: A SPARK OF HOPE

It was with a hollow heart that Arthur gazed upon another Templar's funeral pyre. Hundreds had gathered to witness Matthew's body return to the Light. As the flames had dwindled, so had Arthur's hopes of repelling the enemy. He'd attempted to maintain a stoic self-possession while he fought the tears that were threatening to destroy the illusion. He couldn't show weakness, not in front of his soldiers. Their army's courage hung by a thread. Tomorrow promised another assault, and only six Templars remained. Naberius would pick them off one by one. When they fell, there would be no one left to stop him from taking the Fortress and ravaging the whole of the south.

The pyre collapsed in on itself, sending up a shower of sparks. Around him, the crowd began to disperse, but Arthur remained rooted in place, staring at the embers. He couldn't face the others, couldn't stand to be in his tent with them, pretending to celebrate a life cut short while the enemy waited at their gates.

He saw Wilfred and Elise standing together, heads bowed as they said the final prayers. Using the moment, Arthur slipped away, retreating to the solitude of his tent. He needed a drink. Needed to grieve in his own way, without the weight of other's expectations to make things right.

But when he got closer to his tent, he could see lamplight and shadows moving within. With a growl of frustration, he opened himself to the Angel's Light, ready to face the intruders.

As he shoved the tent flap open, he saw two warriors occupying his chairs while casually passing the bottle of some of his best whiskey between them. Arthur's mouth twitched.

'Templar!' One of them exclaimed, his powerful build straining the seat he was in. The man rose, his blue eyes twinkling as he extended a calloused hand in greeting.

'Cormac,' Arthur said, shaking his hand mechanically while he eyed the bottle being drunk. 'I wasn't sure you'd come back.'

The other man rose, and aside from his fire-red hair, Riordan was the spitting image of his father in his youth.

'And miss all this!' Cormac gestured widely with his hands before offering the bottle to Arthur. 'Sit, drink. Life's short enough without drinking good whiskey when you can.'

'Matthew died today,' Arthur said stiffly.

'That's what soldiers do. They die so the rest of us can keep on living. Until it is our day to step into the Light, we dishonour them if we do not live the best we can.'

Arthur opened his mouth, then closed it again.

The man spoke sense, but it felt … disrespectful somehow.

He looked at the whiskey bottle and reluctantly accepted it from the warrior. He took a sip, the brown liquid going down as smoothly as mountain spring water, its flavour giving way to warm, oaken undertones. Sitting down, he took another sip of the cathartic alcohol, almost tempted to slouch in his chair.

'Feels blazing good to get off those mountains,' Cormac said.

'Would have been easier if the avalanche didn't cut off our way home,' Riordan added.

'Lucky we ran into one of the mountain tribes.'

Riordan laughed. 'I thought we were about to have a fight until they came out with some food to trade.'

Arthur stared. It felt like an eternity since he'd heard someone laugh without a brittle edge.

'When I sent you up there, I didn't expect you to actually pull it off,' Arthur said.

'If you're going to pay me extravagantly, then I have to pull off extravagant feats.'

Arthur felt the ghost of a smile tug at his lips. 'How did you do it? Cause the avalanche?'

'Short version,' Cormac said. 'You know that arsehole you gave me instead of a Templar? Well, turns out his magic hammer has uses.'

It took a moment for Arthur to recall the dark-skinned mercenary, Zahir.

'He did most of it. Now, it took us a while to find the right spot. The enemy advance parties were sprouting up like weeds. Lucky they can't fight worth a damn in snow. Eventually, we found a huge rock overhang, and Riordan here,' Cormac said, hooking a thumb at his son, 'suggested we break it apart like you would a boulder. So our wedges had to be the size of tree trunks – Zahir's hammer was the only thing that could make them budge. It took a good few days before we got that rock to tumble, with Zahir being a miserable goat the entire time, but we got there.'

From a storyteller's mouth, the rendition would have been an epic tale, but from Cormac it sounded no different to shoeing a horse. It made Arthur smile, something he hadn't done naturally since Peter had died.

'Did Zahir make it back?' Arthur asked.

'Aye, he's here.'

'It was a close thing. My father almost brained him more than once,' Riordan said.

'Pig headed demon-shagger deserved it.'

Arthur smiled. 'You seem to have been through it.'

'We could say the same about you,' Cormac said. 'We could see what was going on from the mountains, and I've got to ask you one thing.' Cormac leaned forward, the smell of whiskey on his breath while his blue eye stared directly at Arthur. 'You're a breath away from losing this siege. Half the populace is still living in the southern city. So what in the blazes of hell are you doing trying to defend the outer walls?'

Arthur stiffened. 'I will not be spoken to in that manner.'

'You will if you want to hear sense.'

'I am the First Templar—' Arthur began.

'Which makes you important, but not omnipotent,' Cormac interrupted him.

'I swore I would not give up another inch to the demon's horde.'

'Well, that is epically stupid. You want to lose the war to salvage your pride?'

Arthur stood, pointing towards the exit. 'Get out, I'm not in the mood.'

Cormac snorted and leaned back. 'You'll have to make me.'

Riordan shifted uncomfortably in his chair.

'You really want me to do it?'

'Go on, then.' Cormac smirked. Arthur recognised when he was being tested. He stepped forward, grabbed the older warrior by the shirt, and hauled him to his feet. He spun the man and shoved him towards the exit.

'You've lost the initiative and are letting the enemy dictate the battle,' Cormac said as he was being herded towards the exit. 'If you retreat to the Fortress, you might have a chance.'

Arthur forced a poignant mixture of anger and grief down, holding back the impulse to send the man sprawling out of the tent. Clenching his fists and breathing out harshly, he said, 'Speak your piece, but if I don't like it, you will leave with my boot up your arse!'

'Right. Well, you no longer have the means to effectively cover the outer walls, or respond to Naberius's speed when he can run faster than any of you Templars,' Cormac said. 'Plus, he runs away at the first sign of uncertainty. He's a coward, but a bloody strong one. So you need to lay a trap.'

Arthur paused. 'Go on.'

'Can I have the whiskey back? I've got a hell of a thirst.'

Arthur felt his anger evaporate and he sighed. 'If I like your plan, you can take the bottle.'

'Now we're talking,' Cormac said, taking the bottle back. He took a drink, gave a contented burp, then continued: 'Naberius is the key,' Cormac said. 'Take him out and their army will splinter. You need to draw him in. Goad him into overreaching.'

'A trap,' Riordan said, speaking up for the first time. 'Someplace where we can hit him hard and fast, without all of his army at his back.'

Arthur frowned, turning the idea over in his mind. It was audacious and reckless, but it might be exactly what they needed. He mused aloud: 'We could fall back, let them take the outer city. Rig the buildings with pitch and oil...'

'And when Naberius comes through, spoiling for a fight, we light the place up,' Cormac finished.

It could work, Arthur realized. It would be risky, but they might actually bring Naberius down. As Cormac and Riordan continued their animated discussion of tactics, Arthur's mind raced ahead, already mapping out the possibilities. The whiskey sat forgotten in his hand as he envisioned the northern city transformed into a deadly maze of fire and steel.

'Can you get the others?' he asked, cutting through their conversation, his voice carrying the sharp edge of command that had been absent earlier. 'I want to discuss this with every surviving Templar.'

Riordan immediately stood, recognising the shift in Arthur's demeanour. 'We'll spread the word,' he said, clapping his father on the shoulder. Cormac glanced at Arthur, shrugged as he grabbed the bottle of whisky before following his son out into the night.

Arthur paced the length of his tent, the embers of Matthew's funeral pyre still sharp in his mind. But now, mixed with the grief was something else – a dangerous spark of hope. He pulled out the detailed maps of the northern city, spreading them across his weathered command table. His fingers traced the narrow streets and squares where they might corner their prey.

The surviving Templars arrived within fifteen minutes, their boots crunching on the frozen ground outside his tent.

Wilfred stood close to the entrance, his twin axes leaning against the table. Elise and Rose flanked him. Phillip was the last to join them, informing them that Paul kept vigil on the wall.

'We're pulling back to the keep. They can have the northern city.'

A beat of silence, and then a clamour of voices as they all began talking at once.

'Let him take the walls?' Wilfred asked, then chuckled. 'Finally. I assume you have a plan?'

'Set a trap. Draw Naberius in and kill him.'

'That simple?' Elise asked.

Arthur nodded. 'I want it to be. We'll fall back to the Fortress, let them have the outer city. But not before we turn it into a killing ground.' He outlined the plan, watching their faces as he spoke of pitch and oil, of collapsing buildings and hidden forces lying in wait.

When he'd finished, a heavy silence hung over the tent, each of them grappling with the implications of what he proposed.

'It will require men to stay behind,' Phillip said at last. 'To spring the trap. And to catch the hound.' He met Arthur's gaze squarely. 'I will lead them.'

'Phillip…' Elise began, but he silenced her with a look.

'I have much to atone for,' he whispered. 'Let me do this. Let me strike a blow against the Darkness.'

'I'll stay as well,' Rose said, stepping forward. 'We'll need Templars at each choke point if we hope to hold Naberius in place.'

Wilfred opened his mouth, but Arthur cut him off: 'No, if we're having Templars out in the city, I want you at the keep. If the trap fails, you are our greatest chance to adapt, or hold the line if all else fails.'

For a moment, Wilfred looked as though he might argue. But then he simply nodded.

'Elise, I want you on the walls,' Arthur continued. 'Your javelins will be key in taking out their priests and keeping them off balance.'

Elise grunted. 'Paul will want to be out in the city as well. Three points to hold Naberius in place.'

'But what if he doesn't take the bait?' Rose asked.

'The trap will still decimate their army. If we cannot stop them, I want to cripple the bastards so Zadkiel has a chance to defeat them in the field.' Arthur fingers traced paths through the city streets on the map before them. 'We'll need the pitch and oil distributed all along here.'

As he spoke, the other Templars gathered closer, their shadows dancing in the lamplight. Wilfred was the first to suggest likely positions for the enemy to muster, while Elise pointed out bottlenecks that were optimal places for her archers to work. The Templars each contributed and the plan grew stronger with each addition. Messengers to relay the new commands were continually dispatched in a steady stream. By the end, it felt less like a desperate gamble, and more like it might actually work.

Together, Arthur worked with the others through the night, their voices growing hoarse as they debated each detail. But by the end the plan was set. When at last they had addressed every contingency they could imagine, a heavy silence fell over the tent, the other Templars beginning to withdraw to get what sleep they could before the siege resumed. One by one they left until only Phillip remained, his face shadowed in thought.

'I have not forgotten your warning,' he said after the tent flap settled behind the others. 'I am not doing this because I want to throw my life away. It's justice against Naberius and the debt that he owes.'

Arthur laughed. 'If you are worried about the threat of me hunting you down in the next life, don't be. You are earning your redemption through blood and sweat. You are one of us – a true Templar.'

Something eased in Phillip's face at that, a softening around the eyes and mouth. 'Thank you,' he said simply. And then he was gone, striding out into the night.

Arthur remained behind, staring at the map spread out on the table. The northern city's squares leapt out at him, the three small spaces where they would spring their trap, or hasten their defeat. He never gambled unless it was desperate, but few options remained. If the enemy army got south of the pass, they had no chance, but they had one last gambit, one last chance to turn the tide.

'I hope it's bloody enough.'

CHAPTER TWENTY-FOUR: BEFORE THE STORM

Arthur was drifting once again in darkness. He could feel his bare feet anchoring in the muddy shores of a river; a slight breeze rustled the forest of reeds that surrounded and towered over him. He shivered, though it had nothing at all to do with the chill. Part of him knew he was dreaming, but it didn't stop the helplessness rising in him when every direction appeared the same. He hesitated before striding forward, weaving his way through the field of reeds. The muddy ground sloshed as he walked, the water level never changing. He reached for the Angel's Light, but the power didn't fill him. He closed his eyes and muttered a curse. When he opened them, half the reeds were gone, and a river flowed in front of him. Men and women were lining the opposite shore. The ethereal phantoms watched him with welcoming smiles. Many wore the dress of Zadkiel's church, but most wore the colourful uniforms of the northern kingdoms, and their smiles were no less accepting. Yet when he moved to take another step, one of the ghostly figures stepped forward.

It was Matthew.

Arthus's heart stilled. He looked at the phantoms, and though he knew it couldn't be real, his mind yearned for it to be so. He only needed to wade over the river and he could touch him, but Matthew held up a hand, and twirled a finger, indicating that Arthur should turn around and head back.

Arthur jerked awake with hay in his hair and the familiar scents of leather and horse surrounding him. He'd stumbled into the stables last night, seeking comfort in one of the few places that still felt unchanged by the siege. Ezekiel's stall had offered more peace than his quarters, and he'd fallen asleep against the wooden partition. The horse stood over him now, warm breath huffing against his neck as those intelligent eyes studied him with what Arthur swore was concern. There was something about Ezekiel's presence that always steadied him – whether it was the rhythmic sound of his breathing, the gentle way he'd nudge Arthur's shoulder, or something Arthur couldn't put his finger on. In these quiet moments, Arthur could forget about being First Templar, forget about the weight of command and the thousands of lives depending on him. In here, he was just a man with his horse.

'When this is over,' Arthur murmured, his hand scratching that special spot behind Ezekiel's ear, smiling as the horse's lip quivered in contentment, 'we'll head back to the farm. It's about time I taught Richard how to ride properly – he's old enough now.' Ezekiel's ears pricked forward at the mention of Richard's name, and Arthur chuckled. 'Yes, you remember him. He was barely tall enough to reach your shoulder last time, but he's growing like a weed. Sarah wrote that he's been pestering her about learning to ride. By then, your leg should be healed.' The horse nudged Arthur's pocket hopefully, and Arthur shook his head. 'No more treats, you glutton. But when we're home, Richard can spoil you with all the apples from the orchard.'

'Come, First Templar, can't have you lazing around all day,' Cormac said.

Arthur smiled sadly. His small reprieve was over. He gave Ezekiel one last pat before turning to face the mercenary. 'If I remember correctly, it was you who told me to go to bed.'

'His words were,' Riordan said, '"Can't have the commander fall flat on his face from exhaustion. If you can't see you're about to keel over, I'll knock you out with that mace of yours so you can get some rest".'

'Yes, thank you, son,' Cormac said.

'Have they got everything in place?' Arthur asked.

'Aye, mostly. Many of the city traps were already in place. We ran out of time and some barrels of pitch aren't as well hidden as we'd have liked, but we expected that. Still, half the northern city is ready to explode like kindling.' The mercenary was speaking while he brought over a tray laden with a large bowl of porridge and freshly made bread.

'I know you're used to the rocks that the stew sorcerers try to pass off as bread, but I thought I'd take matters into my own hands.'

'You *made* this?' Arthur asked as he tore into the loaf, whose tendrils of steam spiralled to escape. He tossed the soft food past his lips and closed his eyes. The warm bread practically melted in his mouth.

'Organised it. My best cooking is not burning it,' Cormac said.

Arthur opened his eyes, staring at the barrel-chested warrior. 'Did you get any sleep?'

'Me? Course I did.'

Arthur looked over his shoulder at Riordan, still the uncanny spitting image of his father, who answered for him: 'He took a few hours around midnight, then another two at sunrise.'

'I've spawned a bloody bean counter,' Cormac said.

Riordan grinned.

'The others?' Arthur asked, using the wooden spoon to attack the cinnamon-spattered porridge. The thick, warm oats contained a generous serving of honey.

'The Templars and War Priests are in place and ready to ambush the enemy. The boobytrapped buildings should make them wary of looking at each house. Though we've looked at it from every angle and think they'll be safe, nevertheless—' Corman trailed off and shrugged. 'This is war.'

Arthur swallowed, wondering how many more would be at that river by the end.

'No need to get weepy about it,' Cormac continued. 'It's a gamble, but you're losing, and though it's insane, this plan has a chance of working.'

Arthur took another mouthful, but the porridge had lost much of its savour.

'Archers?'

'Barrels of arrows are ready for them. And before you ask, the catapults have been triple checked. We got the chains off the outer gates and attached them to those metal harpoons. Be just like catching a whale. A great three-headed dog type whale.'

'Have people started leaving the city?'

'The mountains breed a tough bunch. Most are staying until the final call to evacuate.'

Arthur sighed. He was fighting for their freedom, even if it was only so they could put themselves in more danger.

'The Fortress?'

'Everything is ready and in position. Wilfred and Elise are watching the walls. There are times I wonder at the weapon choices you Templars make—Elise looks like a motherly figure until you see that bunch of javelins that are the size of cavalry lances, while Wilfred runs around with two battle axes big enough to fell a redwood.'

Arthur thought about his heavy mace. Most maces were twice the size of a fist, while his was larger than a man's head.

'All they need is their commander, and we're ready,' Cormac said. 'I must admit, I didn't expect you to outrun my ideas and come up with this new battle plan.'

'You disapprove?'

Cormac shook his head. 'Course not. You'd lost the initiative, and would have lost everything if you'd kept letting them dictate the battle. We're probably all going to die anyway, but at least we'll go down fighting.'

'The Light will guide us.'

'Make sure it guides us to victory.'

Arthur sighed, ignoring the man's jest. 'What are your roles?'

'First reserves, with the other mercenaries.'

Arthur nodded. 'Has the enemy been sighted?'

'Nothing yet. I think the lack of anyone on the walls has given them pause,' Cormac said, then nodded to Riordan. The younger man whistled and within moments, men-at-arms were carrying in Arthur's armour stand. He had been mopping up the last of his porridge but now he froze. The First Templar's armour had been polished to an almost mirror shine, its leather straps properly oiled. Though there were still dents and rents, it looked almost ready for a parade.

'It helps if our leader looks the part,' Riordan said, lifting the breast plate to assist Arthur into it.

Moved by the gesture, Arthur allowed the men to help encase him in steel. At the end, he attached the mace to his belt before stepping out into the morning light. He looked up at the snow-capped peaks and breathed in the fresh mountain air, something he hadn't done since he'd first arrived.

'Let's defeat an army,' Arthur said.

'Damn right,' Cormac answered.

They made their way up the winding streets, where Arthur marvelled at how the southern city contrasted with the northern ruins. There was a stoic beauty in amongst the buildings and the cold mountain winds. He felt at peace amid the painted grey stones of the city.

Despite the weight of his armour, Arthur felt light as they made their way to the Fortress. The man-made mountain stood tall, the grey stone meticulously fitted together to create a sheer rock face. The large Iron Gates were propped open, wide enough to allow three wagons abreast to pass through. Their mirror image on the northern side were closed, barred and braced with wood and stone.

As they walked under the vast arches, Arthur surveyed the trans-formed courtyard. Where mess facilities had once stood, a sea of activity now churned. Young soldiers adjusted ill-fitting armour with trembling fingers – grizzled veterans checked bowstrings with prac-ticed ease – squad leaders barked commands while organising their units into practiced formations. The war wives wove through the crowd like threads binding the fabric of the army together: a silver-haired woman staggered under the weight of a basket overflowing with freshly fletched arrows, two sisters darted between groups of soldiers, distributing bread still warm from the ovens, and a young mother balanced a sleeping infant in one arm while using the other to help sharpen spears. Throughout the courtyard, the sounds of steel being honed mingled with murmured prayers and the shuffle of boots on stone as everyone performed the hundreds of vital tasks that transformed an army from disparate individuals into a unified force. Even the children had their roles, scampering between the adults with water skins and messages, their small faces serious with the weight of their duties.

'Warriors of the Light, my brave brothers and sisters,' Arthur called, and every face in the courtyard paused, turning towards him. 'I see the weariness in your eyes, and Light knows I feel it in my bones. But let me share a secret with you, something that Zadkiel has told me in confidence.' He paused, as every eye focused on him. 'Heaven is overrated!'

This elicited a few surprised chuckles.

'With the Angels as our witnesses, let us make a deal. We face this siege head on, fight like our ancestors did, and have people in this life and the next tell stories about the Battle of the Iron Gates. Here, we will make the Angels themselves stand in awe. If we go to meet the Light, let us do it fashionably late and with a few scars to boast about!'

This elicited more laughter from the crowd. They waited, but when he said nothing more, they slowly resumed their work. Though some still wore grim expressions, there were a few hidden smiles amongst them, a lifting of the burden on their war-beaten faces.

'I was worried they had killed your spirit,' Cormac said, slapping him on the back, his armour ringing at the sound. 'But that's the Arthur I remember.'

Arthur turned to Cormac and held out his arm. The man hesitantly took it. 'I think they almost had, but then some upstart turned up, drank my whiskey, demanded I fight again, and then he and his son restored my spirit with a few simple but extraordinary gestures.'

Cormac grinned. 'Sounds like quite a guy. Probably real good-looking, too.'

'The best,' Arthur agreed.

A horn sounded from above. It was soon echoed across the wall.

Their smiles died, as every face looked towards the barrier. Hands tightened on weapons and the children, elderly, wounded and any other non-combatants suddenly hurried about their tasks.

So it begins.

CHAPTER TWENTY-FIVE: FIRE AND IRON

The horns echoed, each in succession, creating an orchestra of blasts that reverberated throughout the southern city. Commanders barked orders, dispatching runners to the reserves, while those on duty assumed their positions.

Arthur drew in a breath, moving toward the stairs that led to the parapets with deliberate calm. Cormac and Riordan followed closely behind him as he ascended. His shoulder pauldrons brushed against the narrow walls of the spiralling staircase, the muted horn blasts echoing in the tunnel of darkness. Small slits provided the only source of light as Arthur maintained his steady pace.

He needed to appear in control. *It will help the morale of the men more than anything*, Arthur thought. Then he admitted to himself that it was also because he hated running in armour.

Brightness curved around the corner, signalling the end of the stairs before Arthur reached it. Blinking against the sudden drenching of light, he saw the stone parapets laid out before him. Archers lined the walls with quivers full to bursting, barrels of arrows interspersed between them. In the same way, catapults were positioned on the towers, their payloads surrounding them. Men saluted as he passed, and Arthur gave a heartfelt salute in return, stepping to the edge.

'Bloody hell,' Arthur growled.

'Templar?' Hadrick said beside him. Arthur glanced at him, no longer seeing the youth, but the capable commander the battle had forced him to become.

'Just forgot how high these walls are,' Arthur said. 'I bet I could spit into the wind and it would float down and hit the enemy.'

'Maybe throw a stone instead, might take one of them out,' Hadrick said with a straight face.

Arthur chuckled, returning his attention forward. A field of grey stone buildings greeted him as he stared over the remnants of the northern city. Those within a hundred feet of the wall had been collapsed so as not to provide shelter to the enemy. While for the next thousand yards the city was relatively unscathed, when it reached the devastation of the outer walls, the smoke-encrusted stone and battered masonry stood as testament to their fight. He drew his gaze back to the rest of the northern city. Despite his scrutiny, Arthur couldn't discern which buildings the sappers had turned into death traps or where their forces were concealed. His eyes moved past the immediate structures to see the enemy marching through the north-ernmost gates.

Horsemen, lightly armed and armoured, sped ahead, weaving through the streets, checking for ambushes or traps.

The front ranks of the enemy formed a shield wall, prepared for a possible cavalry charge or arrow assault. As their numbers continued to pour through the gates, Arthur recognised the azure flag of House Ragat, the gold of Foix, and the black of the Kingdom of Seyan. As more flags joined them, they embodied a tapestry of vibrant colours as their numbers continued to grow like swarms of locusts.

'How did the boys and girls fare after last night?' Arthur asked.

'Worked hard, and got most of the surprises in place. The enemy's not going to like finally getting into the city.' Hadrick said. 'Our soldiers were happy to be doing something else besides manning the walls.'

'It's good to stick it to the enemy again,' Arthur said.

'Too right it is,' Cormac said from behind him, panting and staring at Arthur in disbelief. 'I know you've got Zadkiel's gift, but it's still bloody unfair you can climb these stairs in full plate mail and still look as fresh as a spring daisy.'

'You want the view, you've got to work for it,' Arthur said, then ignored the man's colourful response as he turned back to watching the encroaching army. Enemy commanders were sending squads of soldiers to search the houses. He watched as a group of four kicked down a door and charged in; a few moments later, the entire building tilted, then crashed down in a plume of dirt, burying the squad. The sound of the collapsing building halted the entire enemy army, and soldiers immediately ran to save them. Before the dust could settle, another house started emitting smoke, just as the squad was coming out of the exit. There were shouts of alarm, and those nearest the building backed away before the entire structure suddenly exploded. The building's stones were turned to shrapnel, smashing down any foemen unlucky enough to be caught in the blast. The shockwave was enough to ruffle Arthur's hair as it boomed past his ears.

'By the devil's horns,' Cormac said. 'How'd they manage that?'

'The Light works in mysterious ways.'

'You don't know, either!'

Arthur grinned, seeing the expression mirrored on a few of the men's faces. The mirth quickly vanished, and as he followed their gaze he saw why. Naberius was padding into the city. The demon hound's main head raised his nose to sniff at the air, while his flanking heads scanned the city's edges. His black fur glistened darkly in the sunlight. Next to him, the High Priest appeared in his black robes. Even at this distance, Arthur could make out Guillamere's dreadlocks and the demon-skulled staff. Though he was a tall man, he still barely reached Naberius's shoulder.

'You think he suspects a trap?' Arthur asked.

'Be a fool if he didn't,' Cormac said.

Elise stepped forward, a bundle of javelins hanging over her back. Each projectile was bigger than Arthur's wrist.

'You thinking of trying to stick the dog?' Cormac asked as the woman flexed one javelin, testing its weight. A few of the archers saw and stepped away from the battlements, giving the Templar room.

'No. I want the bastard that killed Matthew,' Elise said, staring hard at Guillamere.

'Aim for his balls,' Arthur said. 'Castrate the bastard.'

Cormac grunted with amusement.

'You two are just as bad as each other,' Riordan said behind them.

'Just need to wait for him to turn away,' Elise said.

The enemy army continued to march, their numbers spreading out and engulfing the city like an incoming tide. As they ranged through the streets, more of the trap houses were set off, making the squads more reluctant to search the buildings they were passing.

'Let's help them along,' Arthur said. 'Hadrick – stage one.'

'Catapults!' the captain shouted, the call echoing across the wall.

The restraining ropes on the catapults were released, the arms flinging forward, launching rubble from their buckets. The height of the Fortress towers gave them range, and though this kind of load wasn't terribly accurate, the sheer numbers of the enemy made it difficult to for them to miss. Entire sections of the opposing host faltered as the rubble rained down on them. After a moment, officers on horseback yelled at the soldiers to get back in line, and their losses were quickly absorbed.

'Now,' Cormac said to Elise.

Arthur's eyes snapped to Guillamere and Naberius. The High Priest was distracted by the nearby devastation wrought by the catapults. Elise glanced at the flag of Zadkiel fluttering in the wind, then back towards the High Priest, judging the distance. She took a step back, her skin beginning to glow with the telltale sign of someone wielding the Light. Taking several running steps forward, she launched the javelin into the air.

The projectile raced towards the heavens, slowing into a graceful arc as its tip angled downward. Arthur watched in awe, as it had to be close to a thousand-yard distance, but it looked like the throw would hit. With less than a second before impact, Naberius looked up. With supernatural reflexes, the beast leapt to the side, knocking the High Priest out of the way just as the javelin struck, piercing the hound's shoulder. The force of it drove the beast back several steps, and his heads alternated between growls and whimpers while the closest head chomped at the javelin, to pull it from his shoulder.

'Did you just hit a demon a thousand yards away?' Cormac asked in disbelief.

'The Light guided my hand, but that Priest has Lucifer's luck.'

Naberius had finally pulled the javelin from its shoulder. The darkness congealed over the hole, and a moment later the wound was gone. The red eyes stared up at them on the Fortress walls as he snapped the javelin in half with his powerful maw.

'Archers!' Hadrick called. The men lined up. 'Loose at will!'

'Eh?' Cormac asked.

'I'm guessing volleys are too easy to defend against,' Riordan said. 'Individual shots will wear them down.'

The archers nocked their arrows, before drawing the strings to their cheeks. Their eyes scanned the opposing army, and they released their arrows at irregular intervals. Though they felled men by the dozen, it felt like they were only drops in a bucket.

'Have they found any of our men?' Arthur asked.

'Not yet. They've searched one of the houses, but the men have picked their hiding spots well,' Hadrick said.

As they watched, the enemy moved inexorably closer to the Fortress walls. Arthur looked for siege weapons. It was only then that he realised they carried no rams, no ladders, no crowbars.

Something doesn't feel right, Arthur thought as he rested his hands on the cold stone walls. He closed his eyes and opened himself to the Light. He needed to be smarter than this. If he faltered here, more would die. Many more. All around him, he could hear the steady beat of marching feet over the walls, interrupted by the twang of bowstrings. He stretched his senses. In the darkness, he was suddenly hit with a wave of understanding.

'Stage two,' Arthur said.

'Now?' Hadrick said, looking at him in confusion.

'Now.'

Hadrick spun. 'Stage two!'

As the call echoed down the wall, a horn rose and blasted one long note. Other horns answered the call, repeating the sound.

Naberius's ears pricked forward, its red eyes scanning the walls before falling to the Iron Gates. His hackles rose and he bared his long fangs as he sprang forward towards the wall. The army quickly scattered out of its path while the hound's lope ate up the distance, moving through the city like the shadow of a giant bird. He reached the Fortress walls within a minute, skidding to a stop thirty yards from the gate.

Naberius's main head sucked in a large breath before spewing hellfire in a pillar of flame. The attack didn't relent; the fiery blast washed over the iron doors like a wave. Arthur recoiled, as did everyone else watching from the walls. He could feel his hairs beginning to singe.

'Muster everyone. The gates won't hold against hellfire for long,' Arthur told Hadrick.

'Battle stations!' Hadrick shouted.

Three quick horn blasts blared, answered by others in the Keep and the southern city. The sounds of pounding feet and movement filled the Fortress and beyond as soldiers in the southern city rushed to the courtyard.

'Elise, slow him down,' Arthur said. The Templar hefted another enormous javelin, looking down at the three-headed beast and nodded.

'Wilfred, with me. Hadrick, you have the walls.'

'First Templar!' They all saluted.

'We're coming too,' Cormac said, joining Wilfred, who had a wild look in his eyes. They journeyed down the spiralling staircase and back into the courtyard. By the time they'd reached the bottom, a thousand men had mustered in the courtyard, with more joining every moment.

'Bring that fucker on!' Arthur shouted as he went to join the front ranks. There was a scattering of cheers among the soldiers, their ranks lining the courtyard, weapons positioned outwards. One soldier approached, handing him a long metal spear with an attached chain that was coiled like a rope. The steel shaft felt cool in his hand as Arthur hefted the weapon. Its point was shaped like a large barbed arrowhead. He flicked it up and down, getting used to the weight before returning his gaze to the gates. If they could pin Naberius down, then it would be the end of him.

His grim smile faded slightly as he looked up.

The solid half-dome doors, made entirely of their strange metal, had begun to glow red like iron in a forge. The heat washed over him as the red spot continued to expand in a perfect circle. Iron slag began dripping from the gates, splashing onto the wood and stone placed there to brace them.

'Stage three, four, and six!' Arthur called.

The orders were echoed through the ranks.

'Which one is which again?' Cormac asked.

'Three is lighting the outer city on fire, four is to try and cage Naberius, stage six is evacuating the southern city,' Riordan said.

'You'd think being a high demon and all, he wouldn't run away the moment things get a bit rough.'

Arthur looked to his left and saw a young man barely old enough to hold a spear standing next to him. He met Arthur's eyes with a grim nod. To his right was a woman old enough to be his mother. Their ranks had been bolstered by those in the southern city, people seeking to avenge loved ones. Arthur wondered if they would survive the next hour.

Arthur turned to the mercenaries. 'Cormac, I want you to take charge of the southern city. Our men will hold the gates as best we can, but I need a steady head to control them if the battle goes ill.'

'Now see here—' Cormac began, stepping forward, his face contorting in outrage. 'We're not about to leave just as the fighting starts.'

'I don't have time to argue. It is your charge, now go do it!'

Riordan laid a hand on his father's shoulder. The man looked utterly mutinous, but he spun dutifully, heading towards the southern city and the remaining Wild Ravens that waited on the other side.

Arthur returned his attention to the entryway, as slag continued to spill from the iron and onto the stone and wood that braced the door below it. Eventually spurts of fire broke through, until a geyser of flame burst into the doorway. Hot molten metal sprayed like water droplets, leaving a huge round hole in the door. The heat from the hellfire felt like an oppressive weight as the black flame shot across the courtyard. It abruptly cut off. A stillness echoed in the air as Naberius's main head appeared at the hole in the gate. Saber-like fangs showed as he bared its teeth, its red eyes fixed on them. Arthur felt his heart still as an icy wave of fear washed over him.

He met those eyes and felt all the rage and anger at the death and misery this demon had caused. His fury welled up inside him like a spring of rainwater after a storm, and Arthur opened his mouth, roaring his defiance. The surrounding soldiers soon joined in, breaking into a crescendo of war cries.

Naberius's head backed up from the hole.

'Steady, comrades!' Arthur called out. 'Today is our moment. The Light has given us the opportunity to slaughter Lucifer's hound!'

The cheers rose amongst them as the men steadied themselves and stood forward, spear points already lowered.

'Stage three ready!' Hadrick called from the parapets.

'Do it!'

Naberius had gained close to a hundred yards from the Fortress. It turned and faced them, before his claws scored into the stone and he propelled himself forward, racing for the Iron Gates at full speed. The last ten feet he leapt into the air, body slamming into the gates. The beams and supports held for a moment before the force of the beast's body broke through them and the remnants of the iron doors slammed inwards, flinging the braces of wood and stone backwards.

The creature stood in the gateway, his claws digging into the ground while its chest heaved heavy breaths. Several of Elise's spears protruded from its hindquarters, but he looked unbothered as its red eyes scanned the waiting Templars and soldiers.

Above them, they could hear the groaning of the catapults as they launched their clay pots into the city.

'Elise!' Arthur yelled, hefting the harpoon. He let the Light fill him and threw the long metal shaft, the chain uncoiling in its wake. It sailed through the air and hit the hound in the chest with enough force to send it staggering back a step. He grasped the attached chain and braced himself as he allowed more of the Light to flow into him. He could feel his strength and speed soaring as he stared at the beast.

Today you die, Arthur thought.

Elise threw her own harpoon, one tied to the very stones of the Fortress. The hound saw it coming and leapt back. Arthur yanked on his hold, but his harpoon ripped free, taking a chunk of flesh with it. Elise's spear narrowly missed him, striking the stones with a shower of sparks.

Behind the hound, the clay pots of pitch smashed into the city, igniting and spreading like wildfire. Strategically placed pitch caches were kindled, with the flames racing across to the main storage points. The first building burst apart like the trap house had, but exponentially more potent. The force of the explosion echoed through the Keep like a thunderclap. Soldiers around him brought their hands to their ears and crouched low, while the shockwave washed over them. The enemy had paused in confusion as the fire continued to spread along the road gutters and into neighbouring houses, causing more of the pitch to ignite. Every chain reaction caused the very ground to rock, the booms echoing out from the Keep and across the mountains in a cacophony of deafening explosions. Arthur was soon bent with the soldiers around him as they waited out the destruction. Time seemed to slow as they were assaulted by one explosion after another. If the effect was this bad behind the walls of the Keep, he could only imagine the devastation amidst the enemy.

Arthur's hand tightened on his mace. The demon was wounded, and one good blow could end this – all of it. His muscles tensed as he pictured charging out alone, smashing through the dazed enemy ranks to reach Naberius. The image of Sarah's disapproving frown flickered through his mind. She always said his courage walked the line between bravery and foolishness. He thought about the plan and how slim of a hope it was. But if he could end the siege here....

The weight of command settled back onto his shoulders like a lead cloak.

'Stage five!' Arthur yelled. 'After him! Wilfred, carve out a path!'

CHAPTER TWENTY-SIX: DARK COUNSEL

*O*ne hour earlier…

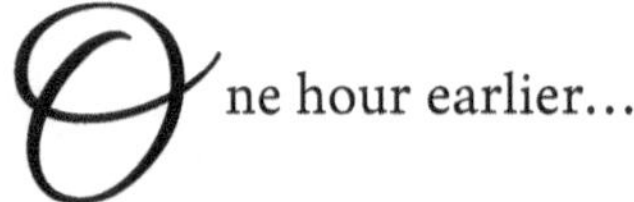

* * *

GUILLAMERE GAZED down at the broken shards of the javelin. He shivered, feeling like the icy breath of death had just whispered in his ear. When he looked up, he saw Naberius – the monstrous three-headed hound that had just rescued him from the grave. He clutched his staff tighter as if to anchor himself to reality. His gaze shifted past the fifty thousand soldiers of Naberius's army as they marched toward the imposing grey Fortress that blocked the pass. He scanned the battlements for Elise, the Templar who had almost sent him to hell. While he looked, the catapults launched another volley of rocks that flew through the air like massive hailstones. The soldiers of Naberius's army raised their shields. Lucifer's favour smiled upon some, but corresponding screams proved others were not so lucky.

The groaning of a building snapped Guillamere's attention back to his immediate surroundings. A nearby house was leaning precariously, while the inhabitants shouted in alarm. Then the entire structure collapsed, trapping the search party within. Commanders bellowed for more soldiers to dig them out. Guillamere's attention returned to the shattered javelin. It was large enough to rival the lance of the most ambitious chevalier.

At least it would have been quick.

'Thank you, milord,' Guillamere said to Naberius.

The hound's eyes were fixed on the battlements before they scanned the road and surrounding buildings.

'I don't like this,' growled Naberius's main head.

'You've disliked everything since Lucifer's death,' the left head said.

'They surrendered the outer city too swiftly,' added the right head.

'I agree, milord,' Guillamere said. The three heads turned to regard him, their ears perking up. Even after decades of service, the sight of those six red eyes focused on him still sent a flutter of unease through his body. But a bead of saliva dangled from the right head's jaw, eliciting a half smile from Guillamere and easing the tension.

'They clung to the outer walls like merchants to their pennies. It is a trap, but whatever their intentions, our men are three days starved. We don't have the luxury of time.'

'So you have said,' the right head acknowledged.

'Perhaps we should speed up our plans.'

'And your thoughts, priest?' inquired the left-most head.

The main head turned its attention back to the city and their advancing army. Flag bearers marched with the vanguard, their standards of red, blue, black and yellow fluttering in the wind.

'A full assault,' Guillamere said. 'They're weakened, outnumbered, and demoralised. Our forces might overwhelm the Templars even without your help. But with your help, we may still keep sufficient numbers to subdue this Ancient power south of the mountains. With that, we may then fulfill Lucifer's last wish.'

That caught Naberius's attention – he had gained the focus of all three heads, their eyes assessing.

'And our original strategy?' the main head asked.

'I'd be surprised if there's even a handful of grain left on this side of the Fortress,' Guillamere said. 'Siege engines are an option, but with hellfire, you could breach the gates within minutes.'

'You presume to order us?' the left-most head asked in his mocking drawl.

'No, milord,' Guillamere replied, a smile tugging at his lips. 'I merely offer sage advice. Whether you heed it is entirely up to you.'

The left head's laughter resonated like ice cracking on a frozen lake. Guillamere was all too aware of the danger lying beneath.

'And if we fail?' the right-most head asked.

'We withdraw. My scouts have discovered goat paths through the mountains. Treacherous and narrow, unfit for an army, but a small group—' Guillamere finished with a shrug.

'I am tired of waiting,' the left head said.

'I want to tear them apart,' the right-side head said.

'Very well, we will be bold,' declared the central head.

'Remember, you owe us your life,' the right head said. 'Ensure you live to fulfil that debt, or we will find you in hell.'

'I am bound to serve in this life and the next,' Guillamere said with a bow.

The hound's six eyes lingered on him for a moment. The main head's mouth was closed, while the left and right heads had their tongues lolling. They all snapped to attention as the beast surged forward, his claws carving deep furrows into the cobblestone. He charged like liquid shadow towards the Iron Gates; the army hastily cleared a path for the monstrous creature.

Guillamere signalled his captain. The man shouted orders and his men moved under his black flag, emblazoned with its demon skull. Their contingent of soldiers and Priests advanced through the streets, joining the main force. Despite the barrage of arrows and stones, their march was as steady as a drumbeat.

Their army halted in the cover of the buildings while Naberius unleashed hellfire on the gate. Guillamere's guard slowed alongside him, their hands on their weapons as they scanned their surroundings. None of these buildings had been searched. A two-story structure caught his attention, seemingly a prosperous carpenter's shop with its ground floor open, showcasing workbenches and tools with living quarters above. Amidst the din of battle and the roar of hellfire against the gate, Guillamere's eyes were drawn to the black liquid flowing down like honey.

Is that Jophiel's fire oil? Guillamere wondered, as his eyes followed their trail, seeing the fire oil on gutters leading to houses up and down the street. It snaked through the city, in and around their army, like an invasive vine. Realisation suddenly dawned on him, and he turned to shout at the captain to retreat, when he heard the catapult winches release another payload. Instead of stones, pots affixed with burning rags sailed through the sky.

'Everybody down!' Guillamere roared.

Men and women, previously entranced by the burning pots as if they were shooting stars, immediately dove to the ground. Those out of earshot saw their movements and tried to follow suit, while some others tried to run. But it was too late – the pots crashed into the city, splattering the burning liquid like blood-red paint.

Burning soldiers screamed while their comrades tried to slap out the flames. The fire found the oil in the gutters and raced along it like lightning across the sky. The blaze, fed by the gutters, licked up into a house fifty yards from Guillamere. Smoke immediately began to billow from its confines, evolving into fingers of flame.

'Stay down!'

The smoke momentarily withdrew, and a moment of deceptive calm ensued. Then fire exploded through the windows and doors, the concussive force blowing the stone out in a blistering explosion. The very ground convulsed as a thunderous shockwave echoed through the air. Flames danced and roared, painting the sky in hues of orange and red. The force of the blast sent men flying. Armoured soldiers clattered against the cobblestone streets while stone debris rained down like hail.

As the dust began to settle, Guillamere peered up from his prone position and before he could fully comprehend the destruction, a second explosion followed. Then a third. The blaze raced through the flowing fire oil, igniting more houses with their devastating explosions. Their army had encircled the traps like water, but as the chain reaction continued to ignite the firehouses in the city, they were being blown apart like a shattered bucket. Each blast sent shockwaves reverberating through his chest and ebbed his courage. Guillamere was reduced to something primal; he curled into a ball and cradled his head.

'Lucifer, watch over me,' he prayed amid the cacophony of destruction. Each explosion rocked him, sending him careening further out of thought and time. In his cowering daze, Guillamere wondered if the Archangels had come for Judgement Day.

Ears deafened, he took a good thirty seconds to realise the explosions had finally stopped. A haunting silence enveloped the city and the pungent smell of sulphur settled over them like a haze. As Guillamere's hearing returned, the screams of the dying filled his ears. The air, heavy with the scent of char and stone, choked the throats of those who still dared to breathe. Amidst the ruins, survivors staggered to their feet, marked by soot and terror. The outer city had been transformed into a hellish inferno.

Guillamere stood, holding onto his staff like a crutch. The ringing in his ears drowned out the screams of the dying. He took a step and stumbled. As he steadied himself, ash and dust floated off his dreadlocks like snowflakes. While the aftermath of the explosion died down, he could see more of his army rising. He wiped his eyes to make sure they were seeing true. Despite the merciless explosions, there were more able survivors than he'd thought possible. Judging from their movements and actions, he quickly estimated there were over ten thousand able bodies. More than enough to overpower the defenders, if the tattered shreds of their morale held.

Then Guillamere saw something that made him feel like he'd swallowed a stone.

Naberius was retreating. The colossal hound was running, his gait uneven, several of Elise's javelins protruding from his rear. Their army scrambled to clear a path, but the slower ones were mercilessly crushed under the demon's claws.

The Fortress's horn sounded, quickly echoed by a dozen more.

'In Lucifer's name, what now?' Guillamere demanded, looking around.

Sounds emanated from the nearby carpenter's house. Miraculously, the place was relatively untouched. A seed of dread was sown as Guillamere saw an unnatural glow of white light from within. He lifted his demon-headed staff, invoking Lucifer's dark power. Shadows cast from the largest buildings to the smallest of cracks surged towards him. As they raced through his staff, they coalesced into a vortex of pure black atop the demon skull.

'Weapons out and be ready!' Guillamere bellowed.

His men exchanged uncertain glances as they eyed the house. They unsheathed their weapons as the door burst open, unleashing one of the defenders' infernal Templars. Clad in polished plate armour, wielding his fabled longsword and glowing like an angel, Paul looked as if he'd just stepped out of a painting. The man's blade moved like quicksilver as he cut down those around him. Behind him charged a cadre of men in chainmail, their broadswords and shields emblazoned with Zadkiel's sacred flame.

War Priests.

Guillamere, commanding the amassed Darkness, split it into two spears of shadow and launched them at the Templar and the foremost War Priest. The force of it caused Paul to stagger as he looked incredulously towards Guillamere. The other spear struck the first War Priest. Though his aura of Light absorbed some of the blow, it still hit him like a battering ram, slamming him back into his fellows.

'They are but men,' Guillamere yelled. 'Their power cannot stand against the Darkness!' Several Dark Priests stepped up next to him. They clutched the emblems around their necks as darkness flowed from them, adding their power to his own. 'Let us finish them in Lucifer's name!'

The unrelenting brushes with death had instilled a recklessness in Naberius's army that Guillamere hadn't expected. His men swarmed the Templar and his War Priests. Outnumbered a hundred to one, the men of the Light were forced backwards. Though Paul's blade cut a swathe through them, for every two he felled, five took their place.

In the tumultuous clash of Dark against Light, Guillamere's spears would strategically strike at the Templar and his clergy. The War

Priests fell one by one, their divine protection faltering against the surging Darkness.

Paul, his blond hair matted with blood and dirt, his plate armour pierced and dented, now carried over a dozen wounds. Yet he fought on, though his aura of Light was dimming. Meanwhile, Guillamere's archers had positioned themselves on the rooftops, their arrows flying alongside Guillamere's dark spears. The Templar roared like a wounded boar.

He is dead, Guillamere thought. *He just doesn't know it yet.*

'High Priest!' his captain shouted. He pointed, drawing Guillamere's attention to one of the main roads. Another Templar, flanked by his own band of War Priests, was carving a path through the city. Guillamere's gaze followed their movement, and he froze, icy fingers of fear slipping around his heart. A huge harpoon was sticking out of Naberius's ribs, while the hellhound fought against the Templar that held the chain.

I need to finish this now, Guillamere thought.

As the archers rained down arrows on the Templar, their points found several gaps in his armour so that Paul now resembled a beleaguered porcupine.

Guillamere moulded all of his amassed Darkness into a single spear, as sharp and potent as a bolt of lightning. With a flick of his staff, he released it. Time seemed to slow as the black spear hurtled forward, meeting Paul's weakening aura. For a moment, it resisted, but the sheer force of the Darkness overwhelmed it, piercing his chest plate, impaling the man. The Templar collapsed.

'Everyone with me – we march to Naberius's aid!'

* * *

CHAPTER TWENTY-SEVEN: THE FINAL LIGHT

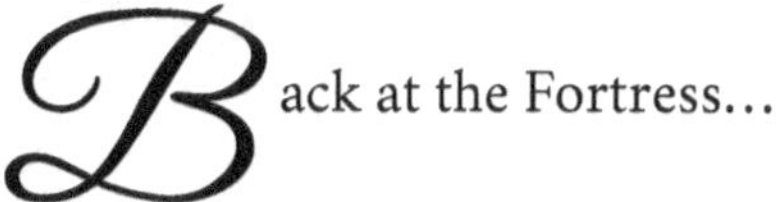ack at the Fortress…

* * *

* * *

WILFRED LOCKED GAZES WITH ARTHUR, brandishing his twin axes and sporting a feral grin. With a loud battle cry he burst from the stronghold, charging into the ember-lit ruins of the northern city. Arthur, imbued with the Light, dashed after him. Their band of War Priests strained to keep pace.

The series of relentless explosions had ravaged the enemy army, and their numbers were scattered like leaves in a tempest. They watched in a punch-drunk stupor as Naberius fled while being pursued by the two Templars and a score of War Priests.

Wilfred's twin axes moved in a relentless dance, cutting through the foe like a whirlwind. Arthur stormed through in the wake of his destruction as the distance between them and Naberius grew. Their superhuman speed paled beside the pace of the four-legged demon. As they ran, Arthur paid no heed to the heat of the blazing city, while smoke and sulphur hung heavy in the air. The First Templar tried to ignore the large number of the enemy still standing.

If they rally and coordinate with each other, this could be a really short counterattack, Arthur thought.

Horn blasts echoed from the Fortress. Even amid their mad dash, Arthur counted three. It marked Naberius's route, letting the Templars know where to converge.

The demon hound was making for the western square – a broad cobblestone plaza flanked by two-story stone buildings. Market stalls covered with wooden awnings lined the ground floors, while residential quarters perched above. Three wide avenues fed into the square: one from the north leading back toward the Fortress gates, another from the east connecting to the merchant district, and a third from the south leading to the fortress. The open space made it perfect for their trap, but those same avenues could quickly become open channels for enemy reinforcements.

As Naberius veered into the square, Rose and a cadre of War Priests surged from a tradesman's dwelling. Radiating with Light, they descended upon the square's foes, springing the trap. Arthur viewed it from a distance and even he was shocked at how effective they were. Rose confronted the high demon with a steel harpoon, its tip glinting in the sunlight, while the War Priests' sudden, ferocious emergence shattered the remnants of the enemy's resolve, driving them from the square.

The hound eyed Rose, his three heads growling and wary. Rose feinted, causing the creature to dodge. This slip gave Rose the moment she needed to throw her harpoon. The steel spear flew, its metal chain uncoiling in its wake. The tip buried itself deep into the demon's flank. Naberius's pained yelp resounded as he faltered, the harpoon protruding from his side.

She has done it, Arthur thought. She'd managed to chain him. Now she just needed to hold him long enough for the rest of the Templars to converge on him.

The War Priests advanced towards the entry point. Their shields and swords orchestrated a ballet of precision and destruction. They cleared the square of enemy soldiers, moving with practised precision to fortify the three entrances. The Light's clergy were the thin line that was set up to hold back the enemy from rushing to Naberius's aid.

Still a quarter mile away, Arthur and Wilfred raced for the square. He could see Naberius trying to leap away, but Rose wrapped the chain around her wrist guard and yanked. The harpoon, lodged deep within the hound's ribcage and ensnared by bone, dragged the demon back to the square. As Naberius whirled to snap at her, Rose looked magnificent, her blond braids flying as she wielded her broadsword, executing swift arcs in the air and valiantly fending off the hound's advances.

Throughout the city, the enemy soldiers were slowly mobilised by the Dark Priests towards the battle. Their numbers were already pressing on the War Priests that defended the square, while in the centre, Naberius and Rose duelled.

Wilfred forged a path for their party, tearing through the enemy as though they were wet parchment. Wielding his mace with lethal precision, Arthur defended the other Templar's flanks. He was all too aware of the hundreds of enemy soldiers that still surrounded them. If they charged, this would all be for nothing. But Cormac's words rang in his mind.

'The enemy has seen you fight for weeks. You Templars are a beacon every time you fight, turning the battle wherever you go. You think a conscripted army is going to rush to face you if you charge out after the Hound? Most of them feel no loyalty to him, at least not enough to risk their lives.'

Whether it was the explosions or Naberius's running like a bloody coward, Arthur was grateful the enemy were keeping their distance.

They were still a mile away, when Rose narrowly avoided the left head's jaws, then slashed forward with her blade at the main head. She almost lost the chain in the manoeuvre.

Just a little longer, Arthur thought desperately. But suddenly he felt a wave of elation as he saw Phillip and his war band tearing through the foe, bursting into the square from its eastern entrance. The

Templar, a blazing ball of Light, charged at the beast. His spear was a metal storm as he cut and slashed at the three-headed hound. Naberius reared up, only to be yanked back down by Rose. One head yelped in pain, a large gash on the creature's shoulder, while the lead head opened his maw to spew hellfire on them.

His legs still pumping and his arms swinging, Arthur was trying desperately to close the distance to the square. Though it was not far, it felt like the width of entire continents. Once he could close the distance, they could finish this.

In the square, Naberius breathed his hellfire, and the fountain of streaming lava engulfed Phillip in a veil of flames. All around the square, the smell of sulphur cut through the breeze while a cacophony of steel sang its song of battle. More of the enemy were recovering and converging on the square, where they tried to strike down the War Priests defending the chokepoints.

Eventually the flames dissipated, revealing Phillip still standing amidst the smouldering aftermath. The man's aura of Light was significantly diminished and his tunic was singed. The Templar stumbled, clutching his spear.

With a blood-crazed scream, Wilfred cut through the last of the enemy blocking Arthur's path to the southern entrance of the square. The foe cleared the road like a retreating tide, giving the War Priests there a brief reprieve while the two Templars burst into the square.

Behind the hound, the War Priests at the eastern entrance buckled under the weight of the enemy. Though their Light-enhanced blades cut down foes by the dozen, the single line of War Priests couldn't stem the tide of hundreds pressing forward. At the northern approach, another score of Priests were faring better, but the enemy was beginning to gain momentum as they fought against them to gain entrance to the square.

Arthur's steel-clad boots rang against the cobblestones as he ran to Phillip's side. Their auras intertwined just as Naberius unleashed its fiery breath a second time.

The hellfire engulfed them, extinguishing sight and sound. It felt as if they'd been thrust inside a lightless cave. The scorching heat washed past as though they'd been dunked in molten rock, and Arthur's reservoir of Light was draining swiftly at the relentless onslaught of the inferno. Then, like the darkness before the dawn, it vanished.

Rose had yanked the chain, pulling the hound away. The beast faltered, but one of his heads grabbed the chain between its jaws and jerked it. The force of it sent Rose stumbling.

Time seemed to slow as Rose dropped the chain, bringing up her broadsword as Naberius bore down on her. A fierce strike rent the air, leaving a deep wound on the beast's cheek, which immediately began to knit closed with dark energy. Then, the primary head clamped down on Rose, his teeth piercing through armour and hoisting her into the air. Rose's defiant cry was cut short as the beast's jaws clenched with a fatal crunch. The woman's sword clattered from lifeless fingers. Naberius flung the Templar away, her mangled body slamming against a building to slide onto the courtyard of stone.

Arthur felt a void open up in him, while simultaneously an inconsolable rage tried to fill it. The sight of Rose's beautiful aura snuffed out as sightless eyes stared skywards, did more to dash his hope than had the entire siege. She had been a beautiful soul, one of the few who had truly earned the title of Templar.

Phillip roared his defiance, running at the Demon in a blind rage.

Behind the hound, the War Priests at the eastern entrance buckled under the weight of the enemy. Soldiers came rushing in, flowing around Naberius like a river around a stone. The demon hound grinned, blood dripping from its muzzle as it backed up into its protective ring.

Arthur knew if he didn't stop it now, the number on the other side of the river would only grow as they haunted his dreams. Then the faces of Sarah and Richard appeared in his mind, and he wanted to look at them again without feeling shame.

He steeled his resolve and charged at the enemy. He swung his mace, the blunt weapon slamming through a raised shield. Meanwhile, Naberius worked at the harpoon, mangling his ribs as he tried to dislodge the weapon. Darkness poured over the wound, albeit slower than before.

Wilfred, embodying the fury of a vengeful Angel, charged at the breach. But even his relentless ferocity was slowed by the overwhelming enemy forces. With a guttural roar of victory, Naberius expelled the harpoon, disdainfully casting it aside as more soldiers surrounded him like a moat.

Just as Naberius looked poised for escape, a javelin flew overhead. The projectile, roughly the size of a ballista bolt, appeared as if from the heavens themselves. Its pointed tip found its mark directly in Naberius's chest.

The power of its divine retribution resonated through the square like a thunderbolt, and it left both allies and enemies momentarily dazed by its reverberating shockwave. Arthur's gaze shot towards the Fortress walls – Elise's luminescent form was unmistakable among the archers. Celebrating, Elise whooped, her figure bouncing with a righteous rage amidst the stunned silence. The soldiers of the Light erupted in cheers, their voices merging in a wave of elation.

Arthur believed the heavens had guided that throw.

Naberius staggered to his feet, his movements laboured and unsteady. Arthur swung his mace with renewed ferocity, each strike splintering the enemy like firewood. He caught up to Phillip, allowing the man to fight freely, his spear moving like a snake, its deadly strikes felling anyone in their way. As they approached Naberius, Arthur summoned the Light until it filled him to bursting with its divine energy—then he unleashed his wrath. The mace club connected with Naberius's leg. Bone snapped and muscles splintered. The foreleg flopped. Despite his injuries, Naberius kept his feet, hobbling back on three legs. Arthur dropped the mace, both hands grasping onto the wooden shaft of the javelin. He channelled the Archangel's power through the weapon. As one head lunged, Phillip intervened, his spear moving so fast it was like a protective thornbush around them. It gave Arthur the chance to direct a powerful surge of Light through the weapon and into the beast's core. The creature collapsed under the intensity of the first pulse. Arthur, unrelenting, amplified his assault, the Light coursing through the javelin with each successive wave. By the fourth one, Naberius lay twitching feebly on the cobblestones.

Arthur felt a surreal pause enveloping him as he stood over the collapsed demon. In that moment, detached and transcendent, he perceived the end of their struggle. Lucifer's hound was on the brink of death.

Then the sounds of battle washed over them, steel clashing, men screaming and blood flowing. Arthur, drawing upon the very essence of his being, funnelled the last vestiges of Light he could muster into the javelin. With a final push, he unleashed a torrent of divine energy into Naberius. The pulse of light surged through the weapon and into the demon, halting its desperate struggles.

He relaxed his grip on the javelin. He'd done it. Naberius's chest had stopped moving. But just as victory was in their grasp, a sudden brutal force struck him from the side. The impact, reminiscent of a hammer's blow, wrenched him from the javelin, sending him reeling. He tripped and fell, his armour clanging against the cobblestones.

The absence of the Light's power left him exposed to his own physical limits. Each movement was a battle against the crushing weight of his armour and the sharp sting of exhaustion.

It was then that he saw Guillamere. A cadre of the black clergy flanked the High Priest of Lucifer at the eastern entrance. Their arrival had bolstered the enemy's ranks, forcing Phillip and the remaining War Priests into a desperate retreat.

Arthur's gaze locked with Guillamere's, witnessing Darkness coalesce around the priest's demon-headed staff, gathering into an ominous orb that hovered like a malevolent storm cloud. With a dramatic gesture, Guillamere slammed his staff to the ground, morphing the orb into a massive spear of shadow.

Arthur pushed through his fatigue and the oppressive burden of his armour to rise to his feet. As the dark spear took form, thoughts of his wife and boy pierced his looming despair. He had made the world a better place for them.

With a final glance at Naberius's still form, he turned to face Guillamere with a defiant smirk. Arthur watched as the Dark Priest commanded the shadowy spear with a lethal thrust.

Diminished to the faintest glow, Arthur's aura offered no resistance as the spear pierced his armour and then his heart. A serene acceptance washed over him in his final moments. He was comforted by the thought that his sacrifice had secured the fall of Naberius.

Then Arthur died.

CHAPTER TWENTY-EIGHT:
SHADOW'S SALVATION

*T*en minutes earlier on the eastern side of the ruined city…

* * *

GUILLAMERE STARED at the now stilled body of Paul. They had downed a Templar without Naberius's intervention, yet he felt no triumph, only a growing sense of dread. The enemy had laid a trap for his master. He shook himself as soldiers rallied to his command, falling into position with parade-ground precision. He looked past them as Phillip's aura of light disappeared amid the buildings at the western side of the city.

As the crow flew, it was less than a thousand yards away, but the aftermath of the explosions had left any clear route through the city in ruins. Guillamere stared at the maze of destroyed buildings and rubble-strewn streets, his eyes picking a path through the hazards so that their army could march up the small rise and follow where Templar Phillip's Light had disappeared to.

Captains shouted orders, and the soldiers marched. Their feet sounded like the beat of a drum. Their orderly procession was in direct contrast to the chaos of burning buildings, scattered rubble, the screams of the wounded, and the silence of the dead. Every fibre inside of Guillamere wanted to urge the men to run, but order needed to be restored. Their army had been decimated by the Templars' trap. Confusion reigned, leaving the remnants of their forces ill-equipped to deal with the Templars' fervent assault. Through intermittent views between the buildings, Guillamere caught glimpses of Naberius's monstrous silhouette. As the hound leapt, snapped and snarled, it filled him with frustrated helplessness. *Does he not understand the threat? Why does he not retreat?*

As they moved through the city, their orderly march brought renewed life to their scattered forces. Soldiers, blackened by soot and smoke, carried bared weapons as they joined onto the end of their train. Their numbers grew with every step. By the time they had crested a rise that brought the western square into clear view, their force had grown into the thousands.

The rest of their army pressed at the square from all sides, their numbers being held back by a thin line of soldiers of the Light. In the centre of the square, three Templars harried Naberius. It was then that Guillamere saw the harpoon protruding from the demon's side. His heart in his throat, he watched as the Amazonian Templar tried to yank the hound off balance. But she made a mistake, and Naberius pounced, catching her in his powerful maw. The teeth clamped shut with a crunch of finality.

A moment later, the Square's eastern defenders buckled under the pressure. The Dark's armies swept into the square, rushing to the aid of their demon lord.

As Guillamere's hope slowly flickered back to life, it was swiftly extinguished as a javelin fell from the sky. Its tip dove deep into the demon's chest, causing Naberius to stagger under its force.

'Charge now!' Guillamere roared. It elicited a swift response from his captains. Their train soon devolved into separate squads breaking like a wave, their numbers rushing forth. War cries echoed around them as the sound of pounding feet echoed through the cacophony. Despite their foes' prowess with shield and spear, they were soon overwhelmed by sheer numbers. As many soldiers were trampled to death as were killed by the blade.

Guillamere ran forward. The black robes of his office and demon-skulled staff commanded respect as the soldiers curved around him. As he stepped into the square, he muttered a quick prayer to Lucifer before planting his staff, and then he drew on the Darkness. As his power gathered, he could see their army slowly snuffing out the Light's defenders. He could see Phillip distracting Naberius's three heads while Arthur grabbed onto the javelin impaling the demon's chest. A pulse of Light surged through the weapon, causing Naberius to falter. The next pulse made the demon collapse.

'No!' Guillamere's scream drove through the battlefield. Raw emotions tore through him, fuelling him as he drew deeply from the well of Darkness. The gift surged into him, a deluge of power filling him to bursting. Then, like a dam breaking, he released it all through the demon-headed staff. Shadows erupted, flowing forward like a tidal wave of inky blackness. The void-like maelstrom struck out, flowing over the square and devouring friend and foe alike. Screams of pain and confusion reigned as Guillamere wrestled with the power. Eventually, he brought it under control, using it to craft a single spear. He then launched it directly at Arthur. The Templar's diminished aura offered no more resistance than loose hay. The spear breached his defences.

Guillamere watched, disbelief mingling with triumph, as Arthur regarded the dark spear jutting from his chest. A rueful smile crept across his face even as his gaze lingered on the fallen High Demon, and he died.

Fuelled by a surge of fury, Guillamere redoubled his offensive, his subsequent assaults driving back the remaining Templars and their War Priests. With Naberius fallen, the enemy withdrawal was swift and fierce. Allied soldiers took off in pursuit, but Guillamere ignored them, pushing his way through the waiting crowd and reaching Naberius's side. He discarded his staff to grasp the embedded javelin. He pulled, but his hands slid from the polished surface. Brushing his sweaty palms against his robes, he tried again. It moved with agonising slowness. Then, in a sudden rush, he yanked it out with a squelching pop. He staggered backwards, almost falling over.

Guillamere was quick to reclaim his staff and call forth the Darkness. As the shadows answered his call, he directed them towards the gaping wound. He hoped that the power would cover and seal the wound, yet like a man dying of thirst, it just kept swallowing the murk that flowed into it like a river. Soon, other priests joined his side, their power joining his own. The continual stream of Darkness disappeared into the wound's void.

Amidst this concentrated effort, a subtle transformation began. Initially imperceptible, the hound's form gradually diminished. Dark fur lightened, his monstrous visage and limbs morphing. The process unfolded with excruciating slowness. The hound's three heads merged, heralding a stark metamorphosis: Naberius's demonic features gave way to a distinctly human form, lying curled and vulnerable. Then his breath misted in the crisp mountain air.

Guillamere's tension dissolved into relief. His staff clattered to the ground as he dropped it, the darkness vanishing. He lifted the hem of his robe and yanked it over to his head. Black cloth in hand, he draped it over Naberius's human form. Without his robe's warmth, he could feel immediately feel the cold bite of the mountain air.

As Naberius's eyes fluttered open, confusion and recognition flickered in his dark gaze. His voice was now barely a whisper.

'You have saved me.'

The laugh that escaped Guillamere was one of sheer relief, a sound that seemed foreign amid the chaos. 'No, milord, it was you who saved me.'

'They have wounded me greatly. I cannot recover in time to join the battle.'

A tentative joy swept through the High Priest that he would recover. He wiped a tear from his eye. 'Our army may yet win, but I will get you to safety first.'

Naberius nodded, his eyes closing.

'You, you and you,' Guillamere said, pointing at nearby soldiers. 'Make a stretcher. We need to get our lord to safety.'

'Where will we go?' one of the Priests asked.

'There are goat trails out there,' Guillamere said with a wave towards their lines. 'We will take our chances in the mountains.'

'And the army?'

Guillamere glanced towards the army, their remnants gathering as surviving captains rallied the decimated forces. 'Will not stop the attack until the Fortress is taken or they're all dead.'

'What will you do?' the Priest asked again.

'Ensure our lord's survival. We will return if you are victorious,' Guillamere said. 'Now see to it.'

'Yes, High Priest.'

Guillamere oversaw the others as they placed Naberius's human form onto a stretcher. Then their small band marched out of the forsaken city and towards the safety of the mountains. Battle horns could be heard behind him as their army assaulted the Keep.

* * *

CHAPTER TWENTY-NINE: LAST STAND

Meanwhile, in the southern city...

* * *

PLUMES of smoke darkened the sky. Riordan's gaze dropped to the Fortress, the man-made mountain standing as a dam in the pass, its grey walls forming a sheer rock face. From this distance, he couldn't tell if the smoke was confined just to the northern city. Yet, since the enemy hadn't breached the southern city, he assumed their forces still held the Keep.

Light watch over Arthur and the other Templars, he prayed silently.

'How long, do you think?' Cormac asked.

Riordan's eyes shifted towards the main road leading down from the Keep. A woman clutched a baby to her chest, her face etched with fear and exhaustion as she stumbled forward, a small bundle of possessions tucked under her arm. An elderly man leaned heavily on a gnarled wooden staff as he hobbled along the street. Children clung to their mothers' skirts, their wide eyes filled with confusion and tears. The wounded lay in makeshift stretchers in horse-drawn wagons, their moans of pain mingling with the creaking of wooden wheels and the clopping of hooves. A young boy, no older than ten, struggled to keep pace with the crowd, his arms laden with a tattered blanket and a small sack of food. They were trickling in from all over the city, creating a myriad of streams that fed into the river of people exiting the southern gates, desperate to escape the impending danger that loomed over their once-thriving city. If the Keep held, they should be safe. Thousands had already passed through, spreading into the open. Some followed the road to the Citadel of the Light, while others ventured into the wilderness or toward the Riverlands.

The congestion of refugees made movement slow. Riordan rolled his shoulders, juggling numbers as he estimated there were several thousand still to go.

'If they were disciplined soldiers, less than an hour. At this rate, maybe five.'

Cormac pursed his lips as he surveyed from his perch on the southern city walls. He glanced towards the Keep. Suddenly he shouted. 'Conner!'

'Yes, sir!' Though the man had enough greys to likely be older than Cormac, he never hesitated when his captain gave orders.

'How many men do you think you'll need to complete the evacuation?'

'Sir?'

'We're not staying. I'm reassigning every able body from babysitting to arse-kicking duties. How many do you need?'

The man assessed the refugees, chewing his lip.

'None, sir.'

'None?' Cormac challenged.

'Did I stutter?'

Cormac grinned, clapping him on the shoulder. 'I like your style. Alright, gather everyone together. We're reinforcing the Keep.'

Conner turned, his voice hoarse as he ordered everyone to line up. They were a grizzled bunch, with more than half of them sporting a visible bandage over arms, shoulders, or legs. Dressed in recently-mended leather armour, or chain mail with broken links, they quickly assembled, spears and shields at the ready.

'Alright, lads,' Cormac shouted, his voice cutting through the murmur of the crowd. 'The southern city is nearly emptied. I'm disregarding orders by not overseeing the last departures, but I don't like sitting here while people up there—' he pointed towards the Keep, '—are fighting and dying without us.'

There were a few grunts and nods from the Ravens.

'I can't make you follow me, but anyone willing should join us as we're making for the Keep.'

'Anyone staying behind will get a spear in the ribs,' Conner said. 'We don't suffer cowards.'

'Yes, sir!'

Their shout drew the attention of the refugees streaming past the gate, who gave them a brief look before being nudged onward by those behind.

'That's one way to motivate people,' Riordan said dryly.

'If it works, it works,' Cormac said.

Following his father, Riordan and the Ravens moved against the flow of civilians, slowly making their way toward the Keep. As they walked, several wounded men and a few women reversed their direction to fall in behind their ranks. By the time they emerged from the throng, their group had swelled from fifty to over two hundred.

Zahir joined them at the front of their train. The man was clad in a green robe, covered by a breastplate adorned with intricate floral patterns. His metal helmet, once boasting a collection of colourful feathers that could have rivalled a peacock's, was now so degraded it resembled a diseased pigeon. His mason's hammer still hung from his belt.

'Thought you'd run off,' Cormac said.

The man's expression darkened. 'I have been paid for this role.'

'To the bitter end, eh?'

'I do not intend to die today. You've wasted enough time; let us join the battle.'

Riordan stepped forward, placing a restraining hand on his father's shoulder. 'It's good to have you with us, Zahir. Every pair of hands helps.'

Zahir grunted.

Cormac exhaled, and though it looked painful, he turned to the mix of regulars and militia that made up their army.

'Any civilians among us, stay close to our soldiers and heed their instructions. To the Ravens, protect the newcomers as best you can. Keep your wits about you, stay alive and let's stop this horde.'

Without waiting for a response, Cormac led the way up the gradual incline toward the Fortress. The moment they entered the Keep's shadow, an orchestra of battle – clashing metal, battle cries in both the common and northern tongues, screams of dying men, and the twanging of bows – enveloped them.

Dark blood flowed through the gutters as they traversed under the archway of the Iron Gates. Within the Keep's yard, a battered line of soldiers of the Light strained to maintain their position, as the enemy numbers contained to push through the northern entrance. Illuminated by the glow of two Templars – one wielding twin axes and the other a spear – they were the bulwark, preventing the line's collapse. Despite their valour, the church's defensive perimeter was dwindling as the enemy poured through the northern gates. The ground was strewn with bodies, over which the enemy stumbled and slid in their advance. Arrows descended from the parapets onto the swelling enemy forces, while another Templar fought along the walls against those who had climbed the stairs. The air was thick with the acrid smell of blood.

Seizing his spear, Cormac bellowed, 'Come men, let's send them to hell!'

With his father in the lead, the Wild Ravens and their makeshift army charged. Riordan, a step behind his father, used his shield and spear to dive into the breach that Templar Phillip had carved into the foe. An enemy soldier turned towards Riordan, the whites of his eyes stark against his helmet's visor. Riordan caught the incoming spear strike on his shield before plunging his own spear into the man's body. The warrior collapsed with a pitiful cry. Riordan yanked his weapon clear to attack the next man.

On the flank, Zahir emerged, his hammer crashing against an

uplifted shield, shattering it and the arm beneath. The victim fell with a scream, and the next strike caved in the man's helmet and skull with a single blow.

The sudden influx of reinforcements made the enemy hesitate, and bolstered the flagging spirits of the church's soldiers. The line held, then pushed forward, aided by the relentless advance of the two Templars. Above, arrows continued to rain down, shattering the enemy's cohesion.

Pushing forward, Riordan aimed to join forces with Phillip, each step precarious on cobblestones slick with blood. He found grim footing atop fallen bodies, striking and parrying to safeguard Phillip as they drove the enemy back through the gates. In a few minutes of battle, the enemy had faltered, retreating into the northern city.

Riordan watched them run into the ruins of the place, where hardly a structure remained intact amid the swathe of smoking debris. Yet the ruins provided cover, obscuring the diminished but reorganising enemy forces. There had to be a few thousand out there, reforming for another assault.

Riordan glanced back and saw Phillip planting his spear on one of the fallen, the aura of light around him flickering like a candle buffeted by the wind. His chest heaved from exertion as he exchanged looks with the other Templar, who was leaning against the wall, twin axes in hand.

'Wilfred, are you alright?' Phillip asked.

Wilfred offered a weary, half-hearted smile. 'Best fight I've ever been in.' A closer inspection revealed Wilfred wasn't just drenched in enemy blood; he was bleeding from at least six wounds Riordan could see. It was a miracle he could even remain standing.

'There's still a few inside the tower,' Cormac said.

'Elise will deal with them,' Phillip replied.

'We'll take care of any trying to flee from the base,' Cormac added, casting a meaningful glance at Riordan. Side by side, they positioned themselves near the tower's exit. The first man came out, trying to attack Cormac. Riordan struck him from the side, and Cormac yanked him out of the way and into the other Ravens, who finished him off. Though a few soldiers survived more than a single strike, the chokepoint made it impossible for them to mount an efficient attack.

Eventually, a soldier came out with his arms up. Cormac drove his spear into the man's chest, then yanked him out of the way to engage the next one. There was no quarter as they killed the enemy coming out of the tower until eventually Elise appeared.

The Templar was wielding a solitary short sword. Her neck was tightly bandaged, though dark red stains were seeping through.

'Are you well, Templar?' Riordan asked.

'Never better.'

Riordan raised his eyebrows, but said nothing. Instead, she looked around the courtyard. The place was a grim tapestry of death that could populate several graveyards.

'We have little time before they regroup,' Phillip called. 'I need barricades at the gates. Elise, how are the arrows?'

'Nearly out.'

'My lot!' Cormac bellowed. 'Scavenge for usable arrows among the dead.'

Riordan's gaze swept over the courtyard, arrows littering the ground like weeds amidst the fallen in a garden of death. He felt detached, his mind insulating him from the full impact of the carnage. Shaking off the numbness, he focused on Phillip.

'The plan. Did it work?' Riordan asked.

Phillip locked eyes with him, a silent exchange, heavy with unspoken truths. After a moment, he answered, 'Though I believe Naberius was slain, we were forced to retreat before we could confirm it.'

'And Arthur?'

'Sacrificed himself for the chance. Along with Rose and Paul.'

Riordan nodded, feeling a pang of grief. Beside him, Cormac swallowed hard, and though he tried to put on a brave face, his father's eyes glistened.

'So, what now?'

'We win, or we die.'

'I like it. Easy to remember,' Riordan said, as his eyes swept over the soldiers still standing. Even with the archers included, their force had dwindled to fewer than five hundred.

'They're regathering—' Wilfred's voice broke the brief silence.

'To the gates!' Phillip yelled.

Those who had been scavenging arrows quickly handed their findings to Elise. With practiced efficiency, she secured them into bundles and hastened into the tower leading to the parapets. The remainder took their positions by the doors, readying themselves among the fallen for the enemy's next assault.

CHAPTER THIRTY: THE PRICE OF VICTORY

The fighting inside the keep had been never-ending, as Riordan's sword bounced off his foe's wooden shield. He stumbled, almost falling, but kept his feet. The enemy warrior wore a mail shirt over his orange and black clothing that covered all but his eyes, though his spindly awkwardness betrayed his youth. His opponent hesitated, eyes wide, failing to exploit the opening.

With an iron-heavy arm, Riordan raised his weapon; the boy lifted his shield. Still holding his sword aloft, Riordan stepped forward, using his superior bulk to body slam the boy, making him stumble. Then his sword descended. Though the armour stopped the edge, the force of the blow broke bone. The boy fell screaming, clutching his collarbone as he joined the hundreds of dead and wounded who lay across the courtyard like felled wheat.

Cormac fended off two more foes nearby. Riordan took a few steadying breaths before moving to aid him, but Phillip was there first. His spear hamstrung one, then with the spear's butt he clipped the other, forcing him to stumble onto Cormac's waiting blade. Though the Templar's power had long since faded, his skill still made him incredibly dangerous on the battlefield.

The courtyard was filled with clanging weapons as the ragged defenders held on. With their current opponents dispatched, Phillip led a counterattack. One assailant backed away at the sight of him, then turned to flee. Others followed, and soon it turned into a rout.

There was no cheering amongst the defenders, no feeling of victory. Several slumped where they were, others swayed with a hollow-eyed exhaustion.

His throat as dry as a desert, Riordan stumbled to a rain barrel at the courtyard's edge. It was empty, with only the moistened wood to taunt him. He breathed back a feeling of defeat.

Then a shout from behind made him turn. Hadrick stood atop the walls, waving his arms frantically. He tried to shout, but his voice didn't carry. Instead, he pointed, but when no one responded, he cursed and disappeared into the tower.

Riordan understood. He readied his shield and sword, moving back into line. The others forced themselves forward beside him, stumbling into a haggard row to meet the next wave.

The edge of Riordan's shield rested on the ground while he leaned on it, waiting for the enemy. None appeared. Eventually Hadrick emerged from the tower stairs.

'They're retreating,' he said, his voice hoarse. 'The last of them are fleeing the northern city, heading for the mountains.'

'It's over?' someone whispered.

'Looks that way.'

'The Priests?' Riordan asked.

'Didn't you hear?' Hadrick swallowed, and it looked like he'd gulped down a stone. 'Elise got the last of them. She made it back but she's not in good shape.'

Riordan felt numb, exhaustion giving way to a bone-deep weariness. He opened his palms, letting his sword and shield clatter to the ground, surveying those around him. From an army over ten thousand strong, less than a hundred remained standing. Some nodded with numb acceptance, while one man began to cry, his shoulders beginning to shake as deep sobs overtook him. It drew others. One patted him on the shoulder while another hugged him. Covered in muck and gore, the man clung to him like a lifeline.

'Come on, son. Fight's not over. Let's save those we can,' Cormac said with a glance towards the stretchers lining the courtyard's edge.

Riordan surveyed the piles of dead and wounded. He began stumbling over the mass of bodies, seeking signs of movement. A corporal's insignia caught his eye. It belonged to a man no more than fifteen. A nasty egg-sized bruise had formed on his forehead. He was unconscious but breathing, and with no other visible wounds. Riordan signalled his father. Together, they loaded him onto the stretcher. Hands clasping onto the worn wooden handles, he met his father's eye and together they followed an inaudible count. With a heave of exhaustion, they hoisted the wounded man, and then, with unsteady steps, they trudged towards the Keep's main hall. Despite the short distance, they rested every twenty yards.

Through the entry hall, they got to one of the larger bunk rooms. The dozens of beds that had originally lined the floor with military precision were now unkempt and disorganised. Half the cots were filled with the wounded and dead. Together, they carried the unconscious boy to the far end, placing him on an empty straw mattress. They adjusted him under the covers before braving the battlefield again. As they left, they saw Phillip treating the other two bedridden Templars, the last of the surviving chosen.

'How are they doing?' Cormac asked.

'Elise didn't make it,' Phillip said, his voice catching. 'She was low on Light but she still charged the last few priests. She got them, but the effort cost more than she had.' He turned his gaze to the fallen Templar. With her eyes closed, she looked peaceful, almost as if she were sleeping. 'She was the heart of us all.'

'She died a hero. As did all the Templars,' Cormac said.

Riordan's eyes moved to Wilfred. The massive Templar lay still as death, his hands grasping the haft of one of his axes, its edge chipped, frayed, and stained almost black with blood. The man who had laughed in the face of overwhelming odds, who had charged into battle with the joy of a child at play, was now a maze of stitches and bandages. Blood seeped through the wrappings despite the healers' best efforts.

His fingers twitched occasionally, as if worried he'd drop his weapon.

'I doubt I'll ever see the like of it again,' Phillip said. 'Even though he was virtually a dead man walking, he wouldn't stop until the last enemy in front of him had fallen. He took thirty men after I thought he'd been down for good. But blood loss eventually did what the enemy couldn't.'

Riordan watched a fresh red stain spread across one of Wilfred's bandages. Despite all the Templar's incredible power and legendary stamina, Riordan knew the warrior would not see another sunrise. The realisation felt like ice in his veins – that someone seemingly as invincible as Wilfred had fallen.

'There's more out there,' Cormac said, nodding towards the exit.

With a sigh of resignation, Riordan joined his father, and together they converged with the other survivors, shouldering the burden of caring for the sick and wounded. The process was slow. Duty alone kept Riordan on his feet as they searched for survivors to carry back to the Keep. He felt a twinge of regret as he ignored the agonised cries of the enemy wounded.

He fell into an exhausted haze, blocking out the hundreds of dead that littered the courtyard. His mind relayed simple objectives: find survivors, then bring them back to the Keep. The monotony of his footsteps felt like the drumbeat of a slave galley. He lost count of the people they'd brought in, but they had filled several rooms with wounded. At one point, Phillip blocked their path back to the courtyard.

'Go to the mess for some food. The wounded can wait twenty minutes,' the Templar said.

Riordan's emotions were muted. He felt no joy or sense of relief as his feet slowly carried him to the mess hall. The tables were filled with trail biscuits and flatbread. Maybe twenty others sat there, chewing in silence.

They washed their hands, leaving a trail of dirt and blood in the once-clean water, before taking the nearest seats. Riordan picked up a trail biscuit packed with oats and honey. Using the side of his mouth, he bit into it and chewed mechanically. The first one virtually vanished. Crumbs fell in front of him as he chewed on the next. Eventually he grabbed some flatbread, dipping it in more honey. As he ate, the sounds of those around him filtered into his ears. Colour returned to the walls; it was like waking from a dream. He was about to stand, but his father shook his head.

'Take a moment, lad.'

Riordan raised an eyebrow.

'You're about an hour from collapsing, no matter how strong your body is. It's time to take a moment. We've done what we can, but if we keep pushing, we'll become a burden.'

With a shrug, Riordan sagged back into the seat and took another biscuit.

'Everyone, listen up,' Hadrick said from the entrance, his raspy voice carrying in the silent room. 'I'm setting up rotations. We're keeping some men on the walls and others to care for the wounded and bring more in while everyone else rests. If you're here, congratulations, you're on the first rest rotation. You have four hours before I'll be switching it around.'

'What about the enemy wounded?' Riordan asked.

'They didn't make it,' Hadrick said flatly. When no one voiced a challenge, he nodded and turned for the exit.

'Four hours?' Cormac said softly, light returning to his eyes. He stood, looking down at Riordan. 'Wait here. I'll be back soon.'

Riordan didn't question him, taking some more flatbread and dunking it in honey. He finished it and was licking his fingers by the time Cormac returned, brandishing several bottles of alcohol, including one bottle of Waterlord whiskey.

'Where did you get those?'

'Arthur's quarters. He always had the best stuff.'

Cormac raised his voice, projecting it across the room. 'Everyone gather round! We're having a celebration!' He planted the bottles on the table, before lining up some wooden cups.

It took a moment for the crowd to grasp his words, then a few more for them to congregate. Cormac diligently gave each person a dram.

'We have fought through hell and killed a high demon in the process,' Cormac said, raising his cup. 'Though we will be hailed as heroes, we all know the truth. It was the Templars, War Priests, and soldiers who fell that are the real heroes. We will reunite with them in heaven, but until then, we drink in their honour!'

A graveyard silence fell as they raised their cups in unison, and then as one they drank. The whiskey thawed some of the numbness that had taken up residence in Riordan's body. As he lowered his cup, he saw his father still finishing his. Beneath his raised arm was an oozing black spot coming from below a rent in his leather armour.

'You're bleeding.'

Cormac lowered the cup and smiled grimly. 'Aye. I am, lad. No, don't get a bandage or needle. It's a gut wound.'

Riordan stared at him, not comprehending.

'It means I am going to die.'

'Don't be stupid, you can't die.'

His father smiled, resting a hand on his shoulder. 'I can, and I will. Before that, I want a final night of drinking with my son.'

Through his cloud of exhaustion, Riordan saw the desperate need in his father. He swallowed his pride. In a moment of clarity, he could see the wisdom in his father's words: Phillip didn't have enough Light to spark a candle, let alone save someone from a gut wound. Even if he did, that strength would save a dozen others.

Tears welled up in his eyes as he nodded in acceptance. His father sat down to pour another cup, and Riordan was surprised he hadn't noticed sooner – the way his father favoured his left side, the tension in his movements.

'So,' Riordan began, a forced smile coming to his lips, 'that bit of praise about the real heroes being the ones who died sounds a bit self-serving.'

Cormac paused as he unstoppered the whiskey with a pop. He chuckled. 'It does, doesn't it?'

* * *

CHAPTER THIRTY-ONE: NEW HORIZONS

ONE MONTH LATER...

Riordan found Phillip in the Fortress, overseeing the reconstruction of the Iron Gates. The courtyard had been cleared and washed, though the grey stones were stained a muddy brown, discoloured by the blood of the fallen. Around them, people moved with purpose, their uniforms crisp and clean. Several weeks had passed since his father's death. Not sure where he would go, Riordan had stayed on, helping the city with its recovery. Phillip was chatting to the other Templar, Oscar. The last Templar had arrived with five hundred soldiers. An irrational anger bubbled within Riordan whenever he saw the man. The Templar's presence could have averted their Pyrrhic victory, prevented so many deaths. He pushed it down, knowing the delay had been out of their control. Yet as he got closer, he could hear them speaking.

'Still no word of Naberius?' Oscar asked, his voice carrying an edge of ambition beneath the concern.

'None,' Phillip said. 'I wish we still had Matthew; he could have tracked anything through those mountains.'

'We need to be ready. The Angeldom cannot be caught so unprepared again,' Oscar said, his eyes gleaming. 'Zadkiel means well, but his heart is too soft. He sees the good in everyone, even our enemies.'

'Easy to say.'

'As the only surviving Templars, we have a chance to reshape things,' Oscar continued, his voice dropping lower. 'To guide the Angeldom down a stronger path. No more hesitation, no more mercy for those who would destroy us.'

'Zadkiel still leads us,' Phillip said, tension evident in his shoulders.

'He does, and he always will.' Oscar's smile didn't reach his eyes. 'But Arthur taught me that sometimes we must act for his own good. The Archangel's compassion is both his greatest strength and his greatest weakness. He needs firm hands to guide him, to make the hard choices he cannot.' He leaned closer. 'Together, the Templars can ensure we are never caught in a vulnerable moment again. Whatever the cost.'

Phillip looked deeply uncomfortable at the direction of this conversation, at the shadow of something dangerous lurking beneath Oscar's words. When he spotted Riordan approaching, relief flickered across his features. He made his excuses to Oscar, who cast an annoyed look at Riordan before moving off, his displeasure at the interruption evident.

'You're leaving,' Phillip said.

It wasn't a question.

'I can't stay here.'

'I understand,' the man said sadly, holding out his hand.

Adjusting his belongings, Riordan reached forward to clasp it.

'Know that it was an honour to fight beside you.'

'And you.'

'Where will you go?'

Riordan avoided the man's gaze and shrugged.

'I won't be needed here much longer,' Phillip said conversationally. 'I've got to head back to the Citadel. I owe Arthur, Wilfred and all the other Templars who had children that are now orphans.' He paused, his eyes distant. "You know, I've been asking myself why I survived when so many better souls fell. Wilfred with his boundless courage, Elise with her endless compassion, Arthur with his unwavering leadership ... and here I stand, the man who once butchered innocents in the north.' He touched the silver flame on his necklace. 'Perhaps that's why the Light spared me – my redemption isn't yet earned. All those who fell had already proven their worth, while I … I still have debts to pay. And watching over Richard, protecting what Arthur died to defend – maybe that's my path to earning my survival.'

He looked up, their gazes meeting. 'I could use men like you with me. It wouldn't be long before you'd get an officer's commission.'

The offer made Riordan hesitate. He met the Templar's concern-filled eyes, then looked around. The uniforms, the power of the Templars, and everything about them made him recoil. They reminded him too much of his father; he needed to get away from it all.

'I'll think about it.'

Phillip smiled ruefully, knowing a no when he heard it. 'The offer will remain open, but may the Light embrace you wherever you choose to go.'

'You too, Templar.'

* * *

* * *

* * *

* * *

GARBED IN GREY WOLF FURS, Guillamere followed their guide through the snowy mountain passes. Behind him, Naberius was clad in black. Beneath his furs was a medium-height man with pale skin and intensely dark eyes. His human form still unsettled Guillamere – to see the mighty three-headed hound reduced to this. Yet this shape had served them well when they'd encountered the mountain tribes. Most had embraced trade. The hostile ones had been met with the wrath of a High Priest.

Their guide stepped up over a rocky outcropping and disappeared from sight. Using his staff, Guillamere planted it like a walking stick and pushed himself up the trail and onto the ledge. A sudden onrush of wind washed over his face, moving through his dreadlocks. Before him lay the southern continent. To the west were the lush Riverlands, home to the Waterlords, and beyond that was the dark forest and Naberius's goal.

'We've made it,' Guillamere said. 'Not in the style we had hoped for but we are here. The Citadel and Zadkiel will, unfortunately, remain untouched.'

'Yes, but I hope it will make them overconfident and blind to our survival,' Naberius said, his voice carrying none of his former thunderous power. 'Our defeat has changed many things. We are in no position to challenge the last Archangel now. But perhaps that is for the best – I had become too rigid in my thinking, too reliant on brute force.' He gazed south. 'This method will give us the flexibility needed to study the power in the south and eventually control it.'

'None of the Archangels, not even Lucifer, have learned how to wield the power of the Ancients,' Guillamere said. 'Only Astaroth had any sort of success.'

'That is what troubles me,' Naberius said, his dark eyes distant. 'If Astaroth ever manages to break free and harness that power....' He shook his head. 'There was always something that made me shrink from trusting her. If she gains control of it, I believe she would challenge Lucifer's right to rule hell herself. That can never be allowed to happen.'

'Is that why you hunt her so relentlessly?'

'No. I do it because Lucifer commanded me to. It was his last charge before Michael struck him down; he saw the threat she posed.' Naberius's eyes hardened. 'We will find a way to subdue the Ancient magic. Then I can fulfill his last wish.'

'To kill Astaroth,' Guillamere finished.

'Let us go,' Naberius said. 'The southern lands await.'

Together they made their way down the mountain. Stealth may succeed where might had failed, and the fate of hell itself might hang in the balance.

* * *

* * *

ARTHUR STOOD STILL, gazing at the faces across the river. They welcomed him as a brother, and yet still he waited. He'd seen thousands of others wade across the river and join the people on the other side. Whether it was through choice or by force, none returned to this side, and Arthur wouldn't take the step until all his comrades had crossed before him.

The irrational part of him that was still human grasped onto the hope that he would see his wife and small boy again soon.

Wilfred came to stand next to him, breaking his reverie. Dressed in a plain white robe, his wild hair neatly trimmed and beard untangled, he was barely recognisable.

'It is okay to let go, Arthur. I am the last. They beat back Naberius – we can cross now.'

'But they didn't kill him?'

'It is no longer our concern. Our part in this battle is done.'

'But my family—'

He thought of Sarah, her smiling face beneath her tangle of brown curls. Of Richard, his bright eyes. He had let them down by dying; shame welled up inside him.

'Phillip will watch over them. Including your horse, Ezekiel.'

'Phillip lived?'

'Yes. The man can fight,' Wilfred said with a grin, before his face sobered. 'Your family will continue to live, as will mine, only because of what we have achieved.'

Arthur stared at the man, the truth of his words sinking in. Acceptance moved like molasses through him, removing the feeling of duty that felt like bedrock within him. Others had to take up the mantle now. As he looked over the river that separated him from the last step into the afterlife, he saw Matthew watching him, smiling with silent exasperation. Beyond him stood Rose, Peter, Elise and all the others who had fallen defending the Gates. Their Light shone more brightly here than it ever had in life.

With a final glance back at the world of the living, Arthur stepped into the dark waters. The current pulled at him like whiskey flowing down his throat, and for the first time since becoming First Templar, he felt truly at peace. His burden was finally lifted. The next generation would have to face Naberius – his watch had ended.

AFTERWORD

Enjoyed Battle of the Iron Gates?

Join my newsletter for exclusive content, early access to new releases, and special offers!

StewAdamsAuthor.com

Continue the story in "Purgatory of the Ancients"!

In the eternal war between heaven and hell, a third power is introduced that upsets the balance.

Ardan is forced to grow up quickly when he witnesses his father's brutal murder. Then a few days later, his mother vanishes amid a myriad of mysteries that plunge Barleron into civil war. As a gifted forest stalker, he makes deals with the Darkness and unwittingly wields the deadly power of the Ancients. Yet through it all, there is something more sinister stalking in the shadows, drawing armies and the powers of Light and Darkness down upon them. Victory here will have ramifications all over the world of Eden, drawing battle lines that divide family and friends. Can Ardan find a way to save the city or will Barleron be another casualty in the eternal war?

Purgatory of the Ancients is the first book in the *Wild Green Flame* fantasy series. If you like fast-paced engaging fantasy, terrifying demons, ambiguous heroes, likeable villains, and biblical supernatural forces, then you'll love the first installment in Stew Adams's page-turning series.

Visit StewAdamsAuthor.com to get your copy of *Purgatory of the Ancients* today!

PURGATORY
OF THE
ANCIENTS
STEW ADAMS

AUTHOR'S NOTE

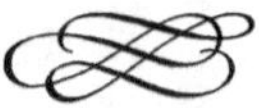

*L*ike every novel it is far from a one person job. I want to thank my incredible writing group, without whom this novella would not have been possible. Their unwavering support, endless patience, and invaluable insights have guided me through countless revisions and have helped shape this story.

First and foremost, I want to thank Christine for her exceptional leadership and her eagle eye for spotting nuances that don't work or flow. Her guidance has been instrumental in refining the story and making it the best it can be.

To Rob, whose boundless optimism and helpful advice have cradled my fragile ego throughout this journey, I am forever grateful. Your encouragement has been a constant source of motivation.

David, thank you for your comedic input, no nonsense attitude and high tolerance for violence has helped craft the battle scenes into something visual and epic. Your commentary on Naberius and Guillamere always made me laugh.

Will, your contributions to the gravitas and underlying tones of the story have been invaluable. Thank you for helping me create a work with depth and meaning.

To Catherine and Clara, who do not have a high tolerance for violence but nonetheless listen as a favour to me, I am truly appreciative. Clara, your assistance with realistic dialogue and general story structure has been crucial, while Catherine your ability to enhance the flow and create beautiful prose has elevated the novella to new heights. Thank you both for bearing through the battles.

Last in the writing group but not least, I want to thank Matt, whose amazing ability to step back and view the whole picture has been invaluable in finding plot holes and keeping me grounded when the story threatens to become a little too far-fetched.

I ALSO WANT to extend a special thank you to Dragan Paunovic for his incredible talent in creating stunning covers. His artwork perfectly captures the essence of the story and draws readers in before they even turn the first page.

And to Tarryn Thomas, my amazing editor, I am eternally grateful. Your keen eye for detail and ability to wield a vast vocabulary without sounding verbose have polished this novella to perfection. Her dedication and expertise have been invaluable throughout the editing process.

Finally to my wife, Mary, like every novel, this is one's for you!

Then theres you, the reader who has kept reading the authors note. You're amazing!

If you haven't had the chance, sign up for my newsletter or send me an email about what you loved (or didn't) about the story!

YOU CAN FIND me at Stewadamsauthor.com